To my mom who will tell everyone she knows, or sees, that her daughter writes books, no matter how many times I shush her!

To my dad who supports me by keeping my books on his shelf, *and* not reading them!

Copyright © 2018 Natasha Madison. E-Book and Print Edition

All rights reserved. No part of this book may be reproduced or transmitted in any form or by any means, electronic or mechanical, including photocopying, recording, or by any information storage and retrieval system, without permission in writing.

This is a work of fiction. Names, characters, places and incidents are the product of the author's imagination or are used factiously, and any resemblance to any actual persons or living or dead, events or locals are entirely coincidental.

The author acknowledges the trademark status and trademark owners of various products referenced in this work of fiction, which have been used without permission. The publication/ Use of these trademarks is not authorized, associated with, or sponsored by the trademark owner.

All rights reserved.

Editor Emily Lawrence

Formatter CP Smith

"You may now kiss the bride," Judge Reynolds says right before Max grabs my face in both of his hands.

"I love you," he whispers, then his lips land on mine, gently and full of love.

My hands go to his waist as I close my eyes and take in the safety of my husband.

"I love you with everything that I am," he murmurs against my lips. I smile and look into his crystal blue eyes.

"I love you more," I say. He lets go of my face and we shake the judge's hand. He grabs my hand and we walk out of his chambers while my chiffon train trails us.

Max proposed to me three hours ago. He got down on one knee and vowed to love me and only me till his last dying breath while I stood there in the middle of the shark reef in the Mandalay Bay. It took me two seconds before I nodded and got down on my knees with him, buried my face into his chest, and cried from happiness. I was completely and utterly in love with him. And not one person in my family knew. Well, none of the men knew. But this isn't about them. This is about me, about Max, about how he took my heart into his hand and treated it like delicate crystal, making sure he bubble wrapped it to keep it safe.

Now here I am, watching my husband dressed in a black tux hold my hand and me in my two-piece lace dress. It is beaded from my collar all the way down. It ties around my neck but leaves my back bare. My arms are also bare. A gold belt ties the second part of the dress, floor-length split chiffon. My legs slip out while I walk, showing off my something blue, which is my Carrie Bradshaw Blue Manolo Blahnik.

As soon as the door to the chapel opens, my chiffon dress blows up almost like Marilyn Monroe's, the hustle and bustle of Las Vegas almost non-existent since we are off the Strip. Someone in the distance must have snapped a picture because his flash went off.

"I think someone just took a picture of us," I tell him while we make our way to the car that is waiting for us.

"Angel, it's Vegas, everyone is taking pictures." He waits for me to get in before climbing in after me. "So, my wife, where do you want to go?" Max turns to me and smiles while his thumb rubs the hand he's holding.

"Back to our room." I look at our hands. "I want to go back with you and lock the door and just be with my husband."

"I was hoping you'd say that." He pulls me to him, his arm going around my shoulder, and I fit perfectly in the crook of his arm.

We watch the city lights come into focus again once we get on the Strip. Walking through the lobby, I hold on to my husband's hand, watching his ring glisten in the light. Max unlocks the door for us. Walking in, I head for the living room that is now turned into what looks like a small reception. Gone are the couches, and in their place is a cast iron square with blush pink roses wrapped all around it. Tea lights make it across. All the furniture is gone. The only thing in this room are blush roses, which are my favorites.

"This place looks like a fairy tale."

Max walks to me, holding a bouquet in his hands. "For you." He hands it to me as our song "Dive" comes on.

"Dance with me?" I ask him as I walk to him.

"Every single day of my life." He wraps an arm around my waist. I hold the bouquet around his shoulders and we hold our free hands to his chest.

He takes his phone out and raises his hand, snapping a picture of us. I'm looking at the camera while he looks at me. "Stunning," he says quietly as his cell phone rings. "Angel, don't freak out." His voice is curt, tight.

I don't have to time to say anything because my phone buzzes with a text from Matthew.

**Allison, when you get this you better call me.**

"Oh my God." I look at him. "What did we just do?" He looks at me shocked, steps back, and away from me.

"Max." I reach out to him while he dodges me.

"A mistake."

I don't know if he's asking or telling. My heart hurts as his eyes go dark. He darts out of the room and the front door slams after him. As I stand here in my wedding dress, a tear rolls down my face, and I look down and see my glistening wedding band.

## CHAPTER 1

## ALLISON

*I can't be late, I can't be late*, I mutter to myself as I run around my new bedroom in Karrie's old brownstone. Karrie is married to my big brother and hockey god Matthew Grant. Well, he's a god now, but he started off as the bad boy of hockey, getting kicked out of the league three years after being drafted first pick. It was the lowest he could go, and he came home with his head hung down and his tail between his legs.

He wanted to sit and sulk, but our stepfather, Cooper Stone, wouldn't let him. Cooper Stone, who actually is the biggest name in history. He holds all the records that all these young kids strive to beat, yet fall short. He was at the top of his game when he met my mom and fell head over skates for her. I say stepfather, but in reality, he's the only father I really know. My parents got divorced when my father had an affair. I was three at the time and Cooper came in two years later. I mean, not only did he fall in love with Mom, he fell in love with me. How could he not? I was the cutest thing ever. We, Matthew and I, were a package deal, a package that Cooper took without thinking twice about it. Slowly but surely, my father started weaning himself out of my life. At such a young age I had no idea really because I was never missing love. Cooper always showered me with it. Hook, line, and sinker. He became even better when Mom gave birth to the twins, Zoe and Zara. Those two are the reason Cooper tries to rule with an iron first. From the first moments they came screaming into the world, they gave new meaning to fiery redheads. My baby brother, Justin, stays in the shadows, quiet, rule abiding, and perfect, but little do my parents know I just found his secret Instagram and that shit is anything but angel like.

So now here I am on my first day on the job and I'm not going to be late. You are looking at the New York Stinger newest Public Relations Representative. I know what you're thinking, that I pulled strings to get the job, and you couldn't be more wrong. I was one month away from graduating when I got a call from Doug, the owner of Cooney Communication as well as the owner of the best hockey team in the world, he is also Matthew's father-in-law, asking me to meet him for lunch. I didn't know what he could possibly want. I thought maybe he needed help shopping for Karrie, so I went. I was surprised to see that it was only us.

*"Hey, beautiful girl," Doug said to me as he got up and kissed my cheek. He had been calling me this since Matthew and Karrie got married almost seven years ago "How is it Cooper hasn't locked you up in a tower yet?" He sat down.*

*"Well, Zoe and Zara just made their latest home school teacher quit when they put rat traps under the table. It's a good thing the woman was wearing shoes." I laughed, thinking about Zoe when she called. "From what they told me, it was a chain reaction and all one hundred traps went off at the same time." I shook my head, picking up my water and bringing it to my lips. "So now Mom says he better brush up on his math skills because he will be teaching them until they can find someone else."*

*"Those two are going to be hellions when they get out into the real world. Either that or they will take over the world. I'm just glad that I shower them with gifts."*

*"Smart man." I put my water down. "Now what is this meeting*

about?"

"Straight to the point. I knew I liked you. I have a job I want to offer you." He folded his hands in front of him.

I sat up straight in my chair. "Why?"

"What do you mean why?" His eyebrows shot up.

"Why me? I'm not even done with school." I pointed out.

"No, you're not, but Mindy has given her notice. Seems that having a husband and carrying a child isn't so easy, so she needs to step back. She will still be with the company as a PR consultant, but..." He looked at me for a reaction, and if I'm honest, I was shocked as fuck. It would be my dream job. Public Relations for one of the original six teams, one that my brother was the captain on. One that just won back-to-back cups. "I need someone, and pardon my words, with balls of steel to handle up to fifty men who range from princesses to cranky. Besides, I trust you."

"I don't know what to say."

"Say you'll think about it. You would start in September when the season starts. One of the perks is that you can stay in the brownstone, since it is just sitting there."

"People are going to think I got the job just because I'm family of sorts," I voiced my concerns.

"Fuck what people think. You are going to have to prove yourself. And I have no doubt that you will." He smiled at me. "Go home, talk it over with your family, then let me know. No hard feelings if you pass on it."

"Okay," I said, not even knowing words were coming out of my mouth. "Okay, I'll do it." I didn't have to talk to my family. I was going to be twenty-three. I could make my own decisions and this was the biggest one I'd ever make.

He clapped his hands, beaming. "You won't be sorry."

I picked up the glass of water again. "Oh, the question is will you be sorry when Cooper and Matthew find out that I'll be traveling with the team of fifty men?" I smile, thinking about them blowing a gasket.

"Now that's a phone call I would kill to be a part of."

Sitting down, I brought my phone out and Facetimed them. I

swallowed as they answered.

"So, princess, what is this meeting about?"

My mom put her hand on his arm. "Cooper, you need to relax."

"So I got a job offer."

"Did you?" Mom asked, surprised at this news. "That's amazing! Doing what?"

I looked at my mom and then at Cooper. "Doug offered me a job with the team as their PR."

Mom's smile went slowly away as the tic in Cooper's head bulged.

"No. Not a fucking chance in hell." He pushed away from the table and disappeared from the screen. "We go way way back to when I was playing; no way should he give you an opportunity without checking with me." His shouting was heard but I couldn't see him.

"Just a second," I said to him. "Hear me out."

He came back holding my mother's hand. "This is such a great opportunity for me."

"You will be traveling with thirty men," Cooper said. "Jock men."

"Actually about fifty, but are you saying that when you traveled with your PR girl you wanted to sleep with her?" I asked him. "Are you saying that Matthew tried to sleep with Mindy every single time? Are you saying that—" I didn't have time to say anything else before he put his hand up.

"That's enough. I would never ever think about sleeping with anyone besides your mother." He kissed her hand. "Never in a million years would I do that to her. But, not all of them are like me or Matthew."

"I know that, Dad, I do, but you have to trust me. Your little girl is growing up." I threw my hands up. "Or actually I'm already grown and I can't begin to tell you how excited I am about this. How about this...if I feel for one minute that someone isn't nice to me I'll tell you or Matthew and then you guys can go in and do your crazy thing."

The rest of the phone call was exactly what I thought it would be. Cooper balked and demanded to see a copy of the contract, where he stipulated that I be put on another floor away from the team, which I vetoed. And, well, then when I called my brother, Karrie told me that

Matthew's vein in his neck ticked for hours.

I rush around the messy room, grabbing my black tight jeans and blush pink silk button-down shirt. Once I button it up, I tie a bow around the collar with the silk that is hanging down. I tuck the front of the shirt in my pants while I roll up the sleeves. I take out my blush suede Louboutins with matching purse from the closet. I smile at my collection of princesses shoes; that is what I call them. When I turned sixteen, Cooper handed me a credit card and called it Cinderella's slipper. I smile thinking how he really treated me like a princess.

Running down the stairs, I get a message that my Uber driver is waiting. Grabbing my sunglasses, I lock the door and rush into the car. I have thirty minutes before I get there, so I apply a coat of mascara, as well as lip-gloss. I pile my hair on the top of my head in a messy bun. By the time we show up at the arena, I'm in the zone. Well, almost in the zone, if I didn't almost trip over a guy walking in my way while he types on his phone.

When we smash into each other, my phone falls to the floor and shatters. "Fuck." I bend and pick it up. My heart shatters like the screen just did.

"I'm so sorry." His voice comes out gravely, deep, rough.

"It's fine." I look up at the man and I'm taken aback. He's wearing a perfect black tailored suit, with mirrored Ray-Bans. His chest is broad and huge while his biceps look like they are going to rip out of his suit a la Hulk. His jaw is clean-shaven and his lips are perfect and plump. Wait, what the fuck is this, plump lips? Who am I? His hair is also perfect as it's cut short on the side and flips over on top. You would think this man just stepped off the cover of GQ. But I know what is behind those glasses. Blue fucking eyes.

I look at what can only be described as a devil in disguise. Max fucking Horton. If there was ever a man I wanted nothing to do with it is him. Yet here I stand in front of him while he reaches out to see my phone, and my hands ache to feel his fingers on mine.

"It's fine." I snatch it and walk away from him while he mutters "bitch" under his breath. And in that moment, I couldn't agree with him more.

## MAX

The sound of the alarm beeping has me leaning over and groaning. Eight a.m. It almost feels like noon to me since I spent the summer up at my house in Canada training every day at five a.m. A log cabin hidden in the woods where the town has a population of one hundred and twenty-five. It was the first thing I bought when I signed my big contract at the age of twenty. It's a place that no one but my sister, Denise, knows about. Four years apart, Denise and I haven't had the easiest life. Our father was in and out of our lives, just as the seasons come and go. Our mother was a mean ass drunk, and let's not forget our verbally abusive stepfather. Think Married With Children but on meth.

    I turn myself in bed and press the button for the shades to open. I lie back in my big king-sized bed as light fills the room. I live in a loft in Soho. One whole floor to myself. I fell in love with this space as soon as I visited. It was an old dusty factory when I first stepped in it. The only thing I kept was the four brick walls. I had a designer come in and she made a miracle happen. Gone were the dusty floors and in their place were all dark wood oak floors all over the house. They match the wooden beams she brought in. She kept the open-floor concept, except when it came to the bedroom. All the way at the other side of the floor it's blocked off by a full wall that hides my bedroom, master bath, and walk-in closet.

The sun is out, with not a cloud in sight. I'm about to get up when my cat shows up. Yeah, I have a cat, but it's a manly cat, a white Persian. Okay, maybe not manly, and it is a girl, but her name is Stanley. "Hey, princess," I say as she lies on my chest and purrs while I rub her ears. She quickly gets tired of me and goes off on her own. It's then I toss my white cover off of me and head to my bathroom. I approach the toilet that is in a separate room and come out to wash my face in the sink. The white and gray marble counter stretches along a big wall with two sinks separated by the 'makeup' part. Something I never approved, but somewhere the designer thought she would be putting her stuff. I walk to the shower, opening the glass door and stepping inside. The inside walls have the same marble as the counter, the white tiles on the floor blending perfectly. Opening the shower, two waterfalls start over me. Leaning my hands out onto the wall, I let the water wash over my back. This summer I added twenty pounds of muscle. Seven days a week, eight hours a day, I pushed my body to where I thought it would snap. I'm coming back bigger and better, especially since this is my last year with New York. My contract is up after this season and I know they can't wait to toss me out on my ass.

Fuck, they would have tossed me out six years ago when Matthew fucking Grant came waltzing in and stealing my thunder. I was a dumb kid back then. The king of the fucking world, at least in my world. I was the golden kid on the team, the one who led everyone till I was the one who almost brought the team down, with just a stupid game.

Not only did Matthew take my place on the team, he turned the team against me. Okay, I did have a hand in that, but I fucking hated it.

One night, drinking by myself in a bar, this hot blonde walked up to me. Puck Bunny, I knew it a mile away. Fuck, just thinking about it I get sick to my stomach. She brought me back to her room, then latched on to my dick like a jellyfish in the ocean. I gave her Matthew's name. Fuck, what a fucking mistake. We spent the night banging each other, only for her to wake up and expect a fucking ring. She genuinely looked shocked when I said I don't do relationships. Her vow to make me regret it should have been my first clue. But how the fuck was I supposed to know she would beat herself up and tell everyone that I raped her? Well, not me but Matthew. The minute the cops came into the locker room, I knew. I had a sick feeling in my gut. I still remember faking sick. I rushed back to my room, got in touch with my lawyer, and together we went down to the police station. Of course by that time, the detectives already knew that Matthew wasn't the one who was with her. Now it fell on me. They charged me with aggravated assault, rape, and impersonation. It was the single worst mistake of my life. After the dust settled and we found out that she pulled this stunt with at least ten other people, I was dismissed, but my reputation was tarnished and destroyed. I tried to apologize, but no one wanted to hear it. So I did what I do best, I went out there and played my heart out. We won the cup that year. I want to say I helped, but my head wasn't in there. I hoisted the cup, but Matthew was the one who led the team. I spent the summer with my tail between my legs, licking my wounds and being like woe me.

Until my sister showed up with a black eye.

*"What the fuck happened to you?" I asked, my blood boiling, my hands clenching into fists as my body became a stone in front of her.*

*"He came to my room tonight," she started talking; she also didn't need to tell me who he was, as I held up my hand, bile rising up my throat.*

*"Did he touch you?" I prayed that she said no, prayed to anyone that would have listened to me.*

*"I fought him," she whispered as the sob she kept back ripped from her and her knees finally gave out. I ran to her just before she hit the floor.*

*I laid her down on my couch and I spent another night in jail that time, but it was worth the look of shock when I showed up at my mother's house and knocked the shit out of my stepfather. While I sat on his dirty, high body as my fists plumaged into his face.*

One week later, I was summoned to New York. So I made peace with the fact that my career was over. I told my agent to go through my contract, making sure I wouldn't end up broke also.

When I walked into the office and Doug was the only one there, I didn't know what to think.

"Sit down." He pointed to the couch and not to the chair in front of him. "Give me one reason to keep you?" it should have been a simple question, but it wasn't. It was a loaded question.

"When my head isn't up my ass, I'm actually a good hockey player." I looked at him square in the eye, man to man.

"No, that is where you're wrong," he said and the confidence I had left my body like a swoosh, "you're a fucking great hockey player. But then off the ice, you're a loose cannon."

"I know what you're thinking," I started, "but this time it really wasn't my fault." He looked over, waiting so I did what I didn't want, I spilled my guts, "My stepfather tried to rape my sister. I couldn't let him get away with it." I shook my head as the thoughts came rushing to my head, and then everything else came out.

The little Canadian boy who had nothing but a teacher and an old hockey coach looking out for him.

Then when I thought that he would give me my walking papers, he did the opposite. He made sure that Denise was taken care of and since she graduated a year ahead of schedule, she got accepted at the top medical college. He vowed that no one would know and he kept his word.

She lived with me while she finished high school and then I paid her way to med school. Now she is the best pediatric doctor out there. The only thing is she never leaves her heart at home, so when she loses a patient, her heart goes with them.

Turning off the water, I snap back into the present. One year, I tell myself. One year to play my ass off and secure another contract. It's a piece of cake. Or is it?

I make myself breakfast while I sit at the island and go through the emails from the team. There is a new PR person who is taking Mindy's place. I scan the email to see if I need to know this and delete it, not caring who the fuck is taking her place. Maybe this will be good. Mindy fucking hated me. She barely used me and all my photo shoots were on my own.

I read the sports section in the paper and then get myself ready. I make plans with my trainer to meet him after the photo shoot. Getting my black suit out, I shrug my shoulders into it as I put on my black Patek Philippe. I walk out to my SUV downstairs. Getting into my black BMW, I make my way to the arena. The streets aren't too crowed today and I make it there in record time. Getting out, I see that I missed a call from Denise, but she sent me a text.

*You think you can get a couple of your hockey players to come visit the hospital? I keep trying to get in touch with the girl Mindy and she never gets back to me.*

I'm texting her back, not looking where I'm going, when I crash into someone. The person's pink phone lands right in front of my feet. I don't have time to bend down and grab it for her. Looking up, I see I've come face to face with an angel. A cliché, I know, but her face is stunning. She's a fucking beauty. I take in her long neck because her hair is piled on top of her head. I know with one pull her hair would fall down over her shoulders. Her eyes are covered with her black glasses. I take in her outfit and know within a second she is all class. Which means this one is untouchable, or better yet, not in my league.

I'm about to grab her phone when she snaps at me and walks away. I don't even know what I did. "Bitch," I say under my breath and shake my head. Walking in, I shake coaches' hands and say hi to some of the guys while I try to find out who the new PR girl is so I can ask her about doing a hospital visit. I turn the corner and see Matthew Grant laugh with the girl I met outside and it all clicks into place. She's fucking Allison Grant, Matthew Grant's sister and Cooper Stone's stepdaughter. Not only is she out of my league, she is in the biggest no fly zone if there ever was one. "Hey," I say, coming face to face with them.

Matthew nods, civil, which is the way we both like it. It's not a secret we don't like each other, but I'm not going to waste my energy on him.

"Did you meet my sister Allison? She is the new PR girl hired to take Mindy's place," he says proudly.

The only thing I can think to say is, "Good to know." Before I walk away and send Denise a text.

*Yeah, looks like the new PR girl isn't going to do the whole hospital thing.*

I put the phone in my pocket, make my way to the locker room, and get into the uniform for the team photo. "One year," I whisper to myself.

## ALLISON

"Okay, everyone look over here," the photographer says, standing on a ladder and taking a picture of the team for the season. Everyone is in uniform, with the captain, which is Matthew, the two assistants, which are Phil and Max, and then the coaches and goalies sitting front and center. I watch them all smile and my eyes drift straight to the one I shouldn't think twice of. He's the biggest jerkface I have ever met, and let's not forget about his shady play when Matthew was arrested. Nope, he is the last thing I need to focus on.

I walk back into the locker room, grabbing the envelopes I prepared to give to the players, even though I emailed all of them. Some are old school and like paper. I place them in each person's mailbox slot. Everyone has at least some paper in it, but Max's is the only one empty with nothing lingering. When I hear the herd coming back to the locker room, I wait in the shadows as they all take their designated seat.

"Okay, before we continue, we have a couple of things to address," Doug says to everyone. "Mindy will no longer be traveling with the team."

Some whisper, some in shock, while others just start peeling their tapes off.

"She'll be in charge at the home office, but you should all meet your new girl. Allison," he says my name and looks around for me.

I step out of the corner and wave my hand at everyone. Some whistle at me while Matthew glares at them.

"Hi, guys, as Doug just said, I'm Allison. I sent you an email with all my contact information. Now I don't know how many of you got them, but I also put a hard copy in your mailboxes. If there is anything you need, you must let me know." I look around the room while they almost hang on to my every move, except Max, who is peeling his jersey off, showing me and everyone what is underneath. He's a work of fucking art. His muscles are so defined you can trace them in the dark with your fingers and know exactly where you are. His chest has no hair on it, but his arms are tatted full sleeves. I try not to focus on it by looking at anything else but that, but my eyes have a mind of their own and swing back to him.

"I'll also be traveling with you guys, so I need to know if you have any preferences for the hotels we stay at. I know some of you share a room, so if you can please discuss things with each other before coming to me." I smile at the guys. "It's not my job to decide who gets the bed by the window. Any questions for me?"

Phil raises his hand.

"Yes?"

"Just so that no one fights over you, are you single and will Matthew be your bodyguard?"

I laugh at him as Matthew shoves him hard to the side.

"Not available." I nod at them. "So if you guys have anything to discuss, I'll be in my office."

I walk out of the room and head down the hallway, past the gym, to my small office with no window. My office is bleak to say the least as it's the second time I've been in here. The walls are stark white, and the brown desk holds my laptop. Tomorrow I'm going to bring in a plant, some pictures, and dress this room up. I'm opening my laptop to make sure I have the travel schedule downloaded so I can make everyone's travel itinerary.

"Knock, knock, knock." Matthew is leaning against the doorjamb.

"Mr. Grant." I lean back in my chair. "What can I do for you?"

"How about you come out and have dinner at my house?" he says. "Kids have asked when you are coming over."

I smile, thinking of them. "How about a rain check? I need to get unpacked and organized before the travel schedule kicks my ass."

"Okay, squirt." He peeks down the hall, making sure no one can hear him. "I swear to God, if any of those fucking chumps pull anything it's over."

I sit up straight and glare at him. "I will remind you that I just turned twenty-three. I will also remind you that I went to college without my family breathing down my neck, and what do you know, I survived." I point at him. "Don't make me call Karrie," I threaten him.

"Calm down there." He stands up straight. "No need to tell anyone anything." He puts his hands in his pockets. "Besides, I've already gotten the talk down from Mom and Karrie, but then Cooper called and it was almost like he was putting a price on someone's head. He basically threatened to call the commissioner and have all females blocked from doing anything with the players."

I laugh, thinking about Cooper and his exaggeration on me working with the guys.

"Hello," Matthew says, bringing me back to now. "You okay?"

"Yes, sorry, I was thinking. Listen, I need to set up some photo shoots. Shoo so I can actually work."

"Okay, kid, text me when you get home."

"Not going to happen, Matthew, but I will see you tomorrow," I tell him. He nods and walks away.

I don't know how long I'm sitting at my computer going over everyone's schedule and placing it on the roster. I have everyone's availability but Max's. I make a note to email him tomorrow morning with a second request. The reason I ask them all this is so I can do some team promo if they are all free, or at least work around some of them. I only stop working when my stomach grumbles, so I get up, closing my laptop, and putting it in my bag, closing off my light. Looking down, I turn to walk away when I run smack into a hard chest.

"Fuck." I hear when I feel hands hold my arms. The scent of woods and citrus hits me. "You need to watch where you're going," he hisses out and the only thing I see is his white T-shirt. Gone is the suit and in its place is his white T-shirt with his name on it and matching pants.

I stand straight and shake his hands off of me. "I'm sorry. I didn't think anyone else was left." I look at him, his hair still perfect, but now closer I can see the ink on his arms, ink that makes my hands itch. He doesn't say anything else but goes the other way to walk around me. "Um, Max, I didn't get your schedule that I requested."

He turns around. "I don't have a schedule, Allison. At least none that should be your concern." He takes two steps away.

"I don't give a shit what you think should be my concern. It's in everyone's contract. If you want, I can forward you the clause. So if you can stop being a dick for two seconds, just send me the schedule."

He walks to me slowly, almost like he's on the prowl. His whole demeanor goes from slouching to standing straight and tall. "I don't need you to forward me shit. I also know that for the last seven fucking years, Mindy didn't give a shit where I went or what I did. You schedule shit for me and send me an email. I'll let you know when and if I'm available or not."

"That's not how I work." I refuse to back down.

"Too bad, princess, it's how I work. Don't like it, why don't you go cry to your brother? Maybe he can fight your battles for you. After all, we all know why you got this job."

My head goes back as if he slapped my face. "I got this job because I'm qualified for this position. Besides, it takes a princess to battle another princess. So if you'll excuse me, your highness, send me your fucking schedule or I'll become the biggest pain in your ass. You'll send me your schedule years after you're gone," I say to him and dart away while he mutters "bitch" again. Not one to give him the excuse twice in one day, I turn around, walking backward. "Takes one to know one." I wink at him, flipping him the bird this time. I walk out of the building, cursing myself for letting him get the best of me. "Asshole." I make my way to the sidewalk where my Uber ride picks me up.

When I get home, I make myself something to eat and climb into bed with my laptop and glasses. I flip open the television while I check Facebook and then Instagram. Then I notice I have an email alert.

*From: Max Horton*
*To: Princess Pain In My Ass*
*Subject: Your Royal Request*
*Here is what you need.*
*I've shared my calendar with you. Work with that.*
*Regards,*
*Princess Max Horton*

I smile at his name. I smile that he answered, but most of all I smile because round one goes to me. Bitch.

MAX

I go to the fridge to get myself another bottle of water, pausing the television on *Game of Thrones*. I don't even have time to open the bottle before I hear my phone ping.

Making my way to the couch where my laptop is out with my schedule, I see it's from Allison.

*To: Biggest Pain in my ASS*
*From: Just Allison*
*Subject: Thank You*
*Thank you for sending me your royal commitment. I will work around them. Please let me know if you change it at any time.*
*Signed,*
*Allison Grant*
*AKA Royal Ball Buster*

I smile and groan at the same time. Fucking chick is getting under my skin. The last time I saw Allison Grant she was just turning seventeen, with her tight jeans and sassy mouth. Now here she is, older and better. I shake my head, trying my fucking hardest not to have her in my thoughts. No way in fuck does she belong here. Her skin is soft like an angel's, her blue eyes, untainted, pure. That is the only word that comes to my mind when I think of her.

I don't bother answering her email. Just leave it alone, I tell myself. Instead, I grab my own computer, going over the things I have planned for this month. A couple of photo shoots with my sponsors. A couple trips to the hospital to volunteer with Denise. I'm about to send my agent an email when I get another one from Allison.

*To: New York Stingers*
*From: Allison Grant*
*Subject: Public Relations Opportunities.*
*Hi All,*
*I will be sharing with you the schedule I have planned for the season. As many of you know, this schedule will or can change according to the team's needs. I will also be scheduling more meet and greet opportunities as the year progresses. If there are any other opportunities that you think we should be doing, please feel free to let me know and I'll do my best.*
*Our first away game will be September 17. As it is just an exhibition game, I know many of you will be not there, so I have arranged for some of the loyal hockey fans to come in and meet the team.*
*Have a great night.*
*Allison*

I close my computer before I'm tempted to answer her, getting up and shutting off the television. I walk to my bedroom, turning everything else off, and diving in. Setting my alarm for six, I plan to work out before the masses come in. It seems everyone is in now.

By the time I walk into the gym at six-fifteen the next morning, I've already been up for an hour. Fucking cat sat on my face. I have to admit it's the most action I got in the last six months. I'm over the girls, the puck bunnies, the meaningless sex. I shake my head and punch in my code to the door. I head to the locker room, my earphones already on.

Tossing my backpack into my cube, I make my way around the logo in the middle of the room. Stepping on it will get you fined five grand. It also curses you. Not one to tempt fate, I walk around it. I'm wearing my shorts with my black socks up to my knees. My gray T-shirt clings to me. My baseball cap on backward, with my earphones blasting Kendrick Lamar, when I turn the corner to the gym, I see the lights already on. Wondering who the hell is in already, I stop in my tracks when I see exactly who is there. Allison.

What the fuck? She's there in her fucking outfit that molds her fucking body, leaving little to the imagination. Her tight yoga pants stretch across her ass as she does jump squats. Her matching yoga top shows off her abs, which are defined. Her B cups bounce just a touch as she kicks up. Her hair is high on top of her head in a ponytail. The back of her outfit is green with crisscrosses.

"What the fuck are you doing here?" I rip my earphones off as soon as she lets out a screech. Then she holds her chest when she sees it's me.

"Jesus Christ, Max, you scared the shit out of me." She bends down to grab her water bottle.

"Doesn't answer my question, Allison. What the fuck are you doing here?"

Her eyes go from open to leering. "I think it's pretty self-explanatory as to what I'm doing here considering this is a gym." Her hands go out and she does a circle.

"I know where we are, Allison. My question was what are *you*"—I point at her—"doing in here?"

Her hands go on her hips, and if she could kill me with a glare, it would be right now. "I work here, Max. I have my badge in my bag if you need clarification, so I can be here."

"Well, you shouldn't be in here with the guys, especially not dressed like that." I point up and down at her outfit.

"Like what, Max, in workout stuff?" She folds her arms, pushing up her perfect tits—wait, not perfect tits, I think one is lopsided.

"You're practically naked and the only ones who use this gym are the boys, so you can't go prancing around naked." I point out to her on my way to my treadmill. My hand flexes into fists and she curses at me.

"You're such an asshole. I think the boys can contain themselves. It's not my fault you can't control your dick."

"Don't you worry about where I put my dick, *sweetheart*."

"Your dick is the last thing on my mind, right after anal bleaching and genital herpes," she huffs out and storms out of the locker room, slamming the door.

I put my music back on and pound the treadmill faster than I think I ever ran before. My temper radiates. I run for about an hour, getting off once my legs start to wobble. My shirt is drenched by the time I finish. Matthew comes in right when I am peeling my shirt off.

"What did you do to my sister?" he asks, his voice irritated.

"Me?" I point to me. "I did what you should have done. She was in here prancing around half naked." He's about to say something, but I continue, "The rookies train here. You think I need the bullshit of them following their dicks and not their heads? You need to talk to her and let her know the way it goes." I shake my head. "You're lucky it was me and not those guys." I point to the group of rookies that just walked in, all nineteen, all ready to bang their way through the night. "Take care of your shit, Grant." I leave before he says anything else.

I do whatever I have to do the rest of the day to avoid Matthew and his sister. I shake my head and think about how it is my fault. I'm getting ready to head home when my sister calls me.

"Hey," I say, answering it right away.

"Hey," she says softly, "you busy?" She sniffles.

"What happened?" I ask, stopping mid-step on my way to my car.

"I lost Cade today." She softly cries. Cade was her seven-year-old patient. Diagnosed with brain cancer at four, he fought a tough battle, but in the end, his little body couldn't take it.

"Denise, I'm so sorry. Where are you?" I ask, getting in the car.

"I'm at The Dive. I feel the need to drink my sorrows away," she says and I hear ruffling in the background.

"I'll meet you there. I can be there in twenty." I start my car and make my way to the Bronx and the little bar called just that 'The Dive Bar.'

It takes me about twenty-five minutes to get there and I park the car in their almost vacant parking lot. I take my cap out of my bag and put it on with the lid coming down low. It's enough I don't have a sweater and my ink is on display. Walking into the bar, I nod at Charlotte, the bartender, who owns this place.

"She's in the back. She's already knocked back a few." She eyes me as I walk to the back and see a wobbly Denise. Which is okay. What isn't okay is the sleezeball who has his arms around her while she holds her pool cue.

"Hey," I say, getting close enough to her.

Her eyes light up when she sees me. "Maxie," she says a name she calls me only when she's blitzed.

"Sup." I nod to the guy as I'm about to lean in and grab a hold of Denise.

"Not so fast there." He grabs her around her waist when she tries to come to me, and it's then I see that he's high as fuck. His eyeballs don't even have a different color, just pure black.

"It's okay. He's my brother," Denise says, now standing straight and sobering up.

"Not so fast there, sweet cheeks, you promised me a good time," he says as I take my cap off and then put it back on.

It's then that Denise tries to get away from him, but he stops her, grabbing onto her wrist, and twisting it so that she yelps out in pain. I pounce on him, punching him straight in the nose, sending his head backward. His hand lets go of Denise, who falls to the floor while he holds his nose that is now spewing blood.

"You broke my fucking nose," he says and spits blood from his mouth.

"Hey, what's going on in here?" Charlotte says with her brother standing behind her. Her brother the cop. Fuck.

"He broke my nose," the creep says, pointing to me, and I lean forward to pick Denise up off the floor, who holds her wrist in her hand.

"He wouldn't let me go." Denise tries to intercept, but it's too late, the damage is done. The phones are out as people start taping what is going on.

I hear someone say, "Holy shit, it's Max Horton."

I try to bring my head down and turn my back, but Charlotte's brother puts his hand on my shoulder. "Sorry, pal, I gotta take you in. He wants to press charges."

"Yeah, no problem," I say and follow him out with my head down, and he holds my arm and leads me out.

## ALLISON

I'm about to walk into the living room carrying my takeout pizza box that I just paid for when my phone starts ringing. I see that it's Doug.

"Hello," I answer, fumbling with the pizza and the phone.

"There has been a situation that has come up. I think we should do damage control before the media gets hold of the story."

I drop the pizza, running upstairs two at a time, getting ready to change. "Yes, where do you want me to meet you?" I say out of breath.

"I'll be at your place in one minute with the situation. We just parked."

Shit, I look down at my outfit. My pants are a light gray, almost a velour kind. With matching tank crop top, I'm wearing a long knitted sweater that I pull together just as the doorbell rings. "Fuck."

I run downstairs, almost fucking tripping on the long sweater. I open the door and gawk as soon as I see who comes in after Doug. Fucking Max.

"I'm sorry we just came here. We have to handle this fast. It's been forty-five minutes since it happened, and I think the news is going to run a story in fifteen," Doug says, walking into the living room, picking up the remote, and turning on SportsCenter. Max doesn't make eye contact with me as he walks through the door, following Doug. He doesn't go to sit. Instead, he goes to stand and looks out the big window.

"So what's the situation that we need to handle?" I ask, walking into the room, standing in the middle of Doug and Max.

"Max just got arrested of sorts," Doug says, putting his hands in his pockets.

"Of course he did," I say under my breath, shaking my head while his head snaps up. "Two days. I've been on the job two days. What was he sort of arrested for?" I ask, folding my arms now as my sweater opens.

"Aggravated assault."

"Seriously. How old are you?" I ask him and turn to Doug. "What could I possibly do with this? He assaulted someone."

"The man was high as a kite," Doug says. "I don't know what you need to do, but we have to put it out before the hounds get it and make it worse than it is."

"Worse than it is, are you serious right now? This is what, his fifth arrest? I'm good, but I'm not that fucking good."

"I'm out," Max says, nodding at Doug. "My ride is here. I trust you to do whatever you need to do."

I watch a car arrive and a girl gets out.

"Seriously, all this for a girl?" I shake my head. "Did you for once just think with your head and not your dick?" I throw my hands up as soon as Doug says my name.

"Told you before, princess, don't worry about where I put my dick. Now do what you're paid to do and make me the knight in fucking shining armor." He slams the door on the way out and I watch him run down the stairs and take the woman in his arms, holding her head, and leaning down to kiss her forehead. I don't stand here long before I turn around.

"You're way off base here, Allison," Doug says, sitting down. "He was arrested for protecting his sister, who was being roughed up by a drugged up man." He punches in some number on his phone, then puts it to his ear. "What do you have for me?" he asks whoever it is on the phone and my head goes back to the window only to be met with the darkness from outside.

"We do as he says," I say. "He's the knight in shining armor. We don't have to give his sister's name, but he came to the rescue of a damsel in distress. Paint him as a hero." I pick up my phone, calling my contact at SportsCenter. "Hey, Erin, do I have a scoop for you," I say when she answers.

"From word on the street, you got a bad boy showing his stripes again," she says right away.

"You think I would call you if I knew that he was guilty? Please, how long have we known each other? Since grade school." I thank my lucky stars that we had sleepovers and I stayed friends with everyone. "He was protecting a woman."

"Is it someone he's dating?" She bites right away.

"You know I won't give you that information." I laugh and turn around to see Doug. "But she was being manhandled by a man who was not only intoxicated, he was high."

"Shut up," she says while she slams her hand on her desk. "You're lying."

"Would I lie to you? I swear. Listen, you run this story, I'll get you first dibs on his interview when he's able to talk about it." Fuck, he better fucking agree to this.

"You got yourself a deal. I just saw some video from the bar. Someone sent it. Your bad boy just became a hero," she says, disconnecting the call.

"That was incredible," Doug says. "Worth every penny." He opens the pizza box. "You still owe him an apology." He grabs a slice, eating it.

"Yeah, yeah, he's right, it's my job," I say with my hand in the air, and we both turn when SportsCenter brings up Max's name.

*"The good deed of the night goes to Max Horton from the New York Stingers. Max Horton stepped in to protect a woman from being assaulted by an inebriated man. We have a video footage, and I have to say"*—the reporter turns to her co-anchor, who is a man—*"who wouldn't want to be saved by Max?"* She laughs and they switch topics.

I close off the television and Doug gets up.

"Okay, kid, I'm out. You did good tonight. Hard, but good." He smiles and walks out, slamming the door lightly.

I look at the pizza box, but my stomach feels ill. I jumped the gun and accused him before I had all the details. I shake my head. I have to be neutral.

I pick up my phone and call the only person I know who will somehow understand me—my mom.

"Hey, sweetheart." She answers right away.

"Hey, Mom," I say softly while I pick at lint that is on my pants now that I'm curled up on the couch.

"What's the matter?" Her voice goes tight right away and I hear her walk away from the noise.

"Nothing." I try to pretend, but a tear sneaks out. "Max was charged with assault today."

"Okay," she says, confused.

"I already deemed him guilty and was not a nice person to him."

"It's normal, honey. After everything that happened with your brother, you don't trust him."

"Mom, that's the thing; it's my job to be on his side of sort, but all I did was stand there and shit on him. When in fact he was protecting his sister."

My mother gasps. "Honey, you had no idea. You can't blame yourself. Did you do your job in the end?"

I nod. "Yes, but I felt like a bitch, Mom. He brings out the worst in me. It's been two days and each time I end up wanting to throat punch him. He complained today I shouldn't work out in the gym because my yoga pants are provocative."

My mother laughs. "Oh, dear God."

"Then I told Matthew and he actually fucking agreed with him," I bark. "Agreed with Douchebag Max."

"Honey, I don't know what is going on, but I do know that you aren't the bitch you think you are. I mean, bitchy yes, but you get that from me."

I laugh at her.

"But now you know to listen to the story before flying off the handle."

"I do. I think I'm going to send him an email apologizing." I sit up, walking to the door, and getting my laptop.

"You do what you need to do," she says softly. "And if he doesn't accept it, well, at least you know you tried," she says right before I hear Cooper in the background.

"What happened?"

I hear her mumbling nothing before coming back to me.

"Now if you're okay, I need to go and save Zoe."

"What did she do this time?" I laugh, thinking about my wild twin sisters.

"She slipped some sleeping pills in her tutor's coffee this morning. Needless to say, we got home to a snoring Mrs. Hendreick."

"Oh my gosh." I laugh out. "Okay, Mom, thank you for this."

"Anytime, sweetheart. Love you."

"Love you, too," I say, disconnecting the call.

I pull up my email on my laptop, composing the email.

*To: Max Horton*
*From: Allison Grant*
*Subject: Tonight*
*Hey Max,*
*I just wanted to say I'm sorry about jumping the gun tonight and accusing you before knowing all the facts. I got them to spin the whole knight in shining armor thing. You will have to grant them an exclusive interview when all charges are dropped.*
*Again, I'm sorry.*
*Allison*

I press send and sit here waiting, for what, I have no idea. I'm expecting him to answer right away. After thirty minutes of me just waiting, I get up, close my laptop, and close up the house. I put on the alarm, a stipulation that Cooper wasn't willing to take no on. It also came with cameras around the house. I walk upstairs doing my nighttime routine, checking my phone one last time, and seeing nothing come in. Sleep doesn't come easy for me that night. I keep replaying the scene in my head all night, tossing and turning, and when my alarm finally rings at seven a.m. I look like I just pulled an all-nighter.

I get up, grabbing my black capris, with a white T-shirt, matching it with a pink jacket. I grab my black ballerina shoes, then my phone, checking it again, and seeing nothing from Max.

I make my way to the office, nodding at people when I walk in. I put my things down and go about finding Max. I peek in the gym and find out he's not there. I check the kitchen, the dressing room, and come up empty. I'm walking back to my office and knock into someone.

I'm expecting to see Max, but it's not him. It's Ryder, a first-year rookie.

"Hey there," he says, smiling. "Looking for something?"

He's dressed in his workout gear with his name on his shirt.

"Yeah, sorry, I was looking for Matthew or Max?" I smile at him. "Have you seen them?"

"I just left Max in the kitchen and Matthew will be here only this afternoon."

I nod at him. "Thank you so much, Ryder. See you around."

I make my way back to the kitchen and walk in when I hear Phil. "Jesus fuck, it's like bad luck follows you everywhere." He shakes his head, walking away from Max, who is sitting down eating his heaping plate of breakfast.

"Hey, I was looking for you," I say to him and his head doesn't come up. He's wearing the same baseball hat that he had on yesterday, and he didn't shave this morning.

"Well, you found me," he says to his food and not me.

I look around and see that it's slowly starting to get busy. "I wanted to just say that I'm sorry for jumping the gun yesterday. I should have listened to your side before I said anything." I trail off because his eyes shoot up, and they are as bloodshot as mine are.

"Forget about it," he says, his voice gruff. "In the end, you did what you're paid to do."

"I think we got off on the wrong foot." I try to say, but he laughs.

"We aren't off to anything. How about this? You stay out of my way and make sure we never have to work together." His tone is hard.

"We work together. We will be traveling together." I cross my arms.

"We don't need to be friends," he says, finishing off his plate. How he could finish that heap in five minutes is beyond me. "You do your thing, let me do mine. I won't assume you're always a bitch and you can assume I'm not always an asshole. How's that?"

I grind my teeth together. "Fine," I say, storming out. "Not always an asshole. His middle name should be asshole," I say to myself, walking into my office and closing the door, leaning on the back of it. "I'm going to do my thing and have him do his. I can do this." I go to my desk and do just that, my job.

## CHAPTER 6
## MAX

The minute I walked out of the house, I thought I was going to punch the side of her fucking house. I knew the minute I sat down in the car and Doug said we were going to Allison's it would lead to this, to her expecting me to be the fuck-up. And, well, she didn't disappoint. I would have let her go on and on, but Doug didn't let her.

I get to the car that Steve, who is Denise's co-worker at the hospital, is driving. As soon as I saw the car coming down Allison's street, I bailed out the door and made it down the steps and to the car. Steve stops the car and Denise jumps out, running to me with tears down her face.

"I'm so sorry, Max." She sobs out in my chest while I hold her head and kiss her forehead. "I didn't even think."

"It's fine. Let's get in the car so we can get the fuck out of here." I walk to the car, getting in the back with her, where she curls at my side as she silently cries. "Hey, Steve, thanks for picking her up."

"Yeah," he says, pulling away from the curb and making his way to my apartment. "Figured you could use the ride."

Denise slowly peels her head from my shoulder. "What happened in there?"

"Nothing. They asked me questions about what happened. Luckily, Charlotte told her brother that the guy has been in there all day drinking and leaving to go smoke or whatever. So they gave me a warning to stay out of trouble. It'll blow over," I say.

"I called Doug as soon as they took you away," Denise says. "I didn't know what was going to happen."

"It's fine. Doug was okay about it. My PR girl not so much," I say, looking at the entrance to my loft and seeing that there aren't any news vans there waiting, which is a good sign. "No news vans. Maybe she actually did her job instead of bitching," I say to myself as I get out of the car. Steve parks in the visitor parking spot and they follow me inside.

"What do you mean?" Denise asks me.

"Doesn't matter," I say when I walk into the kitchen and grab a water bottle out of the fridge.

"It matters to me." She gets on the stool in the kitchen.

"She started throwing my rap sheet in my face." I shrug my shoulders. "Nothing I haven't heard before." I lean back on my counter, crossing my feet.

"You've never brushed it off before." She points at me. "You usually rant and rave about it."

I take off my cap, running my hands through my hair. "Maybe I'm maturing," I say, crossing my arms.

"Maybe." Denise eyes me and then turns to Steve. "You think you could drop me off at home?"

Steve just nods.

"I think I need to sleep for a week and then I might feel human again." She gets off her stool and comes over to me, wrapping her arms around my waist. "You're the good guy." She leans up and kisses my cheek. "Don't forget that."

"Yeah, well, once you fuck up, it's hard for people to see that good in you."

"Hmm." She grabs her bag and Steve guides her out.

I finish my bottle of water and grab my phone to see what mess I got myself into. When I see Twitter the hashtag throws me off #mykindaguy.

The team made an official statement, which I know is one that Allison had to type up. It is basically me as a knight in shining amour. It's been retweeted over a thousand times, and the hashtag is now trending. I shake my head and check my email, seeing one from Allison. I scoff while reading it. Sorry my fucking ass. Only reason she's sorry is that she isn't right. I throw my phone down before I send her a simple fuck you email.

I've never cared if someone liked me, spoke about me, or thought I was a thug. I didn't give a shit, but when she looked at me and threw my rap sheet at me without knowing, it burned all the way to my soul. I stood, ignoring her eyes or the look of disgust. The minute I saw Steve, I bounced. I didn't give a shit. It's been two days and she's already getting on my last fucking nerve.

I peel off my shirt and toss it in the basket. I'm probably holding all this pent-up frustrations because I haven't fucked in such a long time. That is what I need, to fuck. I grab my phone, knowing I can have someone here in ten minutes, but the sane part of my brain tells me to put the phone down and fuck it. I toss my phone, closing off my alarm for the next day. No way am I going to work out tomorrow, at least not at the rink. Then I think about it. Fuck her, fuck them, and their condescending shit. I've paid for my mistakes tenfold and I refuse to make them run me off. Not this time.

Tossing and turning all night, the only thing I see when I close my eyes are her eyes. I give up finally at four a.m., get up, and go to the gym. Go in early, get home early. Maybe, just maybe, I won't have to see her. Maybe. I spend three hours on the ice, by myself. In my own zone. I work on my skating, my stick handling, my shooting. By the time I skate off, my body is soaking with sweat.

"You got here early," Luka, the goalie, says to me, putting his bag down.

"Yeah, couldn't sleep so thought I'd come in." I toss my helmet on the top shelf. I peel my jersey off, tossing it into the basket in the middle of the room. I sit down with just my pants on and bend over, taking the tape off.

"Jesus fuck, how much did you grow this summer?" Luca takes in my chest and arms.

"Not that much." I smile at him and toss my tape at him. "Knew you'd be slacking, so I had to pick up the pace."

"Slacking my fucking ass." He gives me the finger and goes out to find the trainer.

I end up in the shower by myself, which suits me just fine. Getting dressed in my workout gear, I throw my hat on and make my way to the kitchen, knowing the food is being cooked by the smell lingering in the halls.

I fill up my plate, a mountain of eggs, sausage, bacon, and toast. I sit down and I'm about to take my first forkful when I hear her voice.

"Hey, I was looking for you."

I don't even bother looking up.

"Well, you found me." I put a forkful of eggs in my mouth.

"I wanted to just say that I'm sorry for jumping the gun yesterday. I should have listened to your side before I said anything." She trails off because my head snaps up and I'm about to tell her to fuck off, but Denise's voice is in my head. *You're the good guy.* I look at her eyes and see that she isn't bright-eyed this morning.

"Forget about it," I finally say. "In the end, you did what you're paid to do."

"I think we got off on the wrong foot."

I laugh at her. Got off on the wrong foot. That's a fucking joke.

"We aren't off to anything. How about this? You stay out of my way and make sure we never have to work together." Much better than telling her to fuck off.

"We work together. We will be traveling together."

I cross my arms.

"We don't need to be friends," I say, taking the last forkful. I ate so fucking fast my stomach is throbbing. "You do your thing. Let me do mine. I won't assume you're always a bitch and you can assume I'm not always an asshole. How's that?" I throw my fork down.

She grinds her teeth together. "Fine." She storms out.

"She is so hot," Ryder says, sitting down next to me with his own plate while I pick up my plate and am just about to walk away when he adds, "What I wouldn't do to get a piece of that."

My plate slams down hard, making everyone look back at us. I lean in close to his ear. "Have some fucking respect. That's your captain's sister."

His face turns a pale white, his head going up and down nodding. I make my way out of the kitchen, vowing to avoid her like the plague.

And for two weeks, it works out perfectly. I know she's around, but I go the other way when I see her, till the first preseason game when I have no choice. It's a home game and we leave tonight right after we face Toronto. I walk into the arena with my bag over my shoulder. I'm texting Denise when I bump into someone. I don't have to look up to know it's her. I smell her. Her hands go up against my chest, the heat of her palms soaking through my shirt.

"Sorry," she says to me and I make the mistake of looking at her. Her tight skirt hugs her like a skin. She pairs it with a see-through white button-up shirt with a silk cami under it. A black tiny belt ties around her waist.

"Yeah, my fault," I say, going around her and walking away from her. I don't have time for this shit now. I walk into the room and look around. Half of the regular team isn't here as they are still lying with the rooster.

Phil and Matthew walk in. They will both be on the ice tonight, but I'm the only one going on the road trip. I dump my bag and get in the zone. We are all dressed and ready to take the ice when Coach Dan comes in with Doug and some of the coaches and my eyes land on Allison. She has put on a jacket now with polka dots. Her blue heels complete the outfit. I shake my head and put my gloves on my stick and listen to them tell us to go out there and have fun, no stupid tricks since it's not a real game, but let's face it, no one wants to lose.

We line up as the music starts and we bounce on our skates, waiting to finally take the ice. This is my year, my fucking time. I just need a chance to prove it.

## ALLISON

It's not even the big opening day game and I'm a nervous wreck. I had to make sure I put on my bra, then I forgot my phone five times. I walk down the hall, trying to shake out the nerves, and run smack into him. Him. There is no need to say his name because we aren't talking about him. Him who is the bane of my existence. Him who I go out of my way to avoid. Him who fucks with me even in my dreams. HIM. I smack into his chest, his hard chest. My hands go up and I feel his heart under my hands.

"Sorry," I mutter, looking up only for him to just say yeah and walk around me. See, asshole. That is why we aren't talking about him.

Now here we are five minutes before they skate on the ice, almost three hours before we can start loading the bus. My first time going away. I have about a million Post-it notes all lined up in my office. I stand here almost in the corner, watching the guys get up and start to walk out to the ice. If I thought they were big before it's nothing like when they are on skates. Matthew walks in front of Phil, who is in front of him. He motions for me to come to him, so I do.

"Squirt, remember that time in peewee when I used to put my glove in your face for good luck?"

"Matthew, I will fucking put Nair in your shampoo if you put that nasty glove in my face," I threaten him while I look up at him and Phil just pushes him ahead.

"Don't worry, squirt, I'll look out for you." He smiles at me.

"Are we not playing a fucking game?" Max walks past us.

"Ignore him, he gets pissy on game day."

"Well, what excuses does he have for every other day?" I ask under my breath.

Phil laughs out loud. "Fuck if I know."

Fans erupt in cheers, so I know the guys are on the ice. I go to my office, making sure all my things are in order for when we check in. No one has crazy demands, but then again the big guns aren't going.

I make my way up to the team lodge, showing them my badge, and then walking in.

"Auntie Allie." My niece Franny runs to me, jumping into my arms, and wrapping her arms around my neck. "You so pretty." She leans closer. "Did you bring lip-gloss?"

I kiss her cheeks. "No, but how about you come to my office after and make me a picture I can put up?"

She nods.

"Where is my little Vivi?" I ask, looking around for my little niece.

"She stayed home because it's too loud," she says and wiggles herself to go down and join her brother Cooper.

"Hey there, my little man, where is the love for your aunt?" I say, bending to hug him. "Did you guys go downstairs and see them skate?"

They both shake their heads. I look over to see my sister-in-law Karrie talking to her father.

"Hey, I'm going to bring the kids down to see Matthew," I say and she nods.

We walk down the hallway, both of them holding my hands, and we go down the stairs to the glass around the boards. Cooper stands near the glass, slapping it when he sees a couple of players he knows and they smirk at him. I lift Franny up and hold her on my hip as I point at

Matthew.

"There is Daddy," I say and she yells Dada, but just then Max skates in front of her.

Cooper slaps the glass, yelling Max's name. He looks at Cooper, gives him a high five on the glass, and then looks over at Franny, who hides in my neck. He winks at her and shakes his fingers, telling her hello. She smiles at him, and I smile at her. My eyes meet his for the first time in two weeks. It's for a split second, a blink of an eye, but it's enough for my stomach to fall. I don't have time to think about anything because Matthew finally comes to the side of the glass where he leans down and points at Cooper and then blows kisses to Franny, the press capturing everything. Both of them are wearing Grant jerseys, so there is no mistaking that these are his, and well, they look exactly like him. Poor kids. The buzzer sounds, telling us that the Zamboni is going to come on, so we make our way back to the lodge where they tell their mother about seeing their daddy.

I take my spot beside Karrie, who has Franny on her lap as Cooper sits with Doug. No doubt telling his grandfather all about his hockey moves.

"So you ready for the travel?" she asks me and I look away from the ice. "No, not even fucking close."

"That's a bad word," Franny says.

"Oops." I put my hands to my lips. "No, I'm not. I have seven backup plans in case the first six mess up. Seven."

"It'll be fine. As long as they have a bed to sleep in, they don't care." She holds a bag of chips in her hand and Franny eats them one at a time. "I got the memo for opening day. You are going all out there this year. I heard you're trying to get Jay Z to come and sing."

I smile. "Well, he did say he bleeds blue, no?" I look over at the bench, seeing the players that aren't starting take their seat. The five starting players get ready. Matthew is center with Phil on one side and Max on the other. They each skate in a circle around their position. The two star defensemen Jamie and Peter are starting also with Luka between the pipes. Toronto looks ready to rumble and Matthew takes his place as the referee is getting ready to drop the puck and then the music dies and the puck hits the ice.

He wins the faceoff right away, knocking it to Phil, who tries to skate around the forward in front of him, but he loses the puck with a poke check. The young Toronto center man jumps over Matthew's stick to intercept the pass, but Max is one step ahead of him, blocking him from even skating forward. Rookie doesn't see Max and literally bounces off him. The whistle blows and the fans are on their feet while Matthew starts arguing with the ref when he wants to call Max for a penalty, but he doesn't do anything because the linesman comes in and explains what happened.

The change shifts and Dan puts on two other people but keeps Max on there. I see Max talk to the rookies that he is playing with. He says something and they all agree and then the next second he loses the face-off, but then Deegan blocks it at the defense line, passing it straight to Max's blade. It lands with a tock you hear echoed through the building. He looks like he's running on the ice, but he's just that fast. He ducks away from the defenseman, going right when he thought he would go left and then just slaps it in from the blue line. Perfectly aligned to land over the goalie's shoulder and bouncing in the net. The fans get on their feet. Max points at the two rookies while they skate to him and celebrate. They all skate to the bench, high-fiving everyone while we stand on our feet and cheer. The rest of the game is the same. Nothing could stop us and we end up winning five to zero, giving Luka his first shout-out.

When the game finishes, Doug helps Karrie carry the kids to the car with promises to meet for lunch as soon as I'm back. I go downstairs, grabbing my two bags, and lugging them to the bus. I'm waiting for the guys to start loading the bus as I update Facebook, Instagram, and Twitter. I look through the photos taken tonight, finding a couple of Max and posting this with his hashtag #MadMax13.

It takes them about an hour to get in the bus. I sit here in the front with my computer on my lap, putting all the pictures on a USB for a later date. I check my watch and see that it is almost eleven-thirty by the time the coach and Max get into the bus. His hair is still wet, but perfectly groomed. The smell of his aftershave lingers to me. He sits across from me next to the coach, puts his earphones in, and watches something on his phone. I close my computer, storing everything for when we arrive at the airport some fifteen minutes later. I get up as soon as the bus stops, or at least I think the bus is stopping only to jerk forward one more time as I stand in the aisle. I'm ready to go crashing through the window, but two hands hold on to my hips, stopping me from moving. I look down to see his fingers while my heart hammers in my chest.

"Maybe you should wait till the door is open before you get up," he says and I just nod, grabbing my bag, and walking off the bus on shaky fucking legs, but the feel of his fingertips are still lingering on me.

Grabbing my bag, I walk to the plane and sit in the first row. I put my bag next to me and fasten my seat belt. The whole team gets on and we are off the ground in fifteen minutes. My eyes burn by the time we get to the hotel lobby and are greeted by the manager on site. Everyone gets their rooms and I wait for everyone to go upstairs before I pick up my bag, signing everything at the front desk, and going to the elevator. The elevator pings and I get ready to go in, but I stop when I see Max coming outside.

"Sorry." He walks past me and I watch him head out of the hotel.

I stand here wondering where the hell he is going when the doors almost squash me as I get into the elevator, press the button for my floor, and then an arm is pushed inside, stopping the doors from closing. Max steps back inside, a brown paper bag in his hand now.

I press six and he doesn't press anything. Great. "Good game tonight." I try to make conversation while he stares ahead. "Or not," I say to myself.

The elevator door opens and I walk out, looking at the signs as he walks around me, heading down the right side. I pray to God I don't have to follow him, but God isn't listening tonight because I follow him, stopping in front of my door. I take the card out and tap it in front of the door. It turns the light green, but I don't make it inside before Max's door shuts, echoing in the hall.

"Good night to you, too, asshole."

## MAX

What the fuck was she still doing in the lobby? When I walked out of the elevator, I was shocked but ignored her by walking by her.

We landed in Philly earlier than I thought and I had my guy bring me his famous cheesesteak. It's tradition and after the start of the season, I don't fuck with tradition.

The whole fucking game I made myself look everywhere but at the lodge I knew she was in. I thought the minute I skated on the ice I would shut off my head and get in the zone like I always do, but then she's there, by the boards with Matthew's kids cheering on the team. I couldn't avoid it when I skated to her side and little Cooper knocked on the glass calling my name, and then Franny fucking burying herself in Allison's neck. I kept chanting in my head, *she hates you and thinks you're trailer park scum*. And it worked. Well, it worked at the beginning till I scored that goal and sat down looking around, my eyes finding her standing up smiling and cheering. Cheering for the team no doubt. I took the bottle, spraying water on my face, and blocking her out. I did my normal routine after the game, except this time the reports were there asking questions about me saving 'a girl' then it got switched to how fast I'm skating this season. I answered everyone and then quickly showered and walked out and onto the bus, and because I was the last on, the only seat left was right across from her. I put my earphones in and watched highlights of the game. Seeing if maybe I could clean up some parts of my play. Then the bus stopped and I knew it wasn't a complete stop, but Allison stood up and I knew the bus was going to move. My hands flew out before I even had a chance to think about it. I'm pretty sure she is going to have fingertip bruises tomorrow because I was squeezing so hard. But just like that, in a blink of an eye, it was over and I dropped my hand so fast you would think someone told me she was covered in acid.

I made sure I was one of the first in the plane heading straight to the back, even though I usually sit in the front so I can be the first one off. Not tonight. Then when the hotel handed out the keys I was the first one to claim a room, going upstairs and dumping everything, then getting a text from Tony, the sub guy.

Now I'm standing in the elevator with a cold hoagie and looking straight ahead. The elevator doors open and I go straight for my door. She isn't my concern. It isn't my problem that she can't find her room. Isn't my problem that she has no idea where she is going. Nope. I scan my card and see her in my peripheral vision. She is right next door. My door closes before she even gets into hers. What the fuck is going on with me?

I toss the hoagie on the bed, pulling off my tie, and undressing. I think about anything but her. I even think about the fucking weather. By the time I slide under the sheets and unwrap the hoagie, it's cold, soggy, and just tastes bitter. I toss it aside and close the lights, leaving the shade open, having the night light come in. I wait for sleep to come and claim me and it does, but she has blue eyes when it does.

The road trip goes off without a hitch. We win the game on the road, but lose the one the next day, so the ride home is a somber one. No one really talks, but everyone is happy to get back to their own bed. I walk off the plane, getting into my car, and making my way back home.

The phone rings when I'm a block away from home. I see it's Denise.

"Hey," I say as soon as the Bluetooth connects me.

"Hey, yourself. I take it you just got back?" she says to me and I hear papers being shuffled in the background.

"Yeah, I just landed five minutes ago. My body is feeling the pain today, must have been that corner hit from Reddick." I park in my parking space.

"I saw that hit and winced a little. How many times I gotta say don't go into the corner?" She laughs and so do I. You can't avoid the corners or you're known as a little bitch pansy. "Anyway, I'm calling to say I got the tickets to opening game. Should I ask how you scored twenty tickets?"

I laugh. "I called in a couple of favors." And I am not lying. I called everyone that I could think of. Plus, I asked a couple of the rookies to donate to a good cause. "You have three weeks to give them away," I say, grabbing my bag, switching off my Bluetooth, and picking up my cell.

"They are already distributed. It was like Christmas morning in the ward. Lots of happy faces," she says and I know she's smiling. "How many more games do you have to play before the official season starts?"

"There are five more games, but I'm not playing in any of them. So till the opening day I get to train and practice."

"Good, get you ready for the big one. Okay, big brother, I have to go. Dinner next week?"

"Yeah," I say, unlocking my door. "Let me know when you want to come by." I dump my bag on the floor and hang up. Stanley comes to the door and goes through my legs, letting me know that she's happy I'm home. "Hey there, girl, did you miss me?" I ask, rubbing her neck and listening to her purr.

I sift through my mail and go through my email discussing my photo shots with my agent and my endorsers. Adidas has just come on board, so I need to do that one soon. My kitchen table has seventeen boxes on it, all from Adidas. Most need to be signed, so I get myself set up and sign all the shit till my hand hurts. When I notice it's past seven p.m., I get up, grab my gym bag, and head to the gym. Parking at the rink, I get out and make my way inside. Because it was a travel day, I know that no one will be there, which is even better that I won't have to wait for someone or have to chit chat.

When I walk into the changing room, I see I'm right. No one is here. Dumping my bag and changing, I walk to the gym and I'm confused that the lights are on. Stepping in, I see blond fucking hair swinging while she uses the fucking elliptical.

"Seriously, what the fuck are you doing here?" I say louder than I had planned to.

Her head looks over and she's wearing another getup, this one no better than the last one, but at least she isn't wearing those crop top thingies.

"I think it's pretty much self-explanatory as to what I'm doing here," she says as she pants out. "But in case you didn't understand, I'm working out."

"Very fucking funny, Allison." I crush the water bottle that I was holding in my hand.

"Listen, after last time with your temper tantrum I decided I would come at night, so here I am." She picks up her pace and her chest heaves faster now.

"Isn't there a gym that you can go to besides this one?" I ask, walking over to the treadmill. Turning it on, I start on a slow jog and she turns off her machine.

"You know what, I've fucking had it with your bullshit. I've tried to ignore it, tried to walk around you, tried to avoid you, and yet you always seem to fuck with me." She puts her hands on her hips.

"Trust me, the last thing I want to do is fuck you," I say, watching her glare at me out of the corner of my eye. The words taste sour in my mouth.

"Well, thank you for making that clear since I was at home doodling your name in hearts." She walks away then turns around. "And for the record, I wouldn't fucking touch you with a ten-foot pole and someone else's fucking hand."

I pick up my pace, turning to see her standing there. "Is that so, princess?" I smirk at her, knowing she probably wouldn't touch me.

"You're an asshole. You know that, right?"

"I've been told, many times." I shrug my shoulders. "Yet here I am." I put the speed a touch higher. "Playing in the same team your brother said I wouldn't last in. Here I am even with all my rap sheets and convictions. So, princess, if you think I lose sleep over the fact that you don't like me, you're sadly fucking mistaken. You're an afterthought." I put my earphones on, letting her know this conversation is over. Pushing my body faster than I want to, I watch her turn and walk away. I run for over an hour. My legs buckle when I get off and walk back to the changing room. I sit down, drinking my bottle of water, and trying to get my breath under control. The scene from before plays in my head on repeat over and over again. I don't even bother showering here. Instead, I hightail it back home where I shower and eat standing in my kitchen alone.

For two weeks, I make sure I'm never at the rink when she is. For two weeks, I avoid everything that is Allison Grant. The only time I can't avoid her is when there is practice, but I come in and get on the ice and off. She travels with the team, so on those days is when I'm at ease. The rest of the time I'm like a ticking time bomb. But today is home opener. Today is the day the season actually starts and I'll be fucking damned if I let her take over my thoughts.

I take out my new blue suit, white button-down shirt, and a royal blue tie. I place a white handkerchief in the pocket, grab my brown shoes, and take a final look in the mirror. Not too shabby for someone over thirty. I make my way over to the arena, calling Denise from the car.

"Where are you?" I ask when I hear a shit-ton of noise in the background.

"We just got to the arena. Max, this place is awesome. Holy shit," she says while I hear kids in the background asking her questions. "Text me when you get here so you can come meet the kids."

"Okay." I hang up. Usually we don't go out front the day of the game, but this year we have been encouraged to be with the fans. I park my car underground and walk in. The camera crews are already here filming, but I have my Ray-Bans on so they can't see my eyes. I walk in, saying hi to a couple of people while I text Denise and she tells me she's at the fake locker room. I make my way to the main level and I'm blown away by the amount of people there so early before the game. It's only three p.m. and it's already half full. I walk through the arena, shaking hands with some fans and posing for selfies.

There are different stations set up all along the way. There is a kiosk with a big sign that says Which Stinger Player Are You? People are in there answering questions before it tells you who you are more like.

I walk more and see a shooting station. Luka is between the pipes as you try and score on him. The kids are all lining up, bouncing to get their shot. When one of them actually scores, there is a huge light on top, flashing red, and the horn blazing.

I take in Ryder and the other rookie Paul as they sign things and pose for pictures. I see Matthew there with his family and his stepfather, Cooper Stone, who is holding his namesake in his arms.

I walk by the DJ station and see that it is none other than Missy Elliott spinning some tunes. While people stop and take a picture of her wearing Matthew's jersey.

I finally see Denise and her kids when I turn the corner. They are standing in a fake dressing room, each kid posing for pictures in their favorite player's stall. Twenty of them all gang up together in my stall with Denise on one side and Allison on the other. I take her in and she looks like she just walked off the catwalk. What the fuck is she wearing? It's a one-piece pantsuit thing, with silver heels. Who comes to a hockey game with heels? I don't have much to think about before Denise spots me and yells my name, "Maxie." She waves her hand in the air and Allison's face goes from smiling to horror. She is holding on to two kids' hands as they all walk toward me.

"This is so amazing. The kids are having a blast," she says, making sure she has everyone with her.

"Hey, guys," I say, crouching down in front of them. "Are you ready for the big game?"

They all answer at the same time, then they shout out questions and jump up and down when the Stinger mascot walks by, so they run to him and the team photographers start with the pictures.

"They look like they are in good spirits," I say, standing here in the middle of Denise and Allison, who watch the kids with the mascot.

"It's been amazing and Allison has been nothing but amazing. She promised the kids they could go backstage right before you guys go on the ice."

I swallow the lump that is in my throat.

"Is that so?" I ask, putting my hands in my pockets.

"Yes," she says curtly, "it is. Denise, it was amazing meeting you." She turns to my sister. "And you can bet I'll be touching base with you next week with ideas." She smiles at my sister. "I'll have Jason find you guys right before and bring you down to the locker room." I watch her walk away, then turn to my sister, who is glaring at me.

"What did you do? Did you sleep with her and not call her?" She folds her hands in front of her.

"Are you fucking crazy? That is Matthew Grant's sister." I don't have to go on when Denise just mouths an O. "Yeah, so that is why she's like she is."

"Well, she was nice to me and so genuine. So…" She looks over at her kids. "She wants to work with me and the hospital." She smiles at the kids and turns her glare back at me. "Don't fuck this up. Be nice."

I roll my eyes at her. "I am nice." I don't even believe it. But I don't have time to think because it's time to go and get dressed. "See you down there." I lean in and kiss her cheek.

"Break a leg," she says to me and I walk away, shaking my head, and thinking of one thing and one thing only. Apologizing to Allison.

## ALLISON

Game fucking day. For two weeks, I've buried myself in my work. I've avoided even going in and working from home and thankfully there was no issue with it. But today my body is on high alert, knowing I have no choice but to see him. When I saw him in the gym that night, I was shocked, that was for sure, but then he spewed that fucking garbage out of his mouth and I never really hated someone more in my life.

So I grab my pantsuit that I bought especially for tonight. A one-piece blue pantsuit. A little lace in the middle of the collar. I pair it with my favorite pair of silver heels. I grab my leather jacket and put it on since it's sleeveless and I'll probably freeze in the arena. I don't have time to think twice when I hear a beep outside. I run down, grabbing my purse, and seeing the two limos pull up. My family is down for the big game. In one limo, there is Matthew and his family and in the other limo is Mom, Dad, Zara, Zoe, and Justin. The driver comes out and opens my door and I slide in.

"Hey, everybody," I say, seeing my mother smile, but my father is scowling. "What happened now?"

My brother pipes in, "Zoe and Zara asked Dad at what age would he think about using a walker since he's old now."

The twins just shrug their shoulders.

"Not something that is a surprise. Last week he went skating and then sat on the bench for forty-five minutes," Zoe chimes in.

"I think it was an hour," Zara says.

"I had a cramp, and I was coaching." He points at them and my mother looks out the window, rolling her lips together to not laugh at him. He points at the twins. "Don't make me bring boot camp back."

Justin laughs now. "Dad, that lasted two days, two. They complained so much I thought you would pull your hair out."

"What did I do?" he says, lifting his hand in the air. "You two are grounded." Now we all laugh, knowing it lasted maybe fifteen minutes.

"It's okay, Dad," Zoe starts and then Zara continues.

"We will still love you when you're hunched over."

They both nod at him.

"That's enough out of you two," Mom says, then turns to Dad. "I will love you even more." She kisses his lips. "Now it's Matthew's big day and Allison has worked nonstop, so you will behave or no Wi-Fi for a month."

They both look at each other and then back at Mom, knowing she is the one who will actually go through with the threat.

We pull up to the arena and I get out.

"Okay, I'm going to go in and make sure everything is okay. I'll catch you all later." Inside I grab my badge and phone and start walking around. It's just two-thirty, but the festivities are already underway. Luckily, Mindy was here this morning guiding things. I walk around checking everything, smiling to myself when a little boy bumps into me.

"Sorry, lady." He puts his glasses back on straight.

A woman comes up to us, holding him to her. "I'm so sorry," she says and I smile at the boy. I look behind her to see that she is with about twenty kids and four adults.

"I'm Allison," I say to the little boy and then the lady. "I'm the PR for the team. Who are all these fans?"

"Hi, I'm Denise and these are some of the patients from Hudson Children's Hospital."

I smile at all the kids. "Hey there, guys." I look back at Denise. "It's so great that you got tickets."

"Yeah, we have a pretty generous donor that always shoots us tickets. I've tried to get in touch with someone about setting up a players' visit day since some of the really sick kids can't venture out due to their immune system being so low."

The wheels are already turning in my head. "That sounds like such a fantastic idea." I look at the kids. "So who is your favorite player?" I ask them and they all answer at the same time, "Max Horton."

I throw my head back and laugh. "Wow, I'm sure he would love to know that," I say sarcastically. "Why don't we go and take a picture in front of his stall?"

"For real?" the little man with the glasses asks.

"Well, we can take a pretend picture here, but how about I sneak you guys down to meet him before the game?" I think about if he doesn't want to do it there are guys down there who will.

They all cheer and start to walk over to the fake locker room. It looks almost real as each stall has the player's name and their equipment. Their jerseys hang proudly.

"Okay, everyone, let's take a group picture and I can post it on the team website. If that is okay?" I ask Denise, who nods as we all pose around Max's name. I smile as they take our picture and then Denise's phone rings and my smile fades the minute I see him. Max, standing there in a perfectly tailored fucking suit, smiling at Denise. Fuck, it's probably his girlfriend. Great.

I can't hear any of the conversation because the thumping of my heart is echoing in my ears. I excuse myself and say bye to the kids. But as I walk away from them, I can't help but feel his eyes on me. I run into Vivienne, who is with Franny. "Hey." I kiss her on both cheeks.

"You look amazing. And is that a look of love?" she asks me as always.

"Um, is the look of love someone who hasn't dated in what is going on fifteen months?" I kid with her, but not really.

"Well, whatever you are doing you look amazing," she says as we walk together back to where my family is.

"Where is Matthew?" I ask.

"He went down to get in the zone," Karrie says while Cooper holds mini Cooper and shows him different things as Franny reaches out to him also.

He takes Franny in his arms also and turns to the twins. "Old my butt." He walks away, having us all laugh.

We spend the rest of the afternoon visiting all the kiosks around the arena. I check Twitter and Facebook and the hashtag #StingerTown is trending with people posting and retweeting.

"There she is." I hear Doug shout loudly. "This." He looks around. "This is exactly why you are so good at your job."

I smile at him. "Well, thank you, but Mindy did help."

He smiles, not willing to argue his point. "I can't wait to see what you do when the cup comes back."

"Let's work on the season first," I tell him and then the lights flicker, telling us it's almost that time. "I have to go and make sure some special guests are taken care of." I walk away, almost speed walking, my feet starting to ache in these heels. Once I make it downstairs, I see that everything is taken care of and Jason is standing by, waiting as the twenty kids walk around the changing room getting their special jersey all signed. They all have Horton jerseys, another thing I made happen. The smiles are worth being nice to the asshole.

Denise sees me and smiles her thanks as I walk away from the room and go to my office where I sit down and take my feet out of my shoes. A knock on the door has me looking up to see Jason.

"Hey, just letting you know that I escorted them to their seats." He smiles at me.

"Thanks, Jason, and do me a favor," I say, grabbing my purse, taking out my credit card. "Whatever they want is on me."

He puts his hands in his pockets. "No need, it's already been taken care of."

I lean back in my chair. "Really, by who?"

"Max makes sure his sister is always taken care of." He leaves the room. Holy shit, Denise is his sister. I shake my head and get up when I hear Coach Dan yell.

"Let's do this." He walks down the hallway past my office.

I get up, grabbing my jacket, and follow in last. Putting my shoulder against the wall, I try and alleviate the sting in my feet.

"Okay, boys, this is it, opening night. Lots of people put a lot of work into tonight. Allison, I've never seen so many happy fans before."

The team claps their hands while Ryder pipes up, "I think I should take you out and thank you for the team." He wiggles his eyebrows at me while Matthew throws his glove straight in his face.

"Dickhead, she's my sister. No way I'm letting your pencil dick near her."

I lean my head down and laugh at Ryder, who puts his hand up and says, "Big dick."

"That's enough, Ryder." Coach laughs and shakes his head. "I like you, kid, but no way will you survive against Matthew."

The whole room laughs and Paul nudges him sideways. "Okay, let's go out there and make our fans proud to wear our colors." He slaps his hands together.

Everyone gets up and starts lining up. They are starting the announcement of the whole team tonight. Everyone lines up according to numbers, except Matthew, Phil, and Max, who go out last.

I get a list of celebrities that are in the crowd. They range from Jerry Seinfeld to Matt Lauer, but nobody is as popular as Cooper Stone, who gets the biggest applause when they show his face on the Jumbotron. Slowly the players skate out one at a time, leaving just the three of them at the end.

"This is it," Matthew says. "Let's make this a good season, yeah?"

Max just looks ahead, nodding, while Phil looks down, bouncing. They introduce Phil, leaving just Max and Matthew.

"You did good, squirt," he says, winking at me, and the crowd starts to chant Mad Max. "Who the fuck started that nickname?" Matthew says and I don't know what to say.

I don't have to say anything because Max just gruffs out, "Your sister, who else?" He runs toward the ice and skates on.

Matthew shakes his head. "He's such an asshole," he says, and the crowd whistles and hollers when they start talking about Matthew, and then my brother is off, doing the same thing Max just did. When they are all out and the national anthem is being sung, I make my way to the lodge where I plan to sit the whole fucking game and eat a plate of nachos and pizza. I get to the lodge and see that the kids are not watching the game, too interested in their iPads.

"Sweetheart," Cooper says as I walk in. "Hands down the best fucking opening day ever." He grabs me sideways around the shoulders, kissing the side of my head.

"Thanks, Dad." I grab him around the waist. "Now if you don't mind, I want a drink and some nachos." I head to the seats just out of the lodge where I sit beside Karrie, and my mother sits on my other side, holding my hand.

My family, my support system. They are everything. As I look around the arena, I try and find Denise. I finally see her and we make eye contact when I wave at her and she tells the kids, who all turn and wave at me. I smile, thinking about how she can be so nice and her brother is the polar opposite. I look back at the ice when I hear the whole arena gasp.

Max is shoving someone in the corner and I see Phil down on the ice. On his knees. I watch the replay on the screen showing the guy goes after Phil, cross checking him and his skates leaving the ice. Max is circling around with a referee, who is holding him back from hitting the culprit. I don't know what they're saying. All I can make out is "Fuck you."

The referee leaves Max and goes to the guy, ushering him to the penalty box while Max spews, "Watch your back, pussy bitch."

We all see Phil get up and shake his head while going to the bench. His wife is standing up and watching everything to make sure he is okay while she cuddles their three-year-old son on her hip.

The first period is a fight to see who is going to score first, but it ends with zero. The second is worse than the first, with penalties coming left and right but resulting in the same score as the first period. At the start of the third period, Cooper stands up.

"It's going to be a blood bath."

And I wish I didn't feel the same way, but as soon as they drop the puck, you see the aggression from both sides. The same guy who knocked Phil out in the first period goes after Max, only to be taken down as Max bends over and he flies over him. Max turns back around and throws his gloves to the ground, whipping his helmet off. He pulls up his sleeves, ready to pounce, but the referee intercepts and kicks the kid off the ice before he really ends up dead. The hits keep coming, harder and harder, the boards echoing louder and louder. It's really becoming uncontrollable. Cooper is bouncing on his feet with every chance they get and running his hand through his hair when they miss. And then the unthinkable happens when Max puts out his stick to poke check the puck, but it trips up the other player and they send him to the penalty box for two minutes. The whole box goes quiet looking at the time left. Two minutes nine seconds. Short-handed for the last two minutes. He goes to the penalty box with his head down and doesn't watch. Instead, he sits there with his head bent the whole time. They get an offside, which has the whistle blowing for a face-off. There are ten seconds left in Max's penalty. His helmet is back on as he stands up.

The other team wins the face-off and brings it back inside the zone with our four players making a box and not giving them a chance to take a shot. It passes from the left defenseman to the right, but Matthew puts out his stick, knocking the puck out of the zone but leaving it clear for Max, who just got out of the box. He gets the puck and goes on a break away with the defenseman right on him, but his legs move faster since they rested for two minutes. He crosses over to the right and moves his body left so the goalie goes down on the left side, but he quickly shoots from the right, having it go right over his pad. The puck lands right in the back of the net while Max kicks up his one leg and throws his hands in the air. It's a beautiful shot. The arena is wild and everyone is on their feet. Matthew gets to him with a smile on his face, and then the others come where they celebrate and the whole arena chants Mad Max as he skates to the bench and high-fives everyone. The puck drops one more time before the buzzer ends and the game is over.

"Okay, peeps, I have to head down. I guess you aren't coming to the after-party?"

Cooper and Mom shake their heads, but Karrie says yes.

"We are going to take the kids back and Karrie is going to follow with Matthew."

"You guys can stay with me and then we can go over tomorrow morning," I suggest and we all walk out. I kiss Mom and Cooper and hug my sisters and brother before walking downstairs, following the loud noise from their locker room. The press is in there, so I know no one is undressed, so I walk in and smile at everyone.

Paul is the first to talk. "How the fuck did you get Jay Z to come and sing?"

"What?" I shrug my shoulders. "By the way, you each have to sign like fifty jerseys for his charity. You're welcome," I say, smiling as he finishes taking off his shirt.

"Congrats, boys. I'll see you all over at the after-party." I wave at everyone and make my way over to the restaurant that is hosting our bunch. I make sure the club that is hosting us is shut down from the public, that all the stuff is ready. I go to the corner, pulling out my laptop that I brought with me, and post some pictures while I wait for them to trickle in. I see the photos from tonight and I was right. The shot of Max celebrating is fucking amazing. I post it right away with his hashtag Mad Max. A couple of the players turn up first along with the wives or sisters. I put my stuff away as the food comes out of the kitchen. Everyone grabs something to drink and the food right away. I see Matthew make his way with Karrie on his arm. "Hey there, superstar." I go to him. "That was quite a game."

"Yeah, it was a good one, better that we won." He looks around to find a table. "I need to get my girl off her feet. They hurt and I heard we are staying over at the brownstone, so you know what this means, kids free sex."

"Eww," I say, pretending to gag. "I put your bed upstairs," I tell them.

"What do you mean?"

"You didn't think I was going to sleep on the mattress that you guys banged on, did you?" I say as we make our way to a table where I sit down and then Vivienne comes in.

"*Mon Dieu.*" My god, she says. "This place is packed with fresh meat." She wiggles her eyebrows and takes off her jacket, showing off her shoulders in the bustier she wears, pushing up her girls.

"You're naked?" Matthew says as he finally gets some food.

"Not yet, but I see a couple who I wouldn't say no to." She points to Ryder. "*Lui.*" Him, she says. "That's the lucky guy tonight." She pushes off from the table and makes her way over to him like a cougar getting her prey.

I put my head back and laugh. "Poor guy never stood a chance," I say and she starts to talk to him. His eyes almost go in the back of his head.

"Okay, folks, that's it for me," I say, grabbing my bag. "My carriage is turning into a pumpkin. And I may or may not burn these fucking shoes." I point to my feet.

"Wait for us. We will come," Karrie says, but I shoo her away.

"You guys never go out. Stay and enjoy adults." I lean in. "Have sex here so you don't have to do it in my house," I tell them and start to make my way to the door to leave. I'm about to push the door open when it's swung open and there stands the man who is the star of tonight. "Sorry," I say, walking around him and away from him as he holds the door. I walk into the street when I hear his voice.

"What the fuck are you doing, Allison?"

I put my hand down. "Well, Max, this," I say, putting up my hand, "means I need a cab."

"Where is your brother? Jesus," he spits out as he walks to me.

"My brother is having a date with his wife and I'm tired. So seeing as I'm a big girl, I said I was going home." I turn around and put my hand up again. But my bag is almost ripped from my hand. "What the fuck is your problem now?" I ask, but he doesn't answer. He just walks across the street with my bag, pressing a button in his hand, and I hear a beep on the black truck parked across the street from the club.

"Get in." He opens the door for me, tossing my bag to the floor as he waits for me to go to the truck.

"You really should take a course in people skills," I say when I get in front of him. His hair is still wet but perfect and he isn't wearing his tie, so I see his smooth skin under his collar. "You fucking suck, by the way."

"Yeah, so I've been told. Now let me do something nice by driving you home."

I cross my hands over my chest. "You wouldn't know nice if it bit you in the fucking ass and dragged you around," I say to him and he laughs.

"You're probably right, but it seems I owe you an apology."

"Really?" I tilt my head to the side. "What makes you think that? Was it when you barked at me? Was it when you told me I was an afterthought or it might have been when—" I don't finish because he puts his hand up.

"Okay, I get it. I think we both got off on the wrong foot. You hate me because of everything that happened with your brother." This time I put my hand up.

"If I'm honest, you both got the raw deal that time." His eyes open in shock. "But ever since I spoke to you that first day on the job, you have been nothing but an asshole."

"You're right."

I turn around on the street as the sound from the club is getting louder and louder. "Holy shit, did Hell just freeze over?"

"Very funny, Allison, now get in the car so I can do the good deed tonight."

He smiles, like really smiles, and it suits him. Way too much.

"Fine, I'll get in, but I'm still not biting on the whole friend thing." I get in and don't get to finish because he closes the door after me and gets in the car.

"How is this?" He starts the car and pulls out. "I'll bring you coffee the next time and promise if I'm an asshole you can throw it on me."

"Will it be a cold coffee or scalding hot?" I watch him drive, one hand on the steering wheel while the other is resting on the middle console.

"You need to be my friend to find out."

I don't say anything. I just look out the window.

"Seriously, thank you for today. What you did for Denise and stuff, it means everything."

"I like your sister. I can see how much you guys differ." I watch him laugh.

"She's been trying to get together with Mindy for three years, but Mindy didn't give her the time of day, yet five minutes with her and she thinks you hang the stars."

"I would do it no matter who she was." I point out.

"Oh, trust me, I know." He turns onto my street. He stops in front of my house and double parks, so I grab my bag. "How about this? You forgive me for being an asshole and I'll forgive you for making me Mad Max."

"So a truce?" I open my door, getting out. "Don't make me sorry, Max. I would hate to have to kill you. I really like Denise."

He throws his head back and laughs. "See you tomorrow, Allison."

## CHAPTER 10
## MAX

My alarm blares out and my hand comes down and smacks it closed. I grumble and turn on my back to stretch, and my body locks in protest. Fuck, the game yesterday was brutal. My body got beat. I blink my eyes open, looking outside at the sun that is already up. I sit up and my back screams at me. I go to the kitchen and start the coffee then I head to the washroom.

I sit down at the island and make my coffee as I search the Internet, finding the picture of me as soon as I scored. It's a great shot and I see Allison already had it up last night. I watch the replays over again twice, seeing what a great play it was.

I think back on last night and making my way to the event. I didn't want to go, but Coach said it wasn't a suggestion, so I was all for going, showing my face, and then leaving. But when I opened the door and Allison walked around me and then went to hail a cab I snapped. She pushes all my buttons, but after seeing her with the kids and seeing how she was so nice to Denise and what she did for them, I knew it was my time to apologize. It would be a miracle if she didn't give me shit about it, but I gave Denise my word, so I bit my tongue and I admit she isn't that bad.

An email from her comes in.

*To: Mad Max*
*From: Perfect Allison*
*Subject: Last Night*
*I woke up wondering if I dreamed that you were a nice guy last night. I would like a hot coffee today. See you at three.*
*Signed*
*Don't make me throw away good coffee.*

I laugh and answer right away.

*To: Perfect Allison*
*From Max I hate Mad Max*
*Subject: Coffee*
*Would you take cream or milk with that? I'll ask for half of it in milk just in case I say something to piss you off. Chances are fifty-fifty. Kidding. I promise to be on my best behavior.*
*Signed*
*Perfect Max*

I close my computer then and go into the room and pack for the away games. We are going for two days back tomorrow after the game. I pack a suit and then my toiletries. Then my phone rings and I see Denise's number.

"Yeah." I put her on speaker while I shave.

"Guess who just called me?" she gushes out.

"I have no idea, and I have an hour to get to the plane, so."

"Okay, fine," she blows out. "Allison," she says with glee. "We set up a date to meet and go over a plan. She has so many ideas. I think it's going to be so good."

I smile. "Happy that you are finally getting a foot in there."

"Me, too." She covers the phone and mumbles something to someone. "I gotta go. Be safe." She disconnects right away.

I finish shaving, packing my stuff, and tossing it in my bag. It's travel day, so we still have to dress professional. I take out my dark blue jeans, with my white button-down and my navy blazer. I make sure there is enough food and I turn on the water around the house for Stanley. "Be good." I walk out to the car. I stop at Starbucks and order a half black coffee with milk and cream on the side. I park my truck at the airport, seeing I'm one of the first ones showing up. As soon as I get out of the car, I see a black car drive up and Allison gets out. Her hair is piled on her head today, glasses cover her eyes. She's wearing black slacks with a white shirt, but her shirt goes low on the chest. A little too low, but she throws a scarf around her neck to block it. She puts her black leather jacket on covering her arms that are sleeveless. She grabs her bags from the trunk and walks over or actually limps over. I walk behind her. "What happened to you?" I say and she stops and turns, looking at me holding two Starbucks cups.

"Silver fucking shoes happened to me. I swear I will never wear those shoes again." She looks at my hands. "Which one is mine?"

"Actually one is half coffee and the other is milk. I also got cream, but it spilt by the car." I point over to the cup on the floor.

"Fine, I forgive you this time." She smiles and takes the cups from me, then looks down at her bags. "Okay, here, hold these till we get on the plane." She tries to hand me the cups back, but I pick up both her bags and walk to the plane.

When we walk up the stairs, I see that the only one there already is Coach. "Hey, Coach." I nod to him, placing her bag on a chair, and then store the other ones overhead. I walk to the side and sit down near the window. I don't know why I'm expecting her to sit next to me, but she sits across from me and leans back, taking off her glasses and closing her eyes. I grab my iPad and start watching *Game of Thrones*. It takes ten minutes before the plane is all ready to go, everyone arriving at the same time. Ryder walks in with glasses covering his eyes, with Matthew following him scowling. I take one earplug out to hear what happened. Matthew stops in front of my chair, throwing his bag under the seat near his sister, and sitting next to her.

"You are not allowed to invite Vivi anywhere," he says while she laughs.

"I'm pretty sure that guy has no idea what hit him. I think I heard him mention marriage." He turns, looking at Ryder, who is already passed out. Making them both laugh. I put my earplug back in my ear and continue watching till we land three hours later. Everyone gets up and I'm about to grab Allison's bag when Matthew asks her, "How many bags do you have?"

She blinks her eyes open. "Two," she says as she stretches. "But I can carry it."

"Shut up, Allison." He grabs the bags and walks on to the waiting bus.

I make her walk in front of me, but I see her scowling and for once, it's not at me. She walks on the bus and huffs, sitting away from Matthew. I sit behind her.

"Stop being a brat. I used to carry Karrie's bag also."

"Well, considering you were having sex with her, you better have carried her bag. But I can carry my own."

"Fine, carry your bags, but Cooper told me to, so you tell him you don't want me to."

She turns her head, looking out the window. Matthew looks at me and shrugs his shoulders.

When we get to the hotel, I grab my key and make my way upstairs. I open my email and find Allison's number, so I call her. She answers right away. "Where are you?" I ask her when I hear loud voices.

"I'm on my way to my room. What floor are you on?" she asks and I hear her breath struggle. "Fucking bags."

"I'm room five oh nine," I say as the phone disconnects. I look down at my phone and see that it says call failed. I get up and I'm going to head out to eat when there is a knock at the door. I open it, expecting one of the guys telling me where we are going to eat, but it's Allison.

"I'm right next door," she says.

"I was waiting to see if we are having a team dinner," I tell her and she stands there.

"No, we are all on our own." She walks away. "All I know is that I'm starving."

"Where are you going?"

"I'm going to sit my ass on my bed and order some pizza, I guess. I have no idea." I hear her still talking as she disappears around the wall. "Without fucking shoes."

I laugh at her and make a plan. Going to her room, I knock and she opens the door. Her scarf is gone and her shirt falls low, too fucking low for my eyes, so I look away. "I'll get pizza for you. What kind do you eat?"

"Um, Hawaiian," she answers and my eyebrows get close together.

"Is that the one with pineapple?" I ask.

"Yes, and ham. Well done," she adds.

"You want it well done so you don't have to taste that pineapple on it. So gross."

"You're being a jerk." She tries to close the door, but my foot stops it. I look as she goes to the corner where there is a desk.

"What are you doing?" I ask her as she starts throwing stuff.

"Making coffee to throw at you."

I laugh at her then back out. "I'll bring you pizza, calm down."

She glares at me and closes the door in my face. I take my phone out and find out the closest pizza place. Walking to the elevator, Phil and Matthew come down talking to each other.

"Where are you going for dinner?" Phil asks me.

"I'm going to get pizza and then come back," I say to them and I don't know why I don't tell them about getting something for Allison.

"Did you ask Aly what she is doing?" Phil asks Matthew, who is texting away on his phone.

"No, she bitched at me for getting her bag. She's over tired and ain't no one needs tired Allison around. Fuck, if we piss her off she may stab one of us or both," he says and I laugh. Matthew looks at me. "I wish I were fucking kidding."

I shake my head and go downstairs, where Ryder is still holding on to his glasses, and Paul is there with Luka. "Are you guys going out to eat?"

Matthew and Phil say yes as I walk out and they decide where to go and eat. Seeing that it's too far to walk, I turn back and go in as the guys are now walking out.

"Did you change your mind?" Phil says while Matthew is still texting.

"Yeah, I just ordered it. It's easier." I walk away from them and their Uber gets there. I go back upstairs and knock on her door. She comes to the door now changed into pjs.

"Where is the pizza?" she asks.

"I'm just letting you know that it's on its way, so I'll bring it to you when it gets here."

"Okay," she says and I walk away to my own room.

I shrug my jacket off and kick off my shoes. Opening my bag, I grab my shorts, putting them on, and I'm unbuttoning my shirt when there is a knock on the door. I go to the door and open it.

"What are you doing?" she asks, taking in my shorts and shirt.

"Um, undressing." I don't know what is going on.

"Everyone left. Matthew just texted me that he is boycotting me."

"Okay. Do you want to come in?" I move to the side as she walks in and the room is pretty much a bed and a desk.

"I'll sit on the chair," she says and I button my shirt back up. "So tell me about Denise and her project."

I'm only too happy to talk about her. "She runs the pediatric oncology at Hudson Children's Hopstial. It's fucking dire and she loses many kids. It's a hard fucking job."

"Oh my God, that's awful." She crosses her feet underneath her and then another knock comes and this time it is the pizza. I already paid, so I just grab the boxes, handing her the small box. "Your over done pineapple pizza," I say and I sit on my bed and open my meat lovers one.

I'm about to take a bite of pizza when her phone rings.

"What do you want?" she answers. "No, I get it you left me to fend for myself. It's all good." She picks a piece of pineapple off and eats it. I almost gag. "I'm by myself." She looks up at me, and I shake my head and take a bite of pizza, but it almost tastes like pineapple, it's so sour in my mouth. "See you tomorrow." She hangs up the phone. "I'm sorry I didn't tell him I was with you. I just didn't know what to say."

"It's fine," I say, chewing, pissed but not sure why. Did I want her to admit she was with me? Do I need that fucking headache? I'm just barely getting along with Matthew these days. The last thing I need is drama my last year here.

"Are you okay?" she asks me and takes a bite of her pizza.

"Yup, just tired," I say, eating another piece.

"Okay, I'll get out of your hair." She closes the pizza box and moves to the door. "See you later." And the door clicks behind her. I throw my piece on the box and unbutton my shirt, tossing it aside when I hear a soft knock. I get up, opening the door. "I forgot my key on the desk," she says and I stand here with my mouth open and I kind of want to cover myself.

"Um," I say, walking to the desk and picking up the blue card. "Here you go."

She grabs it from me, mumbling, "Thank you."

I open the television, click on the sports channel, and watch the highlight from last night's games around the league. My goal made the play of the night. I take a picture and send it to Denise.

*Your brother is a rock star!*

She quickly texts me back.

*Whose feet smell?*

*Asshole.* I laugh and text her back. I'm about to toss my phone when an unknown number shows up.

*I'm sorry about before. It was rude to not tell him. If it were me, I'd be pissed.*

I smile when I see it's from Allison.

*Like I said, not a big deal. I would have probably done the same.*

*So you would denounce me?*

*Denounce you? What the fuck does that mean?*

I wait, seeing the bubble with the three dots come up and then go away and then come up and then go away. I don't know what the fuck is happening, so I put my phone down when I hear another beep.

*Don't buy me coffee tomorrow or if you do make sure it's cold cause I'm throwing it at you.*

I get off my bed, going to her door, and knocking. I'm really not thinking this out, but she opens the door and she looks pissed. "Are you insane? You just left my room and then went and threw all this denounce shit at me. I have no idea what's going on."

"Well, you acted weird the minute I got off the phone, so I thought you were pissed."

"Okay, listen, I have no idea what got into you from the time you left my room some thirty seconds ago and now, but know this, I'm fine." I turn and walk away before I do something stupid. This whole being friends thing is stupid.

I close the door, look at my phone, and close the volume off, then slide into bed. Maybe tomorrow she'll be normal.

## ALLISON

"So let me get this straight, you hate Max. You guys have been insulting each other for a month, and then last night he gives you a ride home and you guys make peace. He buys you your disgusting pizza and you threw in the word denounce?" Karrie says on the phone.

"Just about."

"*Ma fille*." My girl, Vivienne says out loud.

I sit up in bed. "Oh my God," I yell. "I'm on speakerphone."

"It's Vivienne. You don't even want to know what she did last night, or who she did."

"Ryder. I heard all about it." I lie back down.

"Really? Did he say I rocked his world?"

"I don't know what you did to him, Vivienne, but he was in a trance the whole day."

"It's called vagina magic. My vagina has magic powers," she says loudly and does what sounds like a lightning sound. "Anyway, let's talk about your crush on Max."

"I don't have a crush on Max. He's an asshole."

"Okay, let's go with that," Karrie says. "Just leave it at that and don't poke the bear."

"Poke the bear, are we talking anal?" Vivienne says. "I think a man like Max you need to prime first."

"What the hell are you both talking about?" I shout and go to the wall, pressing my ear against it.

"Vivienne, stop with the anal talk." Karrie shushes her. "I'm saying that I think you should get involved with anyone but Max."

"I'm not getting involved with Max," I say quietly, but something hurts in my chest. "Anyway, I have to go. I'm beyond exhausted." I get into bed. "Thank you so much for the girl talk. We should do lunch when I get home. And you know what, I think I need to go on Tinder."

"On Tinder? No," Vivienne says. "Tinder is not for the innocent."

"You need to go to bed and tomorrow will be a new day," Karrie says. "Love you. Be nice to your brother. He got totally offended he couldn't carry your bags."

"I just want him to treat me not like his baby sister and baby me," I say.

"Just please, go with it," Karrie says and then we disconnect.

I turn on my stomach, looking at my phone to see if he texted me, but he didn't. No surprise there. I close my eyes, but all I see is him, his chest—his wide chest. His ink down his arms, the skull at the end of his arm. His last name on the inside of his arm in big scripture. I finally doze off and wake the next day at noon. Holy shit, I get up and start getting ready for the day. It's a skate day at the rink, so I don't need to be there. I only need to be ready to go on the bus at four-thirty. I grab my shampoo and take a nice, long, hot shower, then try to make the hotel room coffee. It doesn't taste half bad, I think while I curl my hair. I take out my navy blue slacks that fit me tight. I grab my baby blue linen button-down shirt, tucking just the front in, and grab my big knitted gray sweater. I roll the sleeves up a bit, grabbing my leopard ballerina flats to make the outfit look dressy. When my phone beeps telling me it's time to head downstairs, I pack up all my stuff and make my way to the door, opening it, and seeing a coffee cup from Starbucks there in the middle. I don't have time to do anything because Max comes out of his room.

"Hey," he says, giving me a once-over and then bending to get the coffee and picking it up for me. "I dropped this off earlier, but you didn't answer."

"Max, listen." I don't get to say anything else because Matthew and Phil walk down the hall. "Hey."

"You look nice," Phil says. "I have a friend who just became single." He doesn't say anything else before Matthew pushes him.

"You don't get to set my sister up. She's a child."

"She's twenty-three," Max says.

"No one asked you," Matthew says between his teeth while Phil laughs and then Max laughs also. "You want me to set your sister up with his friend?" he asks Max.

"Yes, please do. At least she has a chance at being happy," Max says, walking into the elevator first when it stops on our floor.

"Well, no one is dating my sister," he shouts in the small space as Luka, Ryder, and Paul get into the elevator.

"I'd date her," Paul says, winking at me, and all I do is roll my eyes.

"Thanks, Paul, but I'll be happy to say I'm not dating anyone."

Ryder is the one to talk. "You should go on Tinder."

"Fuck," Matthew says, throwing his head back, and growling out while the guys laugh at him.

I walk out of the elevator with Max at my back. His hand goes to the base of my back and ushers me out. The touch is almost electric, but by the time I turn my head to the side to see, he's already in front of me.

I wait in line as the guys drop their bags under the bus. By the time I get on the bus, the two coaches are sitting in the front seat going over something on their iPads, and across from them is Max. The seat beside him is empty, so I sit down. He's listening to something on his phone, so I peek over and shake my head, seeing he's watching *Game of Thrones*. I don't bother taking my stuff out since it's a short ride to the arena. I'm the first one out of the bus and I grab my bag, waiting to see where to go.

Once inside I walk down the hall looking for a bathroom, when I see two guys I don't know walking down the hall. They both smile at me. I'm about to walk away when I hear one of them.

"Now that's a fine piece of ass."

I roll my eyes and am continuing to walk away when I hear.

"I'll break your fucking teeth."

So I turn around to see it's Max who is still dressed in his suit with his phone in his hand.

"What's it to you, Horton?" the smaller of the two says.

"It's nothing to me," he says and then turns to yell. "Matthew, is it a problem that Duke and Harlot think your sister is a fine piece of ass?"

I turn around mortified as Matthew steps out of the room. "Like she would touch you guys, you fucking wish."

One of them turns around and looks at me. "Oh, she would totally touch me, and I'd love every fucking second of it."

Max starts to advance with Matthew and Phil jumps in front of them. "Okay, this has been fun, but move along."

They both laugh and walk around Matthew and Max, who turn and watch them walk away.

"You shouldn't be walking around the hallways if no one knows who you are," Max says, walking away, shaking his head.

"He's right," Matthew says, also walking away.

I storm to the room and some of the guys are already undressing and don't even bother covering up.

"I was going to the bathroom. How is this my fault? You guys made a big deal for nothing." I leave the room and finally go to the bathroom. I spend the rest of the game in the office they provide me with, watching the game on the screen.

Max is targeted right away by the tall one from before, who I see is Duke. He laughs in his face when the guy tries to push him. It must burn even more when we take the victory 3-2.

By the time the plane touches down everyone is quiet and heading to their car. I pull out my phone when Matthew says, "How're you getting home?"

"I'm calling an Uber," I say, opening my app.

"You're not taking a fucking Uber at two-thirty in the morning, Allison." He curses at me and turns. "Get in, I'll drive you home."

"I'll take her." I hear Max from behind me. "It's on my way."

"Fine," Matthew says and starts to get in his car. "I'm calling Cooper and he is going to buy you a car," he threatens and then slaps his head. "You don't even have a valid license."

"I get it back in seven months," I counter. I seem to have a heavy foot, a very heavy foot, according to all the speeding tickets and loss of my licesnse. I walk over to Max's truck and he laughs at me. I put my bag in the backseat, getting in, and buckling up. "It's getting cold now," I say to him, blowing hot air on my hands.

"I'm just happy for the rest of the month we only go away once," Max says, making his way over to my house.

"Yeah, but we head out every second week in November," I tell him, trying to remember the schedule. "Can I ask you something? What do you guys say to each other on the ice? I kept trying to read the lips, but I couldn't make it out. I mean, with Matthew I know it's fuck and fuck and dick and sometimes blow me."

Max laughs out loud. "That is pretty much what we all say. Once in a while, it'll be like I fucked your sister last night. Mothers are off the table."

"Really, so it's a rule that you guys don't go after each other's mother, but sisters are fair game?" I ask.

"Pretty much," he says and I look out of the window. When we turn on my street, he pulls over at the curb and gets out to come around while I take my bags out. "You need help with that?" He holds the door and I walk away.

"No, I should be good. Thanks for the lift, Max."

I hear one car door close and then I wait for the other while I get my key out, but I don't hear anything. I turn around to see him standing there on the sidewalk watching me. "What's the matter?" I ask, confused, as I locate my key.

"Just making sure you get inside." He crosses his arms.

"Oh my gosh, I'm fine, go."

"Get inside, Allison," he says to me and I know not to argue with him, so I open the door and go in, turning around to wave at him as he walks around the truck, getting in, and taking off.

I fall into bed, curling up into a ball as I fall into a fitful sleep. The next day I check the schedule and I see it's a skate day for the players. I'm about to call Denise to discuss my plan that I ran by Doug. My phone rings with a weird number.

"Hello."

"Hey, Allison, it's Charles Power from Limitless Photos."

"Hey, Charles," I say, pouring myself some orange juice.

"We have a situation. We got all the photos and videos from the photo shoot at the beginning of September, but we can't seem to locate anything for Max. No video and no extra pictures."

"What do you mean nothing? He was there," I say, remembering full well he was there.

"Yeah, I don't know if we are missing a roll of film. This has never happened to me before."

"We need those pictures for the website as well as the video. Let me call him and fix a time that is best for you guys."

"Perfect, thank you," he says and disconnects.

I pull up my texts on my phone, clicking phone next to his name.

He answers right away. "Yeah."

"Hey, it's Aly," I start.

"I know who it is, Allison, I have caller ID."

"Okay, so Charles just called me and he lost your roll of film that they took at photo day. So now we need to reschedule a day to do it again."

"Well, you have my schedule. I didn't add anything else in," he says and I pull up his schedule and see that he is open except for game days.

"How is this Sunday? I know there is a game on Saturday night, but if we do it in the afternoon…"

"I don't book anything on Sundays," he says and I hear water running in the background. "Let's do Monday."

"Yes, that looks good. Okay, I'll fix it with him and then email you the details," I say, then disconnect, call back Charles, and set it up for Monday morning at ten a.m. After I confirm with both of them I'm about to go and get myself something to eat when my phone rings. This time it's Max.

"Yes," I say, opening the fridge and noticing I need to go to the store since I'll be home most of the month.

"I'm leaving in fifteen to go to the rink."

"Okay." Not sure why he's telling me this.

"You need a lift?" he asks, his voice going almost soft.

"I wasn't going in today," I tell him as I check my watch. "It's almost noon."

"Yeah, I know. I was going to go in and just work out a bit," he tells me. "Okay, talk later." He doesn't give me a chance to say anything else when he hangs up.

"What the heck was that all about?" I shake my head, confused on what the fuck just happened.

## MAX

What the fuck did I just call her for and offer her a ride? I'm obviously losing my mind. Maybe I have a brain tumor, so I call Denise, who doesn't answer, so I leave her a voice mail.

"Hey, when you get a brain tumor do you do stupid things and things you would never do? Call me back," I say and disconnect.

I pick my stuff up and head out to the rink. There's nothing like a skating session and workout session. For the next three hours, I skate hard with Alex, Andre, Brendan, and David. We go through plays that Coach makes us do and at the end of it, I'm dripping with sweat as I sit down and drink Gatorade. By the time I walk back into my apartment it's almost seven. I go to the kitchen, taking out stuff to make my supper as Stanley comes out of hiding. I'm cutting up the vegetables when my phone rings and I see it's Allison. I stop midair, not knowing if I should answer or not. It seems my brain doesn't think as fast as my fingers because I press talk and then put her on speaker.

"Yeah," I say, continuing to prepare my veggies.

"I've just spent the last three hours trying to watch *Game of Thrones* and I still don't get the fuss."

I laugh. "Why are you watching it then?" I ask her as I wash off my hands and grab a pan to fry them in.

"I saw you watching it on the bus and every Monday morning my Facebook feed is filled with talks of how this is the best show ever and yet I'm thinking did he just fuck his sister?"

"So, you see it on my phone and want to watch it. Good thing I wasn't watching gay porn." I laugh, turning the stove on.

"Very funny. But honestly, why is this so popular?"

"Because it's fucking good," I tell her, tossing the veggies in the pan. "I don't think I can really explain it. The storylines all intertwine, and which other show is badass enough to kill off the popular people?" I say as the veggies start sizzling.

"I just don't get it, really. Okay, fine, I'll try another couple of episodes and let you know."

I laugh at her. "Okay. Have a nice night."

"Well, I guess that depends on the rest of the episodes. I'll let you know." She hangs up, and two seconds later calls back again. "I'm going in tomorrow morning."

I look at the phone. "Okay."

"Are you?" she asks me and I stand here and wonder why. "I just thought if you are and I'm on the way, you would pick me up, but no biggie," she says, speed talking. "I'll just Uber it. Later." She hangs up without giving me a chance, so I call her back and it goes to voice mail.

"I'll pick you up at nine," I say on her voice mail.

She only answers an hour later with a text while I'm signing shirts for Denise.

***If it isn't going out of your way that would be great.***
***See you then.***

I answer, signing the last shirt. I close up, going to my room, and watching television, or the television watches me because when my alarm rings the next day the television is still on and the remote is on the floor. I grab a pair of sweats and a T-shirt, throwing a sweater on as I walk out the door, adjusting my cap. Once in the car I take off my sweatshirt, seeing it's too warm outside. I make a run to get coffee.

When I make it to Allison's I park in front again and text her I'm here. I wait five minutes and nothing happens, so I get out and go to the door, ringing the bell. Once, twice. I'm about to ring it a third time when I see her running to the door and opening it.

"I'm so sorry. I overslept. My fucking phone died in the middle of the night even when it was on the charger." She turns around and runs up the stairs, and I watch her ass shake.

I have no idea what she is wearing, but my cock has taken full notice. It's like a one-piece booty short outfit, with long sleeves.

"Give me ten minutes I'll be ready!" she yells from somewhere upstairs, then comes out, leaning down. "You can wait in the kitchen if you want or the living room."

I don't answer her and I don't move from the spot at the door. I look down at my cock and scold him. "She's in the no fly zone, buddy." He twitches on his own, basically saying "fair game."

She comes downstairs five minutes later, wearing tight jeans and a T-shirt.

"Did you brush your teeth?" I ask her as she puts on her shoes. She looks over and shows me her clean smile.

"It's the only thing I did. That and deodorant." She ties up her hair in a messy bun. She runs to get her bag and comes back in with her jacket over her arm. "Done."

I shake my head and laugh at her as we walk down to the truck. As soon as she gets in, she sees the coffee.

"Oh my God," she moans. "Lifesaver."

And with the moan, my cock is stirring again. I close my eyes and picture a bat with nails aiming for my junk. We walk in together and each go our own way and for the next six hours I'm busy with practice and working out. I'm walking out of the shower when I grab my phone as I sit down on my bench. I have a couple of texts, one from Denise, another from Steve, and another one from Allison.

I read Denise's first.

**Who told you that you have a brain tumor??**

I laugh and then read Steve's.

**Finally got the tickets to the game Saturday. See you there.**

I answer him back right away.

***Great, see you then.*** I press send when another text comes from Shannon. Shannon is, well, there is no easy way to say this. She is my fuck buddy. We get together once in a while, but it's been over six months since she texted me. Last time she was dating someone. I open her text.

***Hey, it's been a while. Want to get together? I'm free.***

She adds that she's free because she knows I don't fuck with someone who is taken.

***How's Saturday?*** I answer. This is good. This is what I need to let loose.

My next is from Allison and the hair on my neck goes up and my stomach fills with acid. Why the fuck do I feel guilty?

***I'll be in my office till about six, so if you're still here let me know. I forgot my jacket in your car.***

I look at the phone and see it's five-thirty, so I answer her.

***Be there in twenty.***

And I make it there in fifteen as she sits behind her desk, typing away on her computer. "Hey," I say, sitting in the chair in front of her desk, placing my phone and keys on the desk since my shorts have no pockets.

"Hey there. Good day?" she asks, looking up.

"Yes, great, you?"

"I had the best day ever. I actually confirmed our Christmas party and charity event."

I tilt my head back. "Great. I'm so excited," I say and then realize I forgot my wallet. "I forgot my wallet." I get up and walk back to the locker room. It's right there on the top shelf in my locker, so I grab it and say bye to the guys again.

I walk in as Allison is closing down her computer. My phone buzzes right near her and I look down at the same time she does and Shannon's name flashes.

***I can't wait to see you Saturday. I need to let off some steam.*** Followed with the kiss emoji.

I grab the phone right away, but it's too late because she pretty much read it all. "Um, did you need a ride?" I watch her stumble with her computer and her charger.

"No, I have plans. I just need my jacket." She doesn't look up at me and my stomach hurts.

"I'll go get it and bring it to you," I say, walking out and going to the car to get her jacket. Holding it in my hand and walking back, my phone buzzes again. This time it's Allison.

**Had to rush out. Just leave the jacket in my office.**

I tilt my head back and close my eyes. Walking back into the arena and straight to her office, I see that the light is still on, but she's gone. I put the jacket on the chair that I was just sitting in. Placing it down gently, I see two frames on her desk. I pick up one and it's a picture of her with her family. I'm looking at her smile when Matthew comes in.

"Where the fuck is Aly? She just cancelled dinner on us."

I shrug my shoulders, putting down the frame. "No clue. She forgot her jacket, so I brought it back," I say, not adding in that it was from this morning as I walk past him and out. I take my phone and see that Shannon's text is still there along with Allison's.

I text Allison first.

**Your brother is looking for you.**

I press send, waiting. And then I text Shannon.

**Sorry, something came up. Maybe another time.**

Then I toss my phone on the seat and make my way home. Allison never texts me back and the next day she is nowhere to be found. The light in her office stays off the whole day. I know that she has to turn up sometime. The next day is game day, so I know I'm going to see her, but little do I know that it's for a two-second period, and as soon as the game is over, she's gone. I pass by her house on the way home. It's out of my way, but my car just goes there. The house is pitch-black.

I go to the rink early on Saturday, knowing for sure she is going to be there and I'm about to enter her office when I hear her.

"Come on, Matthew, you need to get me tickets."

"I don't have any tickets. You have just as much pull as I do. Why don't you just call the PR that is taking care of the tour?"

"I can't call Ed Sheeran and say, hey, can I have tickets."

I walk away, not sure I want to go in there when Matthew is there, but I know by the end of the night we will be having a conversation.

ALLISON

*This is my girlfriend Shannon.*

My eyes blink open, his voice still in my mind like the dream. I was so stupid to think he wasn't taken. So, so stupid. I turn on my side, thinking about the moment I saw the text and his hand shot out grabbing it. All I could do was blink. My mouth had gone dry, so dry, and my nose started to burn. I knew that if I didn't leave fast it would not be good for anyone.

Okay, fine, I have a crush on Max Horton. Who the fuck doesn't? Okay, I can name a couple of people who don't, but once you get past the big chip on his shoulder, you have someone who is genuine, kind, funny-ish, and fucking hot.

I've avoided going to the arena if I don't have to be there. But on game day, I have no choice, so I show up, do my job, stay out of the way, and take off as soon as I can. But Saturday games are impossible, especially tonight, which we deemed family night. I roll over as I hear my phone ring and see it's Vivienne.

"*Putin.*" Slut, she says in French and I laugh.

"Yes, my leader."

And she laughs. "You need to get us tickets to Ed Sheeran. He is coming next month and tickets are sold out."

"How the hell am I supposed to get tickets?"

"Don't you work for the company?"

"Yes, but I don't do the entertainment side of it. I can ask, though."

"*Quel est le problème?*" What's the matter, she asks right away.

"Nothing, why?"

"You sound different, sad." She picks up right away. "Do we need to bury a body?"

I laugh at her. She would be the first one I would actually call if I had to bury a body. "No. It's really nothing. I'm just tired." I turn in bed and then get up, walking downstairs. "I need to get my schedule for next month done."

"*D'accord.*" Okay, she says. "*Je te verrai ce soir.*" I'll see you tonight, she says and waits for me to say okay before disconnecting.

I sit at the island, picking at two pieces of toast, and drinking my coffee. I check and see that Charles confirmed for Monday morning. I forward it to Max and close it down. My phone rings and I breathe out when I see it's Karrie.

"What's the matter?" she says as soon as I answer.

"Jesus." I laugh. "Nothing, I'm just tired."

"I don't believe you. You're the fucking energizer bunny."

I blow out a breath and finally cave. "I think Max is dating someone."

She laughs out. "As if it's just one person. He was the biggest whore of life a couple of years ago. We had bets going to see how long it would take for his dick to fall off."

"Who won?" I ask and close my eyes, trying to make the nausea go away.

"No one."

"Anyway, it's stupid. I'm a kid and he's, well, he's Max."

"Honey," she says, whispering, "you aren't a kid. You're a woman who likes a man."

"If you do the whole *Notting Hill* scene I'm hanging up."

She laughs out. "I was not going to do that. Hey, how about you come back home with us tonight, spend the day with us?"

"Yeah, I'd like that. Actually, I was hoping to call you later this week, but now that I have you on the phone I'm working with your father on a special project and I'd love the help of the captain's wife."

"Oh, dear," she says, breathing out. "I guess I have no choice, right? Fucking guy for being so good."

"Oh, yeah, baby." I hear Matthew in the background. "You telling Vivienne about the special treat I gave you last night?"

"Ewwww," I say at the same time that Karrie says, "It's your sister."

"I'm going to be sick." I grab my stomach.

"Okay, so sign me up to whatever. What is it for anyway?"

"Kids pediatric oncology."

"Oh my God," she gasps. "We will donate whatever you want. Do whatever you need."

I smile. "Perfect, we will talk about it tonight." Going into my closet, I look at what to wear.

Once I pick out my outfit, I go about getting ready. I don't know why I spend so much time getting ready today. I do my hair almost perfect, and my makeup is on point. I slide my legs into my gray slacks that reach just above my ankle. I grab the cream long-sleeved chiffon top with the ruffle down the front. Tucking it in, I grab a gold belt to finish the look. I grab my gray heels and put some gold bracelets on. The Uber arrives at exactly four and it's past four-thirty when I walk in. I go straight to my office with my overnight bag. Dumping everything in the chair that still has my leather jacket, I contemplate throwing it out.

I shake my head and sit down, opening up all my programs to get the schedule for tonight, when there is a knock on the door. My heart skips a beat, but it's for nothing because it's just Matthew.

"You're coming home with me tonight?" he asks. "You think you can drive back with Karrie for me?"

I lean back in my chair. "Sure, but I need a favor."

"Oh, fuck, last time you did that I was posing for pictures with a chicken." He points at me. "What do you want?"

"I need you to get me Ed Sheeran tickets," I ask, putting my hands together.

"How the fuck am I supposed to do that?"

"Come on, Matthew, you need to get me tickets."

"I don't have any tickets. You have just as much pull as I do. Why don't you just call the PR that is taking care of the tour?"

"I can't call Ed Sheeran and say, hey, can I have tickets." I throw my hands up.

"Sure you can. Call Mindy and ask her."

"I did that already, but she doesn't really like me," I say, lying out of my ass.

"So buy them from a scalper."

I gasp. "That's illegal."

"Well, then I guess you're shit out of luck, considering I don't know Ed Sheeran nor do I have tickets."

"Fine." I roll my eyes. "Get out of here then."

I get up, follow him outside, and walk into Doug, who leans down and kisses my cheek.

"There she is, the one I need to see," he says, looking at me.

I smile at him. "Just the man I need to see," I say as Matthew walks away.

"I take it you got my email," I ask him as we walk back to my office and he takes a seat in the chair.

"I did. I have to say I don't think we've ever done something like this."

"I know. But why not? I know that the Christmas party is usually a family affair, but what if we invited the season ticket holders and some of the big stars who attend the games? Imagine the money that would bring in and the kids it could help."

"I agree and I'm sure the guys will want to help in all that."

"I want each player to adopt a family," I say and Doug looks at me. "We will cap it, of course, unless the player wants to give more."

"I love the idea. When is the visit scheduled for?"

"Beginning of December," I say to him, thinking about yesterday when I told Denise what I was planning on doing. She was overwhelmed.

"Perfect, count me in," he says, getting up. "Is everything set for tonight?" He asks about the party he has set up for afterward.

"Yes, and everyone has said they will be there," I say, thinking of Max and his answer of three people.

"You're good." He walks away, winking. The rest of the night goes by fast. I'm on the phone with the restaurant and finalizing all the little hiccups that come at the last minute.

I bring my bag down to the car, put it in Karrie's car, and walk in as soon as Max walks off the ice with blood pouring down his face. "Oh my God." I shriek and my hand goes to my mouth.

"It's all good, Allison," he says and my heart can't get under control. "It's just a cut." He walks into the room with the doctor and I walk to the door, but the nurse closes it in my face. I turn, looking at the rest of the guys as they walk in.

"What the fuck happened to Max?" I ask Phil, who laughs. "Sherry told him that he fucked his mother last night, so Max knocked him out."

"Idiot," I say to everyone and walk out, going to the after party. When I get to the club I walk in and you have team jerseys hanging everywhere. Tables are set up everywhere with some food in the middle. I look around once and then people start coming in. Karrie arrives with her father.

"This looks so cool," she says, looking around and finally sees the pictures I had posted all around of different players with their family members. "Love this."

Slowly the players trickle in and they introduce me to all their family members. I won't remember tomorrow. I have a water bottle in my hand, but the alcohol is flowing freely. I turn around to go and sit with my family when I see Max walk in. Our eyes meet as he looks around and raises his hand to say hi. I raise my hand and am not sure if I should go to him or not, but then I see him look down and point at me and I see it's Denise. I smile big and make my way to her.

"Hey," I say, hugging her, and she hugs me back big.

"This is amazing," she says. "This is my friend Steve. Steve, this is Allison."

I shake his hand and he looks at me.

"You're the guardian angel?" he says, and I smile and blink. "It's all we hear about."

I move my hand, brushing away the compliment.

I look up at Max and he stares at me. "You look like you got your ass handed to you." I fold my arms. "You have a photo shoot on Monday. How the hell are we going to cover up the black eye?"

"Maybe it'll be a selling point," Steve says. "Badass Mad Max."

"That fucking hashtag." He smiles and a couple of waitresses walk by and smile at him. "Is it seating anywhere?" he asks me and I nod.

I look over and see Karrie. "Hey, Denise, I know it's not business, but I would love to introduce you to my sister-in-law, who is going to be helping me out. If you don't mind."

She looks at Max, who nods. "I'd love to."

I smile and turn around to walk to the table in the back where I introduce Karrie to Denise. They hit it off right away and she sits with them as they make room for them. I sit down and Steve sits on one side while Max sits on the other side. Steve turns to make conversation with me and I watch Max dodge about six girls who walk up to them to take pictures and have him sign stuff. Matthew turns and starts asking Steve questions, so I turn and look at Max, who is looking around.

"Looking for your date?" I ask and I don't know why I do it.

His eyebrows pinch together. "No date, Allison."

I just nod and I'm about to turn away. "What time is it on Monday?"

"Ten," I say

"I'll swing by and get you," he says quietly.

"I'm not coming," I tell him.

"Then I'm not going," he counters. "So you better cancel or change your schedule." He stretches his hands out, placing them on my chair, his hand touching my back. It's a simple thing that has happened with other men a thousand times before, but it's different with him.

"You don't need me there," I counter and he shrugs his shoulders. "I wasn't even there when you did it the first time."

"Allison, it's pretty much either you come or I'm not going."

"Such a fucking princess," I say.

He smiles and laughs. He doesn't move from beside me all night long, and I don't move either till Karrie gets up.

"If we don't leave now we are going to get home after the sun comes up."

"You're right," I say, getting up and standing next to him as he still sits. "I gotta go."

"Where are you going?" he asks, looking around as Matthew and Karrie start making the rounds to say goodbye.

"I'm going to Long Island since we're off tomorrow. I'm going to have a family day."

He nods and I walk around him and say bye to Denise and Steve.

"I'll call you next week," I tell her.

"Yes, tomorrow is the big breakfast at the hospital, so I will be unavailable."

"What is the big breakfast?" I ask.

"Max and a couple of players are coming by and serving breakfast for the kids. They love it." I turn to look at Max, who is just staring at me.

I get in the car with Karrie and we follow Matthew all the way to their house, falling into bed at almost four a.m. My dreams that night aren't of Max and his girlfriend. They're of Max and his smile.

## MAX

"Okay, how about you look over here over your shoulder?" Charles, the photographer, says while he shoots me standing on a stool because he's that much shorter than me. I'm dressed in my gear, minus my jersey. But my mind isn't on the fucking guy. It's on his assistant, Rico Suave, there in the corner chatting it up with Allison.

The Sunday breakfast went off without a hitch. We were all tired as hell that day, but the guys showed up and smiled big. I owe them big time. That night I texted Allison.

*Should I call you tomorrow to make sure you're up or just show up?*
*I don't really have to go.*
*Neither do I.*
*It's your job. I need the pictures.*
*I don't care. I'm not going if you're not there.*
*You better bring me coffee. I'm exhausted.*
*See you later, sunshine.*

Then I pulled up and she was sitting on the steps wearing another pair of skintight jeans that were too fucking tight and a big gray knitted sweater folded up at the wrists and khaki running shoes. She came down the stairs, her sunglasses hiding her eyes.

"I'm beyond exhausted," she said, buckling her seat belt. Then she took the coffee that was waiting for her, smelling it before taking a sip. "Heaven."

"I thought Sunday was a rest day?" I asked her as she took another sip of coffee.

"You would think, but little Cooper, Vivi, and Franny wanted to see if I would wake up when they pulled my eyelid up." She shook her head, "Newsflash, you do."

I laughed at her and proceeded to the rink as she filled me in with stories about her nieces and nephew. We walked in together and she told me to meet her in her office. When I took off my glasses, I winced a bit, thinking. Fuck, it was tight. It was also a dark purple. I got dressed and made my way to her office and she was talking to a short guy when she looked up and gasped.

"Oh my God." She came over and touched my face for the first time ever. Her touch was exactly how I thought it would be. Soft, like an angel.

"It's okay," Charles said. "We can Photoshop that. Trust me, you'll still look big and tough."

So Charles and Allison talked about everything that she needed from him when his assistant finished bringing in his equipment and introduced himself to Allison as Christian. What a pussy name, I thought.

So for the last three hours I've watched him blatantly flirt with her and she just laughs at him and touches him. I'm going to break his fucking hand if he tries to touch her hair one more time.

"Okay, so one more time and try to smile," Charles says, frustrated with the scowl that I've had on my face. "Allison," he calls her and she comes over, folding her arms over her chest. "Does he do anything but scowl?"

She looks at Charles and then at me. "Nope, it's his face. I don't think I actually ever saw his teeth." She points at me and I turn my gloves up and give her the finger. She walks over to me. "You ticklish?"

she asks and I glare at her. "I do that to my niece when she doesn't want to smile. I usually tickle her belly." She brings both hands up and bends her fingers. Her short nails are painted a soft white color.

"If you even try I'm going to shove my hand in your face," I tell her, holding up my gloved hand. "It's still a bit wet from Saturday." I lean forward, snatching her wrist, and she shrieks loudly. Pulling her to me and wrapping my arm around her waist as she bends over, laughing to get away from me. "Here, Charles, a big smile." I smile and Allison moves sideways and turns to look up at me, laughing.

"You stink," she says, standing up in front of me, and I loosen my hold on her as she puts her hands on my arm. She reaches me under my chin with my shades on.

"Look this way," Charles says, snapping pictures of us. "Christian, take the stool to her." He gets off the stool and Christian rushes over to bring it to her. "Now stand on it and put one hand on your hip and the other on his shoulder." She complies. "Perfect, now, Max, turn and look at her scowling."

I roll my eyes, looking at her, while she turns and looks at me, squishing her nose.

"You really need to spray your shit," she whispers.

I lean closer to her. "If you say it one more time I'm going to put them in your bed." I tap her nose with my glove and then she tilts her head back and laughs. All the while Charles is taking pictures.

"Okay, perfect, we are done," he finally says and I walk toward the changing room, turning right before I disappear.

"I'm going to take a shower. I'll be out in ten."

She nods at me, looking at the pictures on Charles's camera

When I come out of the shower exactly fifteen minutes later, I walk to her office and see that she is on her computer doing something and I don't have to ask her what because I get the email.

*To: Best Team in the World*
*From: The best PR girl you'll ever have*
*Subject: Major FAVOR also not a request*
*I have joined forces with Denise Horton who runs the pediatric*

oncology at Hudson Children's Hospital in Brooklyn. We will be assisting her with the following.

*Meet the players day is scheduled November 12. If you notice it is also a travel day. We will travel there later than scheduled. So please make appropriate changes.*

*We will be having a Christmas Wonderland Auction. This will take place on Saturday, December 2. It's mandatory and it will be a black tie event. I will be sending another email in detail about this event.*

*Adopt a family. Each player is going to be adopting a family this year and a list will be given to each of you as suggestions. AGAIN, IT'S MANDATORY (I KNOW HOW MUCH YOU ALL MAKE. DON'T BE CHEAP ASSES).*

*Finally, since we are playing New Year's Day in Buffalo I have rented out the ballroom at the hotel. The party finishes at 12:01. It's also a dry party.*

*That's it for now. See you guys next week.*
*GO, STINGERS, GO*

"You really don't mess around," I say as I finish reading her email.

"It's something that I feel strongly about, so I'm going to do anything I can."

I don't say anything. Instead, I just nod as she closes her laptop and packs it up. We walk out together; no one really paying any attention and no one is there. It's a rest day. Once we get in the car, I do something I know I might regret. I go straight to my loft. "Where are we going?"

"Home. I'm going to cook for you," I tell her, focusing on the road. "Did you have plans with Fabio back there?"

She turns her back to the door. "I did, actually. Is Shannon joining us?"

"Shannon is a friend."

"You mean fuck buddy," she counters and I turn to look at her. "Is that the wrong term?"

I shake my head, not willing to have this conversation.

"You eat salmon?" I ask her and she hums yes.

We don't say anything else until I park and we walk up the industrial stairs to my fifth floor. The door is still the original big brass door. I unlock it and open the door for her to walk in and I hear her gasp.

"I love this." She walks into my open floor plan loft.

I toss my keys on the wooden island in the corner that is the kitchen, opening the fridge, and taking the things out to prepare. "You can go and watch television if you want," I tell her as I place things on the island and she walks around to the stool.

"No, I'm good here." She sits down and then leans sideways. "You have a cat?" She gets off her stool and picks Stanley up. "Aren't you the cutest cat ever?" she says as Stanley takes in all the attention.

She puts her down and walks into the kitchen and I see that she took off her shoes and she is now barefoot. Her toes are painted the same color as her nails. She turns on the water, washing her hands. And then she peels her sweater off, her tank top under rising a bit, and I'm completely aroused. I look down and I can't even begin to hide it. I don't even know if it's possible to hide this. I've never been this hard before. I turn a bit sideways.

"Can you go and see if the cat has food? It's around the couch down the little hall to the bathroom."

"Sure." She walks away, her ass swaying, and it makes it even fucking worse. The jeans are so restricted I'm afraid my cock is going to suffocate and have to be cut off for lack of oxygen.

"Get a hold of yourself. She doesn't want you like that." I shake my head and focus on the fish in front of me, my mind forcing me not to think of the white bra straps that peek out of her tank top, the fact that her jeans are so low, they barely have a zipper.

I place the salmon and veggies in the oven to bake. When I look up, I find her in the living room looking at the pictures I have around the room.

"So you do have teeth," she jokes as she looks at the picture that I took last year when I won the cup. My beard was disgusting and I couldn't wait to shave that shit off.

I walk to my oversized U-shaped brown couch and turn on the television. The replay of my fight last night is playing. I laugh when I see that I almost face-planted as she stands and watches, shaking her head. She comes to sit next to me, putting her feet under her. "Want to watch *Game of Thrones*? I can give you side commentary," I joke with her as I turn on Netflix.

"Great, just what I need, side commentary. This chick fucked her brother and had two kids with him and she's the queen," she jokes, but I put it on and she is more into it than she admits. We end up eating on the couch as one episode slips into the next and then she lays her head down near my leg, her hair spanning across my couch and also my leg. I look down and her eyes slowly close and then blink open till she closes them and I hear a soft snore. I don't wake her up as one hour goes into another and I get up to get a blanket on her. She is now stretched out, one leg bent. One arm is bent over her head, her tank top is rising a bit, and I see a little heart tattoo on her hip. Her other hand is draped around her stomach and Stanley is cuddled at her side and looks at me with a glare when I walk over and cover her.

I look at her, not even sure what to do. I've never had a woman here, ever. Well, Denise, but she's my sister. Other than that, she's the only other female I've had here.

I pick her up finally and carry her to my bed. I'll sleep on the couch. She moans out and cuddles into my chest as I place her on my bed. She turns on her side and blinks her eyes open. "What time is it?" she asks groggily.

"After midnight," I say. "Sleep here. I'm going to sleep on the couch."

"Okay," she says. "Or just sleep here. I won't move." And she just closes her eyes again.

I place my hand on my waist and tilt my head back, asking for a sign, anything to tell me what I'm about to do is wrong, so very fucking wrong, but it feels so fucking right when I get into bed with her and she comes closer. I don't move and start off on my back, but when I open my eyes as the sun comes up, I'm still on my back, but she's wrapped up around me. I don't move except to put my hand on hers on my chest as I close my eyes and drift off again. The next time I wake up I'm all alone as she walks into the room, her hair piled high on her head and she's carrying a tray with coffee and orange juice.

"Morning." She puts the tray down and then climbs into the bed.

"Hey," I say, leaning over and checking the time. "Shit, it's late." I grab the glass of orange juice.

"I know. Good thing I can work from home, so you can drop me off there on your way." She smiles at me and it's then I notice that she really never wears makeup.

"Did you sleep okay?" I ask her, getting up, and taking off my T-shirt. I usually sleep naked. But her eyes open as big as saucers as she looks at me from neck to belly button. "Hello," I say as she blinks again and I laugh.

"I slept like a baby." She gets up and looks at the floor. "You change. I'll wait for you out there." She points to the door and walks out. I know that look. I'm sure I've given her the same look once or twice yesterday. The question is, now what the fuck do I do with that?

## ALLISON

"What the fuck are you watching?" My earphones are ripped out of my ear by Matthew.

"*Game of Thrones*," I answer him and then look around for Max, who is sitting in the back with no one next to him, so I get up and walk down the aisle of the plane, throwing myself in the seat next to him. "Oh my God, she has dragon babies!"

He smiles and closes his phone off. "I thought it was stupid." He eggs me on. We've been on the road for three days now, our only game out of town for a month. I was spoiled because next month I'll be gone for eleven days. I'm dreading it. After I fell asleep in his bed and woke up wrapped around him like a monkey I've tried to pretend I don't really want him other than a friend. The biggest thing is that I've failed at every turn. I know when he's around. I know where he is every time we are in the same room. It's like my body is on high alert for his. He hasn't acted any different toward me, so at least he doesn't feel this from me.

I remember the phone call to my mother two days ago before I left New York.

"Mom, how old are you when you stop having crushes on people?" I asked during one of our FaceTime chats.

"Um, never," she said while Cooper came in the room, opening the fridge. "You always get crushes on people." The fridge door slammed shut.

"What the fuck does that mean?" He came up to the phone. "Hey, honey."

"Hi, Dad." I smiled seeing the look he was giving my mother.

"It means that just because you're with someone or not doesn't mean you stop crushing on people." She turned to him.

"You have a crush on someone, Parker?" He slammed down the water bottle he had in his hand. "Seriously, who the fuck do you have a crush on?"

I laughed because the world could come to a stop and mass-produce only men and my mother would still look for Cooper.

She rolled her eyes at him. "I'm saying that you never stop feeling things and a crush is a feeling."

"Okay, so who do you have a crush on?" he asked again as he folded his hands over his chest. "Tell me!"

"Oh, Jesus, okay, Anderson Cooper." She threw her hand up, just throwing out a name, and Cooper laughed at her.

"He's gay!"

"I have a huge crush on John Snow," I told them, "like I would so have his babies." And apparently that wasn't something you should tell your father.

"Allison fucking Grant, do not talk like that. Where are you? Are you at the rink? Guys hear that and they pounce on women. Is your brother there? Where is your brother?"

"Simmer down there, Pops. No one is fertilizing me any time soon." And that made him throw his head back and groan out while my mother giggled.

"Jesus, these girls are going to give me a heart attack and then they will have a gay stepfather."

We all laughed, but the answer was right there. You never stop crushing on someone, so it was a crush and it would go away.

I get up from the seat without answering him and I'm yanked back down.

"Where are you going?" he asks me.

"I'm not going to sit here while you make fun of me and not tell me what is going to happen." I look at him. "Tell me what happens. Does her hot husband die? I think he dies. He's so hot."

"He's not that hot," he says as the fasten seat belt sign turns on, so I fasten my seat belt and then we are on the ground.

I wait for everyone to get off before I get up and walk down the aisle of the empty plane now with no one behind me but Max. I reach up and start tugging my bag when he hovers over me, reaching over me, and grabbing my bag. His chest is to my back and my heart goes out of control.

"Thanks," I say, looking down and walking down the steps. I fuss with my phone while I walk to the cars.

"You coming with me?" he asks as he walks beside me.

"I could get an Uber in seventeen minutes," I tell him as soon as I open the app.

"Seventeen minutes I could be home after dropping you off," he says, unlocking his car door.

"You're the bestest, Mad Max," I say, laughing at him as he groans.

He drops me off and waits for me to go in before driving off. I don't bother turning on the lights. Instead, I just walk upstairs and undress, slipping under my covers. My dreams are all of dragons and I text him that the next day.

***I think I'm a dragon lady. I'm Daenerys.***

He doesn't answer me and I think that he might be sleeping or even at the gym. I open my computer and start doing my work for the gala that is coming up. So far we are looking at a thousand people attending. It seems that if Doug invites you somewhere, you go.

I finalize all the details with the venue and make appointments with the planner. I look at my phone and see that it's almost six. Where the fuck is Max? Should I call him? *No,* I tell myself, *put down the phone.* And I start making a little supper, but give up a minute later and order myself something.

I'm curled up on the couch watching another episode of *Game of Thrones* when my phone finally rings and I see it's Denise.

"Hey."

"Where are you?" she yells her question, so I pause the television.

"I'm home."

"Come meet me for some pool. Steve is here also."

I haven't been out in forever since all my college friends all moved away.

"Sure," I say, getting up as she gives me the address. I get my leather tights out, pairing them with a V-necked loose wrap shirt. I put a black lace bra under in case it opens when I move, pairing it with a black blazer and my black high-heeled booties. I slap on some lipstick and run out just as my Uber is here. I text Denise that I'm on my way and she tells me she's in the back as we pull up to the little shack of a bar.

I open the bar door, and it's almost all dark. This is an old and dungy bar, and I feel I'm way overdressed. People that look like they live sitting at the bar turn around. I walk to the back where there is a brighter light and as I walk in, I take in the two pool tables with more light. Denise shrieks and comes over, hugging me, and I can smell the booze on her.

"You came." She grabs my hand and pulls me toward the second pool table and I see him. And my heart stops. He's here, dressed in black jeans, a black T-shirt, and his black cap sitting on his head. But that isn't what has my neck burning or my heart beating fast. It's a gorgeous blonde standing between his legs looking at the pool table. His hands are on her hips.

I smile at Denise and hope to blink away the tears that might show up.

"Guys, look who came," she says and then he sees me and his face goes white. His hands fly off the blonde and I wave to everyone saying, "Hi."

She pulls me to the table he's sitting at. "Aly is going to be on our team," she tells her brother and the blonde, who is twirling her hair. "Allison, this is Shannon. She works at the hospital with us, but not on our floor. Shannon, this is the new PR for Max's team." She introduces us and I smile at her. She smiles back at me and leans her hand over the table to shake my hand.

"Nice to meet you," she says and I nod.

"You're here," Steve says from behind me and getting me into a bear hug. "She's on our team." He turns as the waitress brings four glasses of beer. "Take one." He picks one up and hands it to me, and I say thank you and grab it with my shaking hands. I take a sip of the beer that tastes almost like acid as it goes down my throat.

"Come with me," Denise says, grabbing my hand again and dragging me to the pool table where she talks to me about the pool game, but as I look at her and try to take in the words she is saying the only thing I can do is feel Max staring at me. I stand here and smile as fake as I can. For the next hour, I ignore Max and his every move. He gets up to take shots. When he does this, Shannon sits in his chair. More and more people show up from the hospital and I'm introduced to all of them. And I stand here biding my time till I can sneak out.

When I finally get that chance, I whisper to Denise, "I have an early morning tomorrow."

She turns around and nods at me.

"I'm going to sneak out. Say bye to your friends for me."

She nods and hugs me again. "Okay," she whispers as I grab my purse and walk against the wall to the exit where I flag down a cab and only when I'm sitting in the confines of this dark, dirty cab do I let go of the single tear that rolls down my face. Only then do I let my broken heart weep.

## MAX

I knew sitting here in the middle of the poolroom that this was a bad idea. I spent the day trying to ignore the pull to Allison. I picked up my phone over a hundred times and wanted to text her to come over. But I couldn't do it. I knew that if she came over I wouldn't be able to stop myself from doing what I've wanted to do for a month now. Bury my hands in her hair and kiss the shit out of her. I don't even care anymore. I fucking want her, but every time I try and feel her out, she looks down and ignores me.

So I showed up at the bar Denise is letting loose for once and I was drinking my bottle of water when Shannon walked in and I groaned inwardly. I really don't want this right now. I'm sitting on a stool next to the table as she makes her way over to me.

"Hey there, stranger." She leans in and kisses my cheek, and her perfume almost makes me gag. And I swear I feel my cock duck for cover. I smile at her and see that her makeup looks like it's caked on. Why the fuck is she so made up? "What a nice surprise." She dumps her purse on the stool behind me.

"Yeah, it won't be a late night. I have practice tomorrow at nine." I don't but just want to draw the line before she thinks other things. "My turn," I say, getting up and aligning the shot and missing. I shake my head and stand instead and for the next hour, I stay on one side of the room, and when she walks away, I finally go and sit down. I'm not even in my seat for a second when she comes prancing back in. She holds what looks like a martini glass and sits it on the table next to me.

She stands in the middle of my legs. "So when are we going to finally meet up?"

"I have no idea. My travel schedule is crazy for the next couple of months."

"Surely you have one night available," she says and Denise screams out, "You came."

I look over as Shannon turns around and leans on one leg, so I put my hands on her hips to not make her push my leg. I see Allison and my heart stops. She's so fucking beautiful the whole room dims to her. And here I am after ignoring her all day with a girl draped all over me. She doesn't make eye contact with me as I watch her, waiting for her to look at me. Waiting to see if there is something there, and that I'm not just imagining this whole thing.

Denise comes over with her, she introduces her to Shannon, and I see the flicker in her eye as she remembers the name. I try talking to her, but she goes with Denise and for the next couple of hours people keep coming in and she's passed around like she's a fucking piñata at a birthday party. I finally ply Shannon from me as she goes to talk to a couple of friends from the hospital. I spot Denise in the corner talking to a guy that I saw when I went for breakfast.

"Hey, where is Allison?" I ask her and look around.

"She took off," she says and then turns back to talk to the guy.

"What do you mean she took off?" I think it came out harsher than I thought it would.

"She said she has an early morning so she left."

I walk out of the bar, looking left and right for her and come up empty-handed.

Just then, Shannon comes running out. "Oh my God, I thought I missed you."

I don't have time for this, but I also don't have the energy for her. "Listen, Shannon, it's not going to happen," I tell her, grabbing her shoulder. "I'm"—I shake my head—"I'm just not there."

"It's Allison, right?" she asks and I close my mouth and open it again, waiting for the words to come out, denying that it has to do with her and everything to do with me, but nothing comes out, so she continues, "You couldn't take your eyes off her the whole time."

"We work together," I finally say.

"It's more than that. I don't even think you realize it." And she turns and walks back in as I stand here, telling myself to give her the night and then go to her tomorrow, but my heart knows that she can't go to bed thinking I left with her. If nothing else, I need her to know that.

So here I am jogging up her steps. Her house sits in darkness. I ring the doorbell once and wait, putting my hands on the door, looking in, and nothing. I ring one more time and this time I see something. A light turns on from the side and I see her shadow coming closer. She opens the door and my heart stops. Her hair is up on her head. I don't even know what she's wearing because wrapped around her is an ivory cover as she holds it from the inside of her cocoon.

"Jesus, Max," she says and I see her eyes are a bit red. "You scared the shit out of me." She looks down and then back up again.

"I need to talk to you." My hands go into my pockets before I grab her and pull her to me. "Shannon, she…" I stumble when she looks up and I see it, the death in her eye. Everything that I've worked for is gone, because she looks at me like I'm nothing. "I didn't know she was going to be there." I know I'm saying this for nothing because she has already scratched me off her list, already decided I wasn't worth the fight, but I'm going to give it all to her and then I'm going to leave. "I wanted to answer you a million times today, but I didn't have the balls to do it. I tried staying away from you and not getting my hopes high. Fuck, your family hates my guts, and here I am jonesing for you."

She looks at me with a face of shock.

"Anyway, but I didn't want you to think I was leaving with her." I shake my head, now thinking what a mistake this was. "That's all I have to say." And I turn, jog down the stairs, and drive away, the whole time looking at her in the mirror as she stands there looking at me.

The rest of the night is spent lying on my couch, flicking through infomercials. The sun comes up as Stanley sits on my chest, and I pet her. I drift off I think at noon and only wake when I hear banging at my door. I get up and walk over, opening it to see Denise.

"Are you not ready?" she asks me, coming in, and I take in her outfit. "It's Ed Sheeran night." She pulls her jacket down to show me her plaid shirt. "You forgot."

I rub my hand through my hair. "Yeah, I guess I did," I say, walking away. "Let me get changed and we can go." I head to my bathroom and turn on the shower. "I'm going to be thirty. Make yourself at home." I shower and pull out a pair of black jeans and a dark gray T-shirt as I whip my leather off my hanger and put it on. The last thing I put on is my black boots. "Okay, I'm ready." I walk into the room and she closes the television and gets up.

"Steve was really pissed when I took back those extra two tickets." She starts walking for the door. "Who is joining us?" she asks and I look down as I slip my sunglasses on.

"I guess we will find out now, won't we," I tell her, making my way over to the rink, which is now set up for the concert. I still go into the entrance that the players go to and walk down the hallway, but there are so many people running around it's a mad house. We make our way out to the ice, which is now covered with a wooden floor. The lights are dim and the DJ plays some songs as we find our seat two rows from the stage.

"Holy shit. Look at these seats," Denise says, sitting down and pulling out her phone.

I make her sit at the end as I sit with the empty seat beside me. I hold my breath till the opening act comes out. James Blunt sings "You're beautiful" and all I can do is look around at the full arena. Well, full minus the two seats next to me. I inhale deeply, knowing they will probably stay empty. Denise screams as he continues singing when I see the people move back, making way for the person that got the tickets for the seats next to me. Allison. She walks looking down at her feet to make sure she doesn't trip on anything and I know the minute she looks up that she's surprised to see me, as the person behind her pushes her forward.

"What?" She smiles and puts her head down, her hair falling around her.

She whispers to the girl next to her, who tilts her head back and laughs. She smirks at me and I see it's Karrie's best friend Vivienne.

James Blunt leaves the stage and we all clap and Denise looks over and sees Allison. "I knew if he took the tickets away from me it would have to be a good reason," she says and Allison laughs.

"Well, this answers my question," Allison says. "All day I was calling people and thanking them for the two tickets that showed up this morning, and each one didn't know what I was talking about." She laughs as she knocks me sideways. "Well done."

"I'm going to get something to eat and drink," Denise says and Vivienne jumps up.

"I'll come." She follows her out and we watch them making their way through the crowd.

"Allison," I say quietly. "I…" I shake my head, looking down.

"You're just full of surprises, aren't you?" She sits down and turns to me. "Last night…" She doesn't have time to continue because a couple of people have stopped me and asked for pictures. Then when they finally leave Denise and Vivienne come back and hand us both water bottles.

"I know you don't drink when you are training and working, so I got you water," Denise says and she holds up a hot dog and bites into it. "I think it cost me fifty bucks." She continues chewing as I watch her. The whole time I keep looking over at Allison, who is talking to Vivienne, but then the lights go out, and we all stand up, waiting for Ed to come out. And then he just walks across the stage with his guitar as he starts singing.

Allison stops clapping and her hands go down to her sides and they brush against mine. At first, I think it's an accident, but then she slowly does it again as her fingers graze mine. I look down at our hands close together. Her delicate hand moves next to mine, and I take it. I turn my hand around this time, rub my palm down her inner wrist, and snake my fingers into hers. Her hands open up and entwine with mine as Ed Sheeran sings "Castle on the hill." Our hands stand still, both of us afraid to let go, as my thumb rubs her.

It's at that moment I know I'm more far-gone than I thought. It's at that moment I know I can't walk away from her. It's then that I know my whole life I've been waiting for this one fucking moment. I know that whatever hell I went through before it was all for this moment right here.

Our hands hold each other the whole time, both of us almost on edge when his slow song "Dive" comes on. The minute his voice comes out and sings the beginning, I don't think. I just pull her out of the row and walk down the aisle with her running behind me to keep up, but I make my way to the back as I wave to the guy blocking the hallway to where her office is. Thank fuck it's the same guy who works the game because he just smiles and opens the curtain for me to go in the back. I open her door, the lights are off but a small light on under her desk, pulling her in, and closing the door. I look down at our hands still together. My chest heaving, I look at her leaning against the door while she looks up at me and it's there. The look I've been waiting to see, that I've hoped to see. The look that makes me see I'm not the only one in this.

"Max," she whispers.

My eyes go back down to see our hands still attached. I slip my hand out of hers and turn to face her, both my hands going to the side of her head. Her hands go onto my chest.

"Max," she says again and it's almost like a plea.

"Allison," I say, looking down at her. "I tried. Tried to ignore this."

Her hands move up on my chest, softly, slowly. "Kiss me. Please, Max, just kiss me."

And I bend my head as she tilts her head back a touch and my lips touch hers, soft at first. Electricity shoots through me. I move back again. One hand goes to her cheek and my thumb rubs her chin. I lean back down again, this time not going slow. This time my mouth opens and my tongue goes into her mouth as she gasps out. This time my tongue twirls with hers. This time I kiss her with everything I have. My hand goes around her waist and I push her closer to me, and her hands finally wrap around my neck, our mouths never leaving each other. We kiss each other as if it's the last time we will ever see each other. We give in to the months of tension. We give in to the crashing around us, and I pray to fuck we are still standing after this.

## ALLISON

It's happening. Either that or I'm having a stroke and this is my way into heaven.

Since I was little, I used to see the way Cooper would kiss Mom. It would be like the Princes would kiss the Princesses. It's the kiss that you read about in the fairy tales. It's a kiss as a girl you wait patiently for. Each time you kiss a frog hoping he turns into a prince. And this moment right here with Max's lips on mine, with his tongue dancing with mine, I know this kiss right here is what a kiss is supposed to be. A kiss that, if anything happens, I know will be the best kiss of my life.

My day started with me waking up with big red puffy eyes from crying. Crying for actually believing that we had something, crying because he showed up there after all this, poured his heart out, and then just left. He didn't give me a chance to say anything, to tell him that it wasn't just him, that it was me, too. That I was feeling the same thing he was.

After I closed the door I curled up in a ball and chills filled my body, so I shivered on the couch all night wrapped in the biggest blanket I could find in the house as I watched the night turn into morning. My body ached so much it hurt to stand up and as I stand in the kitchen and wait for the water to boil the doorbell rings. I don't know who I expect it to be, but I'm not expecting a man holding a FedEx envelope. I sign for it and open it up and gasp out loud when I see two Ed Sheeran tickets.

I pick up my phone and call Matthew right away. "And you said you didn't have pull," I say as soon as he answers.

"What the fuck are you talking about now?" he asks, confused.

"The Ed Sheeran tickets I just got." I slap them down. "Who the hell would give these? I mean, besides you and Cooper." I slap my head. "Okay, I gotta call Dad." I hang up and call him.

"Baby girl," he says right away.

"Dad, how did you find tickets to Ed? I've been looking for ages," I say.

"I have no idea what you're talking about, but if it makes you happy I did it," he says and I stand here in the kitchen thinking about who the fuck could have gotten me the tickets. "Either way, you are going to bring mace with you, right?" he asks as I roll my eyes and tell him I'll call him back.

The next person I call is Vivienne, who shouts with glee about going to see her future babies' father.

The rest of the day, Max lingers in the back of my head. I need to go and see him, if anything to finish the conversation he started last night. I dress in all black that night, kind of how I feel inside. Vivienne of course gets there late.

"Why can't you ever be on time?" I ask her the minute I got into the Uber she had rode in.

"I had to get the perfect outfit. You never know if he is going to see me and invite me backstage," she huffs out.

"Let's not hold our breath," I murmur under my breath and she doesn't bother answering.

By the time we walk in James Blunt is already singing. We are ushered to our seats as I walk looking down to make sure I don't trip on anything. When I finally get to my seat, look up, and see him, I shake my head, trying not to smile. Of course he did. I'm in a daze till

Ed comes out and I graze his hand with mine. His hot hand makes my fingers tingle, so I slowly do it again, wanting to hold his hand, and as I do it again I feel his hand move, turning his palm over as he takes my hand in his.

And now here I am in my office, lost in him, lost in the kiss. My back arches forward as I try to get closer to him. He moans into my mouth as he presses me deeper into my door as his hands move from my face to my side to cupping my ass and lifting me up, so I wrap my legs around his waist and he slams me back, his hand going from squeezing my ass to up my back to in my hair as his hand fists my hair, pulling my head back, my mouth leaving his, and he bites my neck. I moan out, my eyes closing as my nipples start to perk.

"Fuck." He comes back up and kisses me. This time it's even more hungry than before. When we finally let each other go, our pants are heard in the room as my chest and his go up and down as if we just finished running. "Angel," he says and I whisper out, "Yeah."

"Tell me this isn't just me. Tell me it isn't just me feeling crazy. Tell me it isn't just my world knocked off."

I use my hands to cup his cheeks. "Not just you," I say, kissing him on the lips. My feet uncross and I slip down onto my feet. "I don't want to leave this room." I look down at my hands that are now on his chest, when he uses his finger to raise my face.

"Doesn't matter where we go, Angel," he says softly, "it's me and you." He grabs my hand and opens the door as we walk back to our seats, and now Vivienne and Denise are standing together as they look over at us, both pairs of eyes going down to our hands. But I'm not letting go, and neither is Max, it seems.

The concert finishes and we follow Max, who has his car here. He asks Vivienne where we are dropping her off, but it seems Denise and Vivienne aren't ready to call it a night yet, so he drops them off at the bar. After we say bye to them, he pulls off and makes his way to his house.

"Well, I guess I'm coming over." I smile at him and he takes my hand from the console and kisses it. When he lets my hand go, he keeps holding it in his lap. When we park the car, I get out and he waits for me at the back, grabbing my hand. I smile and try and keep up with him as he walks away. We walk upstairs and he takes out his keys and puts it in the keyhole. "You know," I say with my back against the door, looking at him, "I really like kissing you," I tell him and he leans his head down and I smile as he smiles at me.

"That's a good thing because I plan on kissing you a lot." He sticks his tongue out, licking me. I put my tongue out, meeting his, and he crushes me against the door as I use my hands, going to his waist, and this time I'm the one with my hands on his ass, pulling it to me. And he picks me up with one hand as he kisses me senseless and opens the door. He carries me in while I put my hand through his hair as he groans out and I feel exactly how ready he is on my stomach.

"Fuck, this better not be a fucking dream." He puts me down on his island in the kitchen. I open my legs as he steps in the middle of them. Putting the hair behind my ears, he says, "Angel. Do you need to go home tonight?"

My hand goes to his chest and slides his jacket off of him.

"We leave tomorrow, but." He kisses my cheek, then goes to my neck, and I move to the side, giving him access. "I want you to stay here tonight."

I look at him as he looks up, his eyes clear as fucking day, and he smiles. Well, side smile, smirking. "Okay." I put my hands on his waist. "We should talk about, um." And I look down.

"None of that," Max says. "No more hiding. I want to see your eyes, angel."

"Okay, I don't know what this is." I put my hand up, pointing to him and then to me. "I mean, I know what I want it to be," I stutter out.

"Yeah, what do you want this to be, angel?" He smiles.

"I want to date you," I finally say. "This is stupid." I push him away or at least I try to.

"Oh, I plan on dating the shit out of you. I plan on kissing the shit out of you, also. Just so you know."

"Well, that's good to know since I really want to do all of that." I lean forward, this time kissing his neck. "What do we tell people?" I whisper. "I mean…"

He stops moving and grabs my face. "I want to tell the fucking world, but I want this to be ours for now." He kisses me. "Is that okay?"

"Yeah," I whisper, "but no dating other people."

"I haven't dated anyone in my life."

I laugh at him.

"Banged, yeah."

"Okay, asshole." I push him away again or try, but he doesn't even budge. "No banging anyone."

"Deal. Now let's go make out in my bed." He grabs me. "Or the couch. The couch is closest." He falls on the couch, I fall on him, and we make out for the rest of the night. I wake up the next day to little butterfly kisses on my neck. We fell asleep on the couch in the middle of the make out session. "We have to go," he says. "I'm going to pack and we are going to swing by your house and get your things."

"Okay," I say, turning to my side as he gets up. I close my eyes and then my phone rings from somewhere in the loft, so I get up and walk to the kitchen, grabbing it out of my purse, and see that it's Cooper.

"Baby girl," he says as soon as I answer. "Where are you?"

"Umm, why?" I say, looking to see where Max is.

"Because I just checked and you didn't take off your alarm last night."

I gasp. "Oh my God, Dad, are you spying on me?" I say as soon as I hear my mother, "I told him it was a bad idea."

"Well, I didn't go home last night because I'm at my boyfriend's house," I say as my mother laughs and Cooper growls. I shake my head as Max comes in the kitchen and kisses my neck.

"Who the fuck are you dating? Why didn't Matthew tell me?" he asks loudly, probably running his hand in his hair while trying to pull it out.

"Well, I haven't told anyone yet. It's still new. So we want to keep it private for now. Besides, I don't need you two running him off. I really like him." I look at Max, who puts his hands on his heart while I bow down at him.

"Do I know him? Have I met him? Is he on the team?"

"Bye, Dad, I'm hanging up. Love you. Mom, I'll call you later," I say and he argues with her about knowing who I'm dating.

"So your boyfriend, eh?" he asks, smiling.

"Maybe," I say, shrugging and putting my shoes on. "Let's go."

I finish packing in record time and we are one of the last ones to get to the plane. "Okay, just so you know, I really like you," I tell him.

"That's good because I really like you, too."

He smiles at me and I want to lean in and kiss him, but Matthew is there knocking on the window.

"Jesus," I say, getting out. "What is your problem? You gave me a heart attack."

"Dad says you're dating someone?" he says with his hands on his hips while I laugh. "Don't laugh, Aly, who the fuck are you dating and how don't I know about it?"

"I date, Matthew," I say, walking to the plane with Max by my side and Matthew on the other. "Is it so hard to believe that someone actually wants to date me?" I turn, asking him.

"Max, you picked her up at her house. Did you see this clown she is dating?"

He shakes his head. "Nope, got there and she was already outside." He turns and walks on the plane.

"I don't like this," Matthew says. "Why the secrecy?"

"Because it just happened and I want to see where things go before my two hot heads scare him away."

"Is it someone from the team? I swear to God if I found out one of those imbeciles touched you they're dead," he says, walking up the stairs. "Dead." I hear him talking as I follow him on the plane and see that Max is sitting by himself in the front seat with his earphones in, watching something on his phone. I sit next to him as he looks at me sideways, then looks back at the screen.

Matthew is sitting across from me. "I'm going to be watching you, Aly," he says with his two fingers at his eyes and then moving them to me. "Be on guard."

And Max and I can't help but laugh at him. "This isn't funny."

I smile to myself as I close my eyes and think back on the night before.

## MAX

"One more period and we get to go fucking home," Matthew says from across from me as we sit in the locker room between periods.. We've been on the road for six days. The only ones really enjoying this are the rookies.

"We need this win," Phil says from beside me. "We took a beating in Tampa. We can't lose to Columbus."

"You need to stay out of the penalty box." Matthew looks at me and my eyes glare at him. "Calm down, I know you were protecting Luka, but that's what they want."

"Okay, so next time I'll let them poke check him till the puck goes in and smashes his leg. Got it, Captain." I salute him and get up. Okay, so maybe I'm on edge also. I can't wait to get home and just be fucking normal. This whole sneaking around bullshit is too much. Yesterday we were almost caught dry humping in her room when her brother came knocking. We can't even have a private conversation without someone coming in to ask questions. I grab my gloves and go into the hallway on the way to the ice when I see her standing there, leaning against the wall as she types something on her phone. "Hey."

She smiles, looks around, and then says, "Hey there, pretty boy. You okay?" she asks, seeing something on my face.

"I'm just tired, angel." I haven't had a good night's sleep since we got here. I would fall asleep in her room and then have to sneak back to mine like I'm James fucking Bond.

She looks behind me and then behind her. "How about I stay over at your house tonight?" She crosses her arms over her chest. "Would that perk you up?"

"It's a start." And I'm about to touch her when I hear my teammates behind me, so I smile and walk off.

The third period we are on a roll. It's like we can taste the finish line. Matthew, Phil, and I score one goal each in the first four minutes. I jump back on the ice for what will most likely be my last shift of the game when the goon on the other team cross checks me from the back, making me go flying on my face. Matthew is the first one to grab the guy in a chokehold. I shake my head and look down, seeing blood on the ice. I get up and go straight into the back room, as the doctor is there to put gloves on and the nurse almost closes the door in Allison's face when I speak up.

"Leave the door open, it's small in here." It's a fucking broom closet.

The doctor checks the gash under my chin. "I think we can glue this one," he says and I look up at Allison.

"It's a cut," I say loudly, pretending to look at the doctor, but in fact, I'm saying it so Allison can know. I'm finished by the time the guys walk into the room. I'm showered before everyone else, grabbing my bag, and walking out of the room. I see Allison at the end in a small office closing up her stuff. Looking around to make sure no one is around, I go in, closing the door behind. "Come here, angel," I tell her, standing with my back against the door.

She comes to me. As she stands in front of me, her hand goes to my chin and she touches where the cut is.

"Angel, I'm fine." I put my bag down, grabbing her face, bringing my face down, and kissing her lips. Her breath hitches, giving me just the space I need to claim her tongue with mine. The minute her tongue slides with mine my cock wakes up. Fuck, I'm lying. The minute I see her he gets up. It's like he's singing 'mine, mine, mine.'

My hands get lost in her hair as she presses herself to me, both of us forgetting where we are when we hear the guys walking down the hall.

She pulls away. "Two hours." She rubs her hands on my chest. She finally pushes away from me and I stand up, opening the door, and seeing Matthew coming out of the room looking down. I wait at the door as he stops here also.

"Is your boyfriend picking you up?" he asks and Allison smiles.

"As if I would make him come to that ambush. Nope, Max is taking me home."

"I can drive you home," Matthew pipes in and I know he's full of shit. He's dying to get back to Karrie.

"Isn't Karrie waiting for you?" Allison asks, putting her bag over her shoulder and picking up her luggage.

"Fine, but you." He points at me. "You see this fucking clown I want a picture and I would be okay if you roughed him up a bit."

I shake my head and laugh at him.

"I mean, not like punches, but tell him I'm scary and shit."

"Yeah, you're so scary. I still have pictures of you with eye shadow," Allison says, walking out before us. "Green is not your color."

"I can't say no to my girls." He shrugs his shoulders.

The bus ride is quiet with everyone doing their own thing and the plane ride is even worse. Many of the guys nod out while I watch, I don't even know what I'm watching. I can't concentrate on anything with Allison sitting next to me, her head falling on my shoulder.

When we all make it off the plane we walk to the car, getting in without a word. I pull off as a couple of cars follow me, but I still reach over, grabbing her hand, and she leans in a bit.

"I need to shower before I come to bed," she says, walking into the bedroom, dropping her bag in the corner.

I pick it up and bring it into my closet, placing it in the middle of the room. She follows me, opens her bag, grabs her stuff, and then walks to the bathroom. The need to follow her is like trying to catch my next breath. But she's nothing if not someone who needs to be respected and cherished, even if my balls have turned a shade of blue and I'm pretty sure I've gotten two more calluses from jerking off so much. I wait for her in the bed. I flip through the channels, stopping on the highlights from last night's game.

She walks out of the bathroom, her hair tied again on the top of her head, and she wears booty shorts and a gray T-shirt. It's nothing sexy, no lace, no silk, no garters, yet it's the sexiest thing I have ever seen. She places her knee on the bed and then crawls over to me. She sits on me, her pussy right over my cock, which is ready to start this party. She leans in and kisses me. This time I let her take what she needs.

"So this is going to be really awkward, but I need to tell you something," she says, using her finger to trace some of the ink on my shoulder.

"Awkward I can do," I say, trying to ease her. "What's the matter?" I have to be honest I thought she was going to tell me she got her period. The last thing I expected was what she said.

"So I'm a virgin." She throws her hands up. "I mean, I've done stuff, lots of stuff."

"Not interested in hearing about the stuff you did with other men, angel, when you're sitting on my cock," I counter.

She rolls her eyes. "You are aware that there is a website out there that rates all athletes in the sex area, right?"

I look at her. "What?"

"So say we have sex. I can go onto this website and tell them about my experience and rate you."

I'm shocked. I mean, I knew that puck bunnies all stood together and they all spoke, but to have a website. "Did you read them?" I ask her and she looks down.

"I did and then I couldn't take it, so I blocked the site so I wouldn't be tempted to go back." She looks up. "You're very well rated."

"Again not interested in talking about sex with other people," I tell her, about to toss her off of me.

"Well, since we are dating I thought you would like to know I'm not as experienced as you are." And that is the last thing she says before I flip her off of me and put her under me.

"You're untouched," I tell her, looking into her eyes as she rolls them. "It's not like I didn't have the opportunity. It just never felt—"

I don't let her finish. I just crush my lips on hers, and her legs wrap around my waist, where she locks her ankles at my back.

"I don't deserve you," I tell her in between breathing and kissing her. "I deserve nothing that you are giving me."

She lets my lips go as well as my waist as she says, "You deserve everything."

"I will never force you to do anything you don't want to do," I say as she rubs her finger on my lips.

"You can try, but I'd pretty much kick you in the balls and then cut them off." She laughs, trying to make a joke out of it. "Max. I have never been one to be persuaded into doing things I don't want to do. So if the time is right and we have sex it's going to be something that I decide and not you."

"So we take this one step at a time," I tell her, bending my head to kiss her neck and then suck it a bit. "Is it barbaric to want to put my mark on you? Kind of like she's mine."

And she tosses her head back and laughs. "It's funny you say that because I kept thinking the same thing today when we walked into the plane and the flight attendants were all like 'I can get you what you need.'" She mimics the girl. "Ugh, really, bitch, he doesn't need coffee. It's fucking midnight."

"You're jealous?" I kiss her.

"You have a website that rated your dick. It doesn't get worse than that."

"You are not allowed to bring that fucking shit up anymore," I say, biting her lower lip, and then sucking it into my mouth. "I haven't had sex with someone in over eight months."

"What?" She opens her mouth. "Impossible."

"Angel, that is the last of it," I tell her, rolling her on top of me. "No more fucking talking. I'm tired. I finally get to spend the night fully sleeping without trying to tiptoe down the fucking hall with my shoes. By the way, next time, adjoining rooms."

"I can't request that. It'll be like a flashing 'I'm getting it on with

Max'," she says and then thinks about it. "That isn't a bad idea."

"Tomorrow. I need sleep and you need to get off me or my cock will think it's time to play and it's not."

"Want me to take care of it?" She smiles and wiggles her eyebrows at me, laughing in my chest at the end.

"Good night, angel." I kiss her as she turns on her side and I turn into her.

"Um, Max, I can't sleep with that thing in my back," she says quietly. "I mean, I'm a virgin, but you know."

"Shut up, Allison," I say, turning around and squishing my cock into the mattress, and I swear I hear him groan. It takes me about two minutes before I finally fall asleep. I don't even know how long I sleep. All I know is I wake up and the bed is empty next to me, so I get up and go about finding my girl. I walk around the wall and hear her.

"Hey there, princess." She is talking to the cat. "Did you have fun while we were gone?" She picks her up, kissing her face, and bringing her into the kitchen. "Did you have a big party with your cat friends?"

And my cat is listening to every single word she says as she takes out some food and puts some on the plate. The cat jumps out of her arms and walks away while Allison starts the coffee and opens the fridge, taking out the milk as she looks up. Her hair is down now.

"Morning," she says as she opens cupboards to find two cups. She finally finds them on the fourth try. "Coffee or orange juice?"

I walk to her, taking her in, standing in my kitchen, barefoot again, one foot on top of the other. Her camisole strap is falling down on one shoulder, showing me that she isn't wearing a bra. I grab her by her waist and put her on the counter again, putting her hair over her shoulder, leaning down, and sucking right where her camisole starts, right above the swell of her breast.

"Max," she whispers, looking down at me as her legs dangle.

I lift my head, looking down at the red mark. "Perfect," I say then kiss her good morning.

## ALLISON

"Let's go, people," I yell, running down the hall at the rink. It's the day that we go and visit the hospital. It's been two weeks of 'dating' and I'm fit to be tied. I can't get enough of him. We can be watching television and I look up and crawl on his lap just to kiss him, because I fucking can. We've mastered dry humping and kissing. We spend the majority of time at his place, since it's our safe haven of sorts. Plus, I wouldn't be surprised if Cooper got the cameras hooked up to his phone. "How are you guys not ready? It's been forty minutes." I look at my watch, seeing that they all arrived here forty minutes ago. "The bus is waiting," I say as the guys start walking out.

We are traveling again after the hospital, so everyone met here as it's easier. "Here, wear this." Matthew throws his jersey at me and I look down at it. "So they know you're with us."

"I don't need to wear your shirt," I tell him, opening up my jacket and showing him the T-shirt I have underneath is of the team's logo. I won't take off my jacket because then he will see that it's Max's name on the back. When I walked in the kitchen this morning wearing it, well, you can say my guy was more than happy because it led to a heavy make out session, "Fuck you make me lose control." He whispered. "We don't have time for this."

As my tongue mixed with his. "I can help you,' I said as my hand cupped his cock over his jeans, rubbing up and down, his moan drowned out by mine.

"Next time," he said as I laughed at him trying to postion his cock in his pants before walking out to the car.

Now here we are all heading to the bus on our way over to the hospital. Once we get there we all make it to the fourth floor where Denise and Steve are there waiting for us. She comes to me, hugging me, and thanking me for doing this.

"Shall we?" she says. "Half will be with Steve and half will be with me," she adds as half of the guys go one way and the other half go the other. Max and I both follow Denise. "The first patient is Katie, thirteen. She has Lymphoma. Diagnosed six months ago and is in her second round of chemo. She just shaved her head again, and she is having a hard time with it."

I walk next to Max as he walks in first with eight other guys.

"Hey there, Katie," he says and the other guys all follow his lead as he sits with her and they talk about everything. She asks them all questions.

"How many of you have a girlfriend?"

Denise and I stand by the door and giggle. Such a girl question. Most of the guys say no because they are mostly the rookies and are 'playing the pussy' as the guys call it. When it's Max's turn, I stand here waiting for his answer.

"I have a girlfriend."

The rookies all howl at him.

"Ignore these rats." He smiles.

They spend ten more minutes with her and then Denise takes them to the next one.

I wait for them to walk out before giving her a team bag so she can put all the stuff in.

"He's so cute," the little girl says as her mom smiles beside her.

"He's my favorite."

I look around to make sure it's just me, then lean in, and wink at her. "Mine, too, but don't tell anyone." I walk out and by the time the tour is over all the men are silent. Denise thanks them and hands them a thank you card that they made for them. Everyone gathers around Denise and we do a group photo. I don't know where I should go and stand, so I go to the right and then look behind me and feel Max's hand on my shoulder, as his other hand rubs against my other. We smile for the picture and then make our way to the bus. As soon as we pull off the talk starts. Everyone thanking God that their kids are healthy. It's a little thing, but I have some of the rookies ask if they can go back. It makes my heart burst with pride that I did something so good.

On the bus Ryder is the first to speak up, "Aly, you think that I can go back when I have free time?" he asks from the back of the bus.

"I'm sure that could be arranged." I look at him.

"Thank you," Phil says next as Matthew nods his head. "We have never done this and it was so nice to be with the kids."

"It was beyond awesome," Ryder says, "seeing all those kids fighting for their lives. It just goes to show..." He looks out the window and everyone is lost in their own thoughts.

We get on the plane again. Everyone is bustling about. I sit down, Max sits next to me, and we watch *Game of Thrones* together. Once we get to the hotel we all get our keys and I make sure everyone is okay before going up to my room. As soon as I open my door and drop my bag, I hear a knock coming from the door in the corner. Getting up and opening it, I see it's Max.

"How the hell did you manage this?" I ask him as he comes into my room and puts his hand on my face before taking my lips under his. My hand goes to his waist as I pick up his shirt, putting my hands on his skin. He lets go of my mouth, groans out, and puts his head back. I'm about to rip his shirt off of him when someone knocks at my door. Max steps back into his room as I close the door and yell, "Coming." I swing the door open to find Matthew there.

"Jesus, what the hell were you doing?" he says, looking at me up and down. "Your hair is messed up and everything." He puts his hand on his mouth. "Oh my God," he shrieks out loud as Max opens his door and comes outside. "Were you having face sex?"

"What the hell is that?" I ask him as I pat my hair down, and when I see him still staring, I tie it up.

"It's when you FaceTime, but have sex doing it. FaceSex." He looks at Max. "You do that, right?"

Max shakes his head and tries to hide his smile.

"You were doing face sex with your asshole boyfriend," Matthew says angrily.

"Why is he an asshole?" I tilt my head to the side.

"What guy dates a girl and doesn't meet her family?" he asks me back.

"A sane one who doesn't have to deal with his girlfriend's neurotic family members." I smile back and he frowns. "What do you want?"

"I want to go for dinner. Most of the team is going and we want to treat you to dinner as a thank you for today." He looks over at Max, who has just stepped out of his room and is taking in the scene. "You in?"

Max nods.

"Okay, well, I have to go make myself less flushed." I wink at him. "Let me tell my guy I'll call him back." I close the door as Matthew yells and Max laughs. I open the door a second later as Matthew points at me.

"I'm telling Mom and Dad about your face sex."

"Yes, you should and then explain to them what it is and how you know about it. By the way, I am never touching your phone again." I shake my head with a grimace as I turn to walk and grab Max's hand. He slides his fingers with mine and I jerk my hand free, forgetting that Matthew is right in front of us. I look at him as he looks at the floor and shakes his head.

We get in the elevator and follow everyone to dinner. It's a sports bar and they are all watching another game on the television. We don't sit with each other and I'm a little pissed about it. It just gets worse as the night goes on as the waitresses all hover over the guys, Max included, and I get up and leave. I whisper to Matthew that I'll see him tomorrow and walk back to the hotel. I get into my room and get myself ready for bed. I close off the light and the side door opens.

"Where the fuck did you go?" He stands there, taking off his hat, and tossing it on the desk.

I lean up on my elbow. "Obviously you're confused as to what I'm doing considering I'm in my hotel room in my pjs going to bed."

He stands there with his hands on his hips. "What's the problem, Allison?"

I glare at him. "I don't have a problem, Max, I was tired. So I came back. What's the matter, did all the attention get to you?"

"You're jealous." He smiles and I flip the covers off of me to stand up, forgetting that I'm wearing just my white lace cheeky panties and matching lace bralette, standing up.

"I was so not jealous," I say to him. His eyes rake over me and I look down and then look back up.

"You're naked." Are the only two words he says. "I can see everything."

You can't really see anything. Okay, fine, you can see my nipples a bit and, well, my vagina is on display. "Who cares? You're my boyfriend. Does me standing here offend you? Is it because I'm not bigger in the boob area, or is it because I'm too skinny?" I throw my hands up and I'm almost tackled into the bed, as I feel exactly what he's going through right in the middle.

"We can't do this," he says, shaking his head. "Not like this."

"Max, I'm going to say something right now and I hope you get offended." He looks at me confused. "I'd really like to go past the kisses stage. For the love of God, grab my tits, my ass, fuck," I say breathless and try to buck him off of me, but obviously he's like an ox. "Fine, stay there. I'd like to touch your penis, but I'm afraid that you don't want me to."

He gets up on his knees. "Okay, number one, I wasn't interested in anyone at that restaurant, except my girlfriend who was sitting five fucking tables over. Second, you're fucking perfect. All of you is perfect. Your tits are fucking perfect. I've jerked off to the thought of them at least five times this week, and it's only fucking Wednesday." He pulls off his shirt. "And my penis really wants to be touched, like really really, but I don't want to pressure you. So I go at your pace."

"Max, any slower and we are going to be senior citizens finally going to third base." I smile, sitting up, crossing my legs. "Don't freak out." I lean over and unsnap the button on his jeans.

"Well, we need to speed things up a touch."

"Yeah, we need to speed things up a touch." I look at his heated eyes as I pull the zipper down slowly and I don't know what I'm expecting. It's almost like a jack in the box. You wind it and then wait for it to pop out at you, but nothing happens because his white Calvins hide what I'm after.

"Angel." He puts his hands on mine. "If you touch my cock right now I'm going to go off like the fireworks on Fourth of July and it's not something I want to happen the first time you touch me."

"Max, I just want to touch you. I want you to touch me." I take his hands and place them on my tits. "Touch me," I whisper to him. "Show me you want me."

His eyes go dark before he pushes me back on the bed and my legs open for him.

"By the time tomorrow comes you won't question it anymore," he says as he starts kissing my neck softly, one side, then the next. My head goes from right to left, giving him the access he needs. Both his hands go into the straps of the camisole and pull them down at the same time, my breasts springing free. "Perfect." He leans down and takes a nipple into his mouth and his hand squeezes the other one. My head goes back as my back arches off the bed. My legs squeeze his hips. He moves to the other breast and takes that one also, but he twists the wet nipple he just left. I moan out as the tug makes my toes curl. "I need to leave a mark here." He goes right next to my nipple, sucking it in. "Mine." He kisses down my chest to my belly, his hands still twisting and playing with my nipples. My breaths are starting to come in pants now. My legs fall to the side, opening for him. His hands leave my breast as he rubs one finger over my lace-covered pussy. "You're wet." He rubs and the friction hits my clit, almost sending me over the edge. "Not yet, angel." He runs his finger and my legs open more.

"Max," I plead. "I need…" And I don't finish because his mouth lands open-mouthed on my pussy, as his tongue laps me up and down, the lace blocking most of the feeling. "Take it off," I say, lifting up my hips.

He gets on his knees, puts his fingers in the side of my panties, and peels them down so slow, I groan out, watching his eyes get dark blue. I watch as he sees me for the first time. I look down to see what he's looking at and I see my little strip of strawberry blond, right above my clean lips. Glistening, that is the only word that comes to mind when I see that my lips are still wet from his kiss. I close my knees for him to take the panties off, but he tears them apart instead. "What the hell?"

"No one is ever going to see you in those." He grabs my knees and throws them to the side. "Untouched." His fingers go through my folds and he wets the middle finger and then brings it up to my clit. "Never," he says to himself. "No one." He circles my clit with his rough finger. "I don't know who or what I did to deserve this." He moves his circles a little fast, my stomach getting tight, as I watch him watch his hand. "Cherish." He lets my clit go, goes down, and slowly enters his finger into me. The tightness must get to him because he hisses out, "Forever." And I raise my hips now, wanting it all in me, wanting more.

"I need…" I close my eyes and let my body get used to his finger and then another, then I feel his mouth on my clit as he takes it in his mouth, sucking it in. I look down at his head between my legs. My hand goes into his hair as his eyes come up to look at me and he bites me now. My pussy coats his fingers even more now as he pumps it faster and faster. He's all around me. I'm surrounded by him and my senses are going through the roof. His finger touches something inside me as my breath stops and I know he's touched my G-spot. "Right there." I pull his face more into me as his fingers don't stop, and I can't stop the feeling. I'm ready to let go. I can't push it off and I don't even try. I close my eyes and my pussy clenches his fingers and my clit grows a bit, and his teeth grazing over it makes me come again. My legs close around his head as he hums out. I ride the wave till I'm at the end of it, but he doesn't let up. My clit is so sensitive it hurts to touch, but then it craves it. I try pushing his head away from it, but he fights me, biting down. I yell out.

"One more," he says and I have no idea what he's talking about because usually it's over by now, but the orgasm is lingering. Coming closer and harder than I think is possible, and the second he releases his teeth from my clit and flicks it with his tongue I come again. This time I do it groaning out as my toes curl and my legs go limp. He crawls up onto me, his body hovering over me, as I push his hair off his forehead. "I liked that a lot." I rise up to kiss him, tasting myself and him. A taste I can learn to crave. I roll my tongue with his till his taste is back to only his, till I leave him and myself breathless. "My turn," I say with a wink and his eyes never leave mine.

## MAX

"My turn." She smiles at me and claps her hands together. The only thing on her is her bra in the middle of her chest. She gets on her knees, this time coming to me as I take her in. Her hair is all over the place, as her cheeks are still pink from her two orgasms and my mark on her tit. Her perfect tit that sways from side to side as she crawls on her knees to me. "I know we aren't supposed to talk about all the sex you had before, especially not now with me about to cup your junk." She looks down and then up again. "I haven't given that many blow jobs," she says softly, and the only light on in the room is from outside. I'm almost tempted to go close the curtains so no one can look inside at her, but she looks at me with full blue eyes, her lips plump from me kissing her. "I mean, if we are honest, I've given two.," she says and I stop her with my finger.

"I can say without a doubt I really don't want to hear about you giving someone head. Not now, and pretty sure never fucking again," I say with my teeth clenched.

"Okay, fine." She shrugs and kisses my neck and then sucks in.

"Since you marked me, can I mark you?" she asks me and I don't give a shit if she fucking spells out her name in hickeys.

Her hands go up my arms softly. "Do you know how many times I stared at your tattoos wondering what they meant, wondering which one you got first, wondering if it hurt?" She kisses my shoulder and then her tongue comes out softly. "I wanted to trace them with my tongue," she says, leaning down and kissing my pec, and then she twirls her tongue around my nipple before biting down. "And the name on your bicep," she says as she kisses each letter. "I've wanted to touch it."

"I got that when I was eighteen and drunk," I tell her, watching her trace it with the tip of her tongue, my cock getting harder and harder. "A couple of the guys in the team thought it was a good idea. I just went with it," I hiss out as she sucks in a little and then bites.

Her hands go to my waist as they go into the elastic of my boxers, my cock so fucking hard I could drill through fucking cement houses. She looks up at me and slowly peels them off my hips. My cock finally springs free and points at her, and I swear the fucker smiles. Her eyes go down to look at me. I'm not shooting smoke up my ass, but I know I'm not lacking in the cock department. I mean, I'm human and if any guy tells you that they haven't measured themselves, they are flat out lying. "Oh," she says, looking back up. "I can definitely work with this." She winks at me and I throw my head back and laugh. Only this girl can make me laugh while trying to suck my dick.

I look back down at her as she uses her hand to grip my base and go up, the pre-cum leaking out, and I think she is going to use her finger, but instead she leans down, getting on her hands now, and licks the tip with her tongue. I almost shoot right there as her hot tongue twirls around. Her ass is in the air as she leans down, taking my cock in her mouth. I move the hair from her face to see how she takes me in. She moves her head to the other side as she takes me deeper into her mouth. She uses her hand to fist it and go up and down in the same motion as her mouth, each time taking more and more of me in till I'm buried all the way in her. Fuck. I throw my head back and my hips take over as I hear her gag a bit. Putting my hands in her hair, I hold her head as she fucks me with her mouth. I watch her as she looks up at me, innocent, pure, and fucking mine.

She groans out and the vibration shoots to my balls. I see her ass moving from side to side and one hand is buried in between her legs.

"You touching your clit, angel?" I ask her as I pump into her mouth as she nods and takes me back in. Her spit drips down my balls. "Rubbing it in little circles?" I ask her as I see her close her eyes. "Finger your pussy," I tell her as my balls start to get tight, ready to fucking blow. Her mouth goes faster on me and she finger fucks herself. "Angel, I'm about to come," I tell her, waiting for her to get off my cock. Fuck, I'll be happy to come on her tits if I have to. But she doesn't let me go. She just does it faster and faster and moans out as she comes all over her fingers and I come down her throat. I thrust softly as I grunt out my release. Closing my eyes, I spill into her. I've never had someone suck my cock like this. She took as much pleasure in it as me. She wanted to suck it more than I wanted her to and that makes it so much fucking hotter. Plus, my girl is dirty talking what she needs while giving me what I need. When she finally lets go of my cock, it's almost with a plop.

"That was—" she says and I don't let her finish as I pull her to me and my mouth shuts her up.

I slide my tongue into her mouth and my cock, which was almost going back down, stands back up, waiting for an encore. We spend the night trying to one up each other. I've never come harder than when she sat on my face and gave me a hand job at the same time.

Fuck, I don't even know what time we went to bed, but I was dragging my ass on the ice the next morning, and the guys thought I brought someone to my room when I took off my jersey the next day and saw four hickeys on my chest. Four.

"Someone got lucky," Phil says.

Ryder chimes in, "Was that your girl I heard yelling all down the hall last night?" He laughs as he rips the tape off of his leg. "Steve and I were running up and down the hallway trying to find it." He laughs and I just shake my head. "Was it the blond waitress who was all tits over you?"

"She was not," I say, pulling off my skates. "She was like that with everyone."

"Um." Luka puts his finger up. "I'm still waiting for my fucking water." And we all laugh. "And my food, for that matter. When I asked her for my burger she looked at me like I was bothering her."

I shake my head and go into the shower where Matthew sees me,

"Jesus, did you go to war with a Hoover?" he asks and I shake my head as I turn the shower on. "Jesus, she fucking scarred you near your penis. That, my friend, is her marking you. No one's going to suck your dick now that it's got purple shit near it."

I look down and see the little devil got my hip.

I get back to the hotel ready for a fucking nap and when I open my door I toss the key down on the desk and walk into hers as she sits in the middle of the bed on the phone, her white bra back in its place. I see my mark under it.

"Yeah, okay, I'll get back to you," she says as she hangs up. "I guess you didn't speak to your sister?" she asks me as I flop down next to her, taking off my baseball hat. "So apparently she is invited over for Thanksgiving this year, since her and Karrie are like best friends now and well," she says but stops and leans over to kiss my lips. "Missed you," she says against my lips and then gets back up. "Denise said that she usually hangs around the hospital with you and you cheer people up, so now my whole family is coming to the hospital and having a big dinner."

I look over at her. "They are going to love that." I pull her hand down so she's over me and she smiles as her hair covers our faces. "Kiss me," I say and she does, no questions asked. "You marked my dick," I say when she sits up again, and she shrugs her shoulders. "Your brother saw it."

"He saw your dick?" she asks and scrunches up her nose.

"And the guys drilled me on who I was banging last night because apparently your yelling was heard all the way down the hall." I laugh as she opens her mouth and covers her face, mortified. "I guess from now on we have to do all the yelling in my room."

"Holy shit, what did they say?" she asks me and I'm debating whether to tell her or not.

"They wanted to know if it was the blonde from the restaurant," I say as she glares. "I need a nap if I have to play tomorrow. I'm totally fucking spent," I say, turning around as she slides back down and her phone rings again.

"Oh, by the way," she says before answering, "I'm telling my mom about us."

I don't even know what to say as she answers her phone. I listen to her go on and on about a dress she is getting custom made for the gala as my eyes close and I fall into a peaceful sleep with my hand draped over her legs.

Five days later and we finally touch down in New York. This road trip is going down as the worst road trip of my life. We got our asses handed to us, twice from Chicago and Nashville. Not just a little jab. They fucked us so hard we are all still walking funny. I walk off the plane and to my car, waiting for Allison to come, but she walks toward Matthew's car and smiles at me. I nod at her and make my way home. I've dropped off my bag, fed my cat, went through all my mail, and she still isn't here. I pick up the phone and dial her.

"Where are you?" I ask as she picks up.

"I'm home doing laundry," she says and flicks the television off in the background.

"You could have done your laundry here," I tell her as I look around and she laughs.

"I haven't been home in six days. I had to do laundry and I have no clothes at your house. Besides, aren't you tired of me?"

"Why?" I counter. "Are you tired of me?" I grab my keys, walking out of my loft, and down to my car, opening the door.

"No, but I wasn't sure."

"Pack a bag, angel, I'll be there in fifteen," I say as I make my way over to her house. "I don't give a shit if you bring your wet clothes with you. Besides, I want to hear how loud you really yell when I make you come." I smile as I think back on the times she put a pillow on her face to drown out her moans.

"Fine," she huffs out. "Twist a girl's arm."

And when I pull up to the house she's sitting on the stoop with a small bag packed. I pick her up and some food, and then on the couch I spread her legs and eat my dessert, listening to her moans echoing through my loft.

We have one home game and then we leave the next day to North Carolina, then right back home for Thanksgiving. I'm on my way in for the home game when Denise finally calls me back.

"Where the hell have you been?" I ask her as soon as I pick up.

"I've been going nuts. This gala is going to be the best thing since they put chocolate on pretzels," she says with so much enthusiasm. "And the Thanksgiving meal is going to be amazing. Karrie is a god send. She has jumped in with both feet, not even batting an eye."

"That's great," I say as I walk down the hall to the dressing room.

"So you and Allison?" she finally asks and I smile as I look at her door that is open, but the light is closed, so I know she isn't here yet.

"Yeah," I answer, looking around. "It just happened."

Denise lets out a laugh. "Maxie, there was so much sexual tension with you two it was off the charts. You're welcome, by the way."

"Why is that?" I ask as I see Allison walk down the hall with Matthew behind her. She's wearing a skirt. She never wears a skirt. This one is tight, with a black button-down and a white blazer.

"Well, if I didn't invite her that night you would still be walking around with your head up your ass."

"Well, Shannon there didn't help, by the way."

"Yeah, well, it pushed you both, so. Are you still going away for Christmas?" she asks as I look down.

I always stay for Christmas Eve, but Christmas morning I get in my car and drive the five hours to my house.

"Yup, my place the eve. I leave in the morning."

"Perfect, I'll arrange everything," she says as someone calls her in the background. "Okay, I gotta go. See you in two days." She disconnects and I go into the room, suiting up for the game.

I warm up by working out and then making myself a peanut butter sandwich as Allison walks in, looking around.

"Is Matthew here?" she asks, and I shake my head. I want her to come over and kiss me. I want to drag her in the back and find out exactly what she's wearing under that skirt. "Okay," she says, stopping in front of me.

I look up at her as her eyes laugh.

"You seem to have a mark next to your name there." She points to my bicep that has my name scripture on it, with two hickeys next to it.

"Yeah, forgot about those. What's with the getup?" I ask her as she looks down.

"I had a staff picture to do. Do you see my garters in this?"

And my eyes glare at her as I grip the knife my hand was holding.

"Have a good game," she says and sashays out of the kitchen and right before she pulls the door open I say, "Don't fucking change."

She looks ahead and nods.

"Not even the shoes," I say as the door closes behind her and I eat my stuff.

I get on that ice like a bat out of hell. I deke, I push, I smash into the corner as I count down the time till she's on her back. I wait by the blue line as Matthew passes the puck back to the defenseman, who shoots me the puck landing in the middle of my blade, and cross over to go into the zone. Knowing I don't have a shot, I pass it back to the defenseman as we start the box, passing back and forth till I slide into the middle as Matthew accepts the pass and shoots it at the net, sliding into the goalie's legs since I'm standing in front of him as a diversion. He points at me as we skate to the bench to high-five everyone. The rest of the game is the same with our line creating four more scoring chances. I finish the game off with that they call 'A Gordie Howe' hat trick, a goal, an assist, and a penalty. I get on the plane, not even looking in the back because Allison is sitting in the front and her skirt is riding high and there is no way in fuck anyone else is sitting next to her. Putting my bag in the overhead, I sit down next to her, and take off my jacket, putting it beside me to cover her legs. She glares at me as I smile at her and bring my phone out. When we get into the hotel, I open my door and see that there is no adjoining door.

I take my phone out and call her right away and she answers almost breathlessly.

"Yes."

"Where are you?" I ask her, opening my door, and looking down the hallway.

"I'm on the second floor," she says and I walk to the elevator and press the door. "They were sold out on the fifth, so they stuck me on the second. Two fourteen."

"I'm coming," I say, hanging up, and then pressing the button down. It's taking forever, so I walk to the end and take the stairs down three flights. I knock at her door softly and she opens it.

"Hello there." She smiles lightly as I wrap my arm around her, drag her to the bed, and find out exactly what she has on under her skirt, as I have her legs draped over my shoulders wearing just the fucking heels and her garter. I spend the night making her scream.

ALLISON

"I'll be outside in five," Max gruffs out in the phone.

We got back last night and he was none too pleased when I told him that I was sleeping at my house. He pouted like a two-year-old. I grab a scarf around my neck as I run down the stairs to the front door, putting my black Tory Birch shoes on to complete the outfit, which is black tight jeans and a team T-shirt, with my leather jacket. I grab my purse and phone and walk out the same time that Max arrives. I open the door and see him in jeans and his leather jacket with his Ray-Bans on.

"Morning," I say, getting in, and putting my seat belt on. "What?"

"I haven't seen you all night and you don't even kiss me when you see me?" he says with his back to the door and one hand on the steering wheel while the other rests on the middle console.

"Well," I say, leaning over, and pecking his lips. "Morning."

"Seriously?" He whips his glasses off. "Allison."

"Max," I counter him as he whips his belt off and leans over, his hands cupping my face as he kisses me, his tongue twirling with mine. He turns his face to the right, bringing my face even closer to his, and he consumes me. He takes what he wants from me, leaving me breathless and achy. "Well then," I whisper when he leaves my lips, trailing kisses to my chin and cheek, and then biting my earlobe as I groan out.

"Kiss, Allison," he says, buckling back up, and making his way to the hospital.

We get out of the car and I reach for his hand as he turns his palm toward mine. We walk toward the door and jump when someone honks and I drop his hand as he yanks it away from me. We look toward the beep at my father and mother getting out of their car with Zoe, Zara, and Justin followed by Matthew, Karrie, and their kids, Cooper, Franny, and Vivi. Pulling up is Doug also. We wait for them to walk to us as Max puts his hands in his pockets.

Zoe and Zara run to me and tackle me with hugs and kisses. I miss these nutcases.

"You look like a fucking rock star," Zara says as Zoe looks at me. "You also look like you're in love." And then she puts her finger down her throat. "Groddy." Then I see the second they get a look at Max because their eyes bulge out. "Who is this?"

"This is Max," I say, turning to Max as if it's nothing. "He plays with Matthew. These are my sisters, Zoe and Zara."

Max is about to nod hello when Zoe walks up to him, putting out her hand, so Max shakes hers then she turns and whispers, "Ohhh, Max. Big hands, big feet. Big—"

I put my hand over her mouth before she finishes that sentence.

Zara meanwhile walks up to him, getting on her tippy toes, and leans in to hug him. The look on his face is priceless and he doesn't move his hands from his sides. Because growling behind is Cooper carrying Vivi.

"Would you two for once in your life not make my teeth clench during the day?"

They both shrug and walk away holding Franny's hand.

Cooper comes to me and kisses my cheek. "Happy Thanksgiving, princess," he says as I lean up, hugging him.

"Happy Thanksgiving, Dad." And then I see my mom, so I hug her tight. "Hey, Mom."

She turns to Max and smiles at him, walking to him, and hugging him. He bends down and hugs her also with one hand as Matthew arrives with his arm slung around Karrie.

"Are we not going in?" he asks and Max nods and turns away, walking ahead of us as I walk next to my family.

"So, Matthew," Zoe starts, "just so we are clear." I look at them as they walk backward, facing Matthew and Karrie.

"If Allison can get lifts from your arch enemy, does this mean I can have a crush on him?" She laughs as Zara nods her head and turns to high-five her.

"Girls." My mother stops walking, making everyone stop, my father putting both hands to his face.

"First of all, he isn't my arch enemy," Matthew starts as I look down at my feet and he continues, "and second of all, all he is doing is giving her a lift."

"So, it's a go." Zoe and Zara both clap and then run into the hospital where I see Max get to the elevator and the twins pounce on him, asking him question after question.

When we finally reach Denise's floor she whelps out, running to us. "You guys, you have to see this," she says as she pulls Max with her and walks down an empty room at the end of the hall. It's set up like buffet style, but there are five tables of food and desserts. While four chefs, and I mean chefs, all donning white aprons and high hats walk around checking stuff. I look at Denise, who has tears running down her face as she hugs Max's waist. She looks over at us and then at Karrie. "I have no words and I don't think I can thank you enough."

"It's nothing," Karrie says as she smiles. "Now what else can we do?"

"We can go meet the families that have come out today," Denise says as she leads everyone away from the room and in fifteen minutes, my family has taken over the third floor. Zoe and Zara are busy playing princess with three of the patients, as Justin, Cooper, Franny, and Vivi play Uno with two other patients. Well, at least they try. Justin just lets them do what they want. I take my jacket off, tossing it in the corner with everyone else's, as I walk down the hall looking for someone, but mostly looking for Max.

Max, Matthew, and Cooper are in the room with a little boy, talking hockey as they sign his autograph book. I walk into the room as he turns to look at Cooper and then at me. "She's so pretty," he says, pointing at me. He must be nine years old.

"She is," Cooper says as Matthew rolls his eyes. "That's my little girl."

"My dad says if I want to marry a girl I have to ask her father. Can I marry her?" he asks Cooper, who laughs and says, "Anytime."

I turn to walk away and Matthew yells, "Why are you wearing a Horton shirt?" He puts his hands on his hips.

"Well, considering we are here for his family, I found it fitting," I say as Max looks down and then up, smirking.

"Whatever. I'll let it slide for this one time, but you're a Grant," he says as I walk away and when it's time to eat I make my way to the room and see that my sisters have sat down on each side of Max as he looks up and almost glares at me as I take a seat in front of him. My mother comes to the table and sits as does Cooper. We all wait at the table as the families walk in and take in their Thanksgiving feast. We get up and applaud them all as they stand there with hands over their mouths and shocked expressions. I beam with pride, smiling over at Karrie as she wipes away a tear as Matthew pulls her to him and kisses her head.

We sit down to eat as one of the fathers stands up, "We wanted to." He dabs his eyes as tears start to form, "I think I speak for all the parents here when I say every day we walk into the hospital and our child is okay it is a thankful day. But what you guys did today," he shakes his head, "shows us that we have so more to be thankful for." He raises his glass and says, "Thank you." We all raise our glasses as we sit down and eat.

As soon as everyone gets up and leaves to go to their rooms, the day no doubt exhausting everyone. We get up and start helping put things away. When everything is back to normal we all get ready to leave, stopping in to say goodbye to Denise.

Stepping out of the elevator, Cooper says to me, "You coming over to our house, baby girl?"

I shake my head. "Nope, gotta date with the BF." I smile as I walk outside. My mother looks down and smiles.

"Well, why the fuck didn't he come and meet us today?" Cooper hisses out then looks at Mom. "I don't like him."

"Honey," she says, tapping his arm. "Let it go."

"You know, don't you?" He points at her as she shakes her head.

"Well, at least let us drop you off," Cooper says as the twins run to Max and give him a hug and he awkwardly leans down, tapping their shoulders.

"Not a chance in hell, Pops," I say, walking toward Max's truck. "Besides, Max is driving me home and I have to get my bag." I then turn around to walk backward. "But I'll see you all tomorrow."

"Max, if you see this tool, get his license plate number!" Cooper yells while Mom pulls him to their car.

I get in as soon as Max opens the door lock. I don't even get buckled in before he is taking off, going down the street, and turning randomly into a side street. "What is—" I don't finish because he's over the console and his lips are on mine. My hands reach out to touch him.

"Angel," he says quietly, dusting my lips with kisses, soft kisses, light kisses, perfect kisses. "Your sisters are fucking nuts." He smiles as he kisses me. "I think one tried to touch my cock with their foot."

I throw my head back, laughing.

"It's not funny."

"They think you're hot." I push him away. "Don't let it go to your head. They are both fighting over Ryder," I say as he starts the car, making his way to his loft. "I'm so tired I might sleep till four tomorrow."

"The night is just beginning."

I look at him as he winks at me.

"Besides I need to show you what I'm most thankful for." He laughs as he takes me home, shows me exactly what he's thankful for, and I thank him all night by yelling out his name again and again and fucking again.

When we arrive the next day, he takes off as soon as we walk into the rink. I get a text from my mother telling us they are already there in the shop, so I make my way upstairs. Zara and Zoe are wearing a Horton jersey. I put my head in my hands and laugh.

"Those two are in love." I hear my mother from the side of me. She stands there as she watches them try on baseball hats. "I hope you know what you're doing," she says, still looking ahead at the twins, her voice low. "I know we don't get to choose who we love, but I just want you to be careful."

"Mom," I say, "no one said anything about love."

She cups my cheek. "My beautiful girl, you wouldn't risk everything you know if you didn't love him." Her smile comes out. "His history with the family is a big hurdle that you will have to overcome. You have to just prepare yourself, whose side you will be on. Because"—she shakes her head, looking down—"if you can't stand by his side, wholeheartedly, let him go."

I swallow as the words rip through me. Let him go. Just the thought hurts me. Not seeing him smile, hurts my heart; it's an ache that goes deep, an ache that no matter how many times I rub my chest I don't think it can go away. She sees me rubbing my chest.

"That's love." She grabs my shoulders as she pulls me to her and I bask in the security of my mother's hug. I've felt this security with three people in my life—my mother, my brother, and Cooper. And now the same security comes from Max.

I struggle with my thoughts throughout the whole game, the lingering feelings staying there in the back of my head during the whole week leading up to the gala. I've been going nuts this whole week, so I haven't seen Max that much. Till the night of the gala when I'm rushing around my bedroom in my strapless bra and matching panties as I get ready. Max is picking me up in ten minutes and I haven't put on my dress yet. My hair is tied at the side in a messy side bun with loose, wavy strands falling out. I take the one of a kind dress off the hanger. It's a beautiful soft pink, fully embroidered. It dips low in the front and comes in at the waist tight and then flairs off with ten layers of crinoline. I step into my dark pink satin high heels as the doorbell rings. I grab my shawl and hold the back of my dress as I walk downstairs to the door, opening it to the back of Max, since he is looking out onto the road. His black tux falls perfectly as he turns around and sees me. He's beautiful. I know we shouldn't call a man beautiful, but he is. He looks at me and grins as

I turn around and ask him, "Can you zip me?"

He comes in, closing the door as he zips the zipper to the middle of my back, then he leans down and kisses my shoulder. I turn around to face him and I see the circles under his eyes.

"Did you not sleep good last night?" I ask him. With everything going on with getting things ready, we haven't really been together this last week.

"I know we have to go." He looks at the limo parked outside. "And I know I'm going to sound like a needy bitch right now, but"—he struggles with his words—"is this it? You're distant and I know you said it's because of the gala and the stress but"—he shakes his head—"if you need to end this or just need to walk away…" He swallows and I see his Adam's apple move. "I get it."

My hands get clammy as I open and close them. My heart beats so hard, I feel like it's going to beat out of my chest. "What?"

"You've been distant since Thanksgiving." He places his hands in his pockets. "I know your family means a lot to you," he starts and his voice goes low. "I get it. Trust me, if anyone is going to understand anything about family loyalty it's me. So I get it if it's too much." He shakes his head. "So if this is the end or whatever, just know that I get it."

"The end," I whisper as tears come to my eyes. "Are you breaking up with me?" My shawl that I was holding with my purse falls to the floor and my hand flies to my stomach because I really think I'm going to be sick. I look down at my hand that is shaking as all the memories fly through my mind. The nights on the couch making out, laughing, watching television. The nights of us cooking together. The nights of us forgetting about cooking because our hands were too busy on each other. The nights of falling asleep in his arms. The mornings—the lazy ones, the rushed ones. It's like a running movie clip in my mind. "I'm going to be sick," I say as he reaches out to me and I yank my hand away from him. "You need to go."

"Angel."

"No!" I yell at him, the tears falling over my lids. "You don't get to fucking break up with me and then call me fucking angel." I use my thumb to catch the next tear that is threatening to fall.

"You're the one breaking up with me!" he roars out. "You're the one who is distant and not even there. Making excuses and shit." He points at me.

"Me, what are you talking about? I've had a lot on my plate, Max, and a lot rides on tonight."

"Well, what the fuck do I know?" He throws his hands up. "I've never done this, Allison, so when you started pulling away—"

"I was." I throw my hands up. "I don't know getting in the zone," I say and this time he lunges forward and grabs me around the waist with both hands, bringing me close to him. "I was not ending this," I say finally in a whisper.

As his head leans down he whispers, "Last chance to walk."

I lean in closer to him and right before our lips touch I say, "Irresistible."

And in that moment, I know my mother was right. I am in love with him. Hook, line, and sinker, as they say, but I also know I choose him. I will stand next to him in a fucking tsunami as I hold on to his hand. His kiss isn't hungry, it isn't rushed, it is soft, delicate, like he is savoring every single second, as one hand leaves my waist to go up and hold my face close to his.

We stand here the both of us holding on to each other almost in fear that the other person will disappear when we hear a knock at the door and then it swings open.

"Are we going?" Denise stands there as she wears a black, full-length dress that has a split down the middle. "You look like a fucking princess in that dress." She laughs as I bend to pick up my shawl and purse.

I close the lights as my hand holds on to Max's as we make it into the limo and we make our way over to the gala.

MAX

I hold her hand in mine the whole way there, not letting it go for a second, because I know once we get into that gala I won't touch her till she comes home with me tonight. I know it isn't what we planned since her parents are staying at her house, but no way in fuck I'm not bringing her home. Once I see that we have arrived I pick her hand up and kiss it before getting out. I wasn't ready for the whole red carpet photo session. The only good thing is she will be right there. I get out first as I lean in and hold my hand for Allison and then Denise.

We walk in together as the ladies pose on each side of me. Reporters scream my name, as we don't speak to any reporter before walking in. Making our way through the lobby of the hotel, we see almost everyone is dressed up to the nines. We also see a slew of celebrities that are all walking in and waving hello. Once we get to the ballroom the music is already coming out of the doors.

"Here we go," I say to them as my fingers brush with hers. My pinky wraps with hers right before we walk in and then stand here, taking it in. I'm blown away. The whole room is a soft blue and wherever you look is something about winter. Snowflakes hang from the ceiling all are lit up. Tables are all around with white silk tablecloths and huge white flowers. We walk in a bit more as my hand goes to her lower back.

"Look out," Denise says and we look up as Zoe and Zara come to us. Both are dressed in baby blue dresses that hug their every curve. I shake my head, watching Cooper behind them.

"Max," they both say.

"We flipped a coin and I won the first dance," Zoe says as Zara folds her hands over her chest.

"He's saving the best for last." She follows as Cooper comes to Allison.

"You look beautiful." He kisses her cheek. "Is your guy coming?"

"Nope, he's traveling this week, but he's due back tonight so." She turns and says, "I came with Denise and Max."

"Honey," Parker says beside Cooper, "that dress is perfect for you."

"Thanks, Mom."

Cooper sees someone he knows and waves at them. "There is Ken." Then he looks at Allison. "His son is just out of med school. We should set you guys up."

"Dad"—she shakes her head—"I'm happy with my guy, but thanks. I'm going to get some champagne. Tonight we celebrate."

Denise smiles and nods, following her to a waiter who is handing out champagne.

"When does the dancing start?" Zoe asks, winking at me.

"Look, there is Ryder." I point to them and they both whip their heads around and look at him.

"Dibs," they both say at the same time, speed walking to him.

"I said no to those dresses," Cooper says, looking at Parker. "Why, why, why do you go behind my back?"

"Pick your battles, Cooper. It was that or a mini dress. I chose the lesser of two evils," Parker says. "Why don't you go and bid on some silent auction items? I see a nice condo in the Rockies that would be a great getaway."

He leans in, kisses her lips, and smiles, walking away to the auction table.

I stand here with Parker and she looks at me with a smile. "Now I'm going to do what I told myself I wouldn't and that is give you the third degree."

I put my hands in my pockets, waiting to hear it.

"Pick your battles, Max. If you know you won't fight tooth and nail for her—"

I don't let her finish. "With all due respect, ma'am, there are two people in this world I would fight for. One is my blood, my duty. The other is your daughter." I shake my head. "I don't really care if you or anyone in the family likes me or not, or thinks I'm not good enough for her." I laugh, a bitter laugh. "I know I'm not. Trust me, I wake up every day knowing that I'm not good enough for her."

She puts her hand on my arm, squeezing it. "You're a good man, Max Horton. Regardless of your past mistakes." She leans up, kisses my cheek, and then walks away as I look and see that Allison is being introduced to another guy in a tux. Cooper laughs with them, and her eyes fly around the room, searching something, and I know what that is the minute her eyes meet mine and she smiles at me. I turn, walking to the bar, and ordering a water bottle. I'm here for a minute or two before Phil joins me, then Ryder, Luka, and Charlie.

"This is going to be the longest night of my life," Nico says. "Aly owes me for this. I'm all for going to the hospital, but getting dressed up in a monkey suit."

"Shut up," Phil says. "It's for a good cause."

"What is?" Matthew asks, coming to the bar, and ordering a water bottle also.

"All of this," Phil says as he points all around. "This," he says and then points to the pictures of the patients both past and present, both in the middle of treatment and some that are in remission. "Go put your name down on some of those prizes."

"Fine," he grumbles. "It's for the kids."

I drink a gulp of water when Zoe comes running to me. "Max. I'm sorry," she says breathlessly. "I'm not going to be able to give you the first dance."

Matthew throws his head back and groans.

"I got another offer." She winks at me and turns to walk away.

"Those two are going to give my father a heart attack," he says as someone comes on and tells us to get to our places as the ceremony will start.

I walk to my table that Denise is at and sit down next to her. I see Matthew come to the table with Karrie, along with Doug, Cooper, Parker, and the seat next to me stays open.

"Vivi is going to be so pissed she missed tonight," Matthew says, taking a sip of champagne that they put in front of him. "I think I saw that Charlie dude."

"Which Charlie dude?" Karrie says, looking around when the seat next to me gets pulled out before Allison sits in and pulls herself in. "Oh my God, is that the *Sons of Anarchy* guy?" She points to the man who is in fact Charlie Hunnam. "Shit, give me your phone." She knocks Matthew's arm, taking it from him, and snapping a picture. "He's on my safe list," she says as Matthew snatches the phone from her.

I have one hand on Denise's chair and the other on my leg as the MC starts talking. And then the tablecloth is moved, covering it as Allison puts her little hand on mine. We sit listening to the MC talk about the hospital and all the good that the money collected tonight will do. She lets everyone know about the silent auction that is going on.

"So what do you guys think? Should we get this party started?" she says as people clap. "The dance floor is now open."

When the song "All of you" starts Doug asks Denise if he could have the first dance to thank her. Karrie gets yanked up by Matthew. Cooper pushes his chair out as he holds out his hand for Parker and then looks at us.

"Oh, I see Lincoln." He points to the guy that was talking to her before.

I push my own chair out. "I got it," I say gruffly as Allison gets up and follows me to the packed dance floor. My hand wraps around her waist the same time her hand wraps around my shoulder, and I hold her hand in the other.

"Smooth," she says, looking down and laughing. We spend the rest of the night with stolen touches as I sit at the table watching the girls dance till finally they both collapse next to me.

"I'm ready to go," Denise says.

I nod and text the driver who has been on standby the whole night.

"Me, too," Karrie and Parker say as Cooper and Matthew say, "Finally." Under their breath.

"Oh, look," Allison says as she looks at her phone. "Okay, people, my guy is home early." She picks up her glass of champagne, downing whatever was left. "It's been fun, but—"

"You can't hide him for that long, Aly," Matthew says.

"Leave her alone." Karrie slaps his arm. "She'll introduce you when she's ready," she says as Matthew grunts out.

I walk out, going to the door as Denise and Allison say goodbye to everyone. I see our limo guy and put my hand up to him as I walk over and get in. The car door opens and both girls get in, closing the door after them, and laughing.

"This was so much fun," Denise says, coming on the bench I'm sitting on as we switch places and Allison scoots closer to me, shivering.

"It's getting cold."

I take my jacket off and put it around her shoulders as she lays her head on my shoulder and that is the last thing she sees. Her eyes fall closed and when it's our turn to get off I'm carrying her all the way upstairs to bed. She stirs when I take her shoes off and a bit while I peel the dress from her body. I crawl in next to her and her body turns into mine as she places her head on my chest, throwing her leg and arm around me. I fall asleep to her soft snores.

"What do you mean you're leaving?" she yells the next day as we sit at the island in my kitchen. Her in my shirt from last night and me in boxers. Both of us with wet hair since we took a long shower. I've never gone this long without having sex with someone that's done pretty much every possible thing that I could think of. I know she's ready, but I don't want to just fuck her. I'm one hundred percent not fucking doing it in a hotel room, that's for fucking sure. At least not her first time.

"Well, I usually take off Christmas morning," I say as I place the eggs in her plate. "We aren't back on the ice till the twenty-eight."

"I'm with my parents on Christmas morning," she says, crossing her arms over her chest. "It's traditional."

I shrug my shoulders. "Well, it's tradition that I have Christmas Eve with Denise and then early Christmas morning I load up and take off. It's a five-hour drive."

"So are you saying that you aren't going to be home till the twenty-eight?"

"I usually come back the night before the game. So I'll be back around the twenty-seventh."

"It's our first Christmas together," she says out in a whisper. "You don't even have a tree." She points to the living room.

"Allison, if you want a tree we can get a tree," I tell her as I put my own eggs on my plate. "Whatever you want, angel."

"Well, are we going to exchange gifts?" she asks and I nod as I take a couple bites. "When?"

"We can do it on the twenty-fourth before you go to your parents," I say and all of a sudden, I'm not sure I'm hungry anymore. I look over at her as she picks her eggs in her plate. "We can go shopping today if you want."

"Okay," she says, not looking up as she eats a bite. "We leave tomorrow, so I can order all the decorations online for when we come back in three days."

As soon as we finish, we go out looking for a tree, which is a big mistake. Where I want a small one, Allison is the bigger the better and full. It takes two guys to strap it to my truck and it takes us an hour to drag that fucker upstairs. The amount of pine needles is like we have two trees.

"Isn't it perfect?" she says as Stanley jumps on the couch looking at it with a glare. "Where is your computer?" she asks as she sits on the couch. "I'm going shopping." She totally does because when we get back from Boston there are over fifty boxes waiting in my living room.

I pick up my phone, taking a picture of all the boxes, and send it to her.

She sends me a text with a thumbs-up. I undo my bag, throwing my clothes in the washer when a knock on the door echoes. Opening it, I see it's Allison.

"I couldn't wait," she says with glee as she walks in. "Oh my gosh." She puts her bag down on the counter. I walk over to the drawer in the kitchen, taking out the spare key. "Look," she says as she takes out an ornament of *Beauty and the Beast*. "It's so pretty, but first, lights."

"Here." I hand her the key to the door, my hand holding it out. "What's the matter?"

"Is that a key to your house?" she asks, taking it from my hand, as I nod. "Um." She looks at the key in her hand, turning it over and over, her head coming up and smiling at me. "You like me."

I lean down, kissing her lips. "Yeah, angel, I like you," I tell her as my thumb rubs her cheek.

"Good," she says as she tosses it on her bag. "Now can you get me a ladder? I need to put the lights up."

And after what takes two hours, but feels like two weeks, four thousand lights are draped around the tree. Four thousand. "I think this is a fire violation," I say, watching some of the lights blink.

For two weeks, she keeps ordering Christmas stuff, so much stuff it looks like a picture from one of the catalogues. I place her gifts under the tree after we get back home from the last game before the holidays. There are more gifts under the tree than I know what to do with. I think I'm responsible for about twenty of the fifty.

She spends the twenty-third with me as we spend the night hugging, kissing, pinching, pulling, and devouring.

"Happy Christmas Eve," she says as she wakes the next day.

I look at my watch and see it's past noon. "Merry Christmas, angel." I hug her and then she shoots out of bed.

"Presents!" she yells as she runs into the living room.

I get up, following her, and sitting on the couch. "Can we get coffee first?" I ask as I walk to the coffee and press the button.

We exchange gifts, the silly ones first. I get her a key chain with an angel on it, a scarf that she was going on and on about, a thick winter jacket with a fur hood for when we go to Canada in January, and some UGG boots. She gets me a scarf, a kickass jacket, and the best one yet a picture frame of us taken on the couch as she looks at the camera and I lean in and press my nose to her cheek. I get up, putting the picture in the living room on the main table in the middle. Bending down, I pick up the three small boxes that I saved for the end.

She smiles as she unwraps the smaller of the two and her mouth opens as she sees the red Cartier box. Opening it, she gasps as she sees the rose gold bangle I got her.

"Max. This is…" She doesn't finish as she puts it on her wrist. "It's too much." She touches it as she picks up the same size box and unwraps it to see another red Cartier box. She looks up at me and shuts the box once she opens it. "Are you crazy?" she asks as she opens it again this time to see the rose gold wrap bracelet. "Holy shit, this is the bracelet that everyone is talking about." She takes in the bracelet that looks like a nail that is twisted. Her tears come now. "This is too much."

"Angel." I grab her and hug her. "You forgot the last one."

"I don't want it. Return it," she says, pushing it away from her.

"I can't. It's engraved," I tell her as she now grabs the box and unwraps it to find a stainless steel and rose gold Rolex. She buries her face in my neck. "You didn't see what I wrote," I say as she unburies her face and takes it out, turning it over.

We have never spoken about feelings, so I don't know how she is going to take my declaration.

*I love you more every second.*
*12-23-17*

"To this day, I have never regretted anything I've done in my life, nothing. But with you, being with you, I regret almost everything. I regret that fucking rape charge. I regret giving Matthew's name. I regret thinking I was so much better than him and everyone else."

"Max," she whispers as she moves closer to me. "You don't."

"But you see, I do." I kiss her lips. "I never ever thought it would backfire the way it did. My life was spiraling down and nothing could have stopped it till I hit rock bottom. But when those cops came in that room and arrested your brother, I was never more sorry about anything in my life. It was a mistake that I would take back in a heartbeat." I take in a breath. "It's because of that mistake we are going to overcome the biggest obstacle of all: your brother."

"You were young and stupid. I know you," she points to my chest, "I know the man you are, the man that you strive to be, and that man would never hurt someone purposely. When it's time, we will do it together." She says as she leans forward, "no matter the outcome. I'll be there."

She gets up to give me my box. "Open it." I open it and see the same color box. I smile and find a stainless steel watch. Taking it out, I turn it over and smile at her engraving.

*The best moment is yet to come. Angel*
*12-23-17*

"It's perfect," I say as I put it on my wrist and she cuddles into me. I hold her close, knowing I won't do this for a while. The door rings and I look at the time. "That's the caterer," I tell her as she gets up and goes into the room to get ready.

She comes out with her bag packed. "I called an Uber since the guy is here," she says as she wraps the scarf around her. "You better call me." She walks toward the door and grabs her new jacket. "I'm going to miss you." She leans into me and kisses me, and I hug her close.

"Merry Christmas, angel," I say to her right before she walks out the door. "I love you," I whisper at the closed door.

## ALLISON

"I'm here!" I yell out as I open the door to my parents' house in Long Island carrying in my bag, dumping it at the door. They really should think about moving here permanently soon. "Hello." I kick off my new UGGs and hang up my new jacket as I smile at the bangels and the bracelt and watch that I put on and refuse to take off. I walk through the doors and see the winding staircase all decorated. Lights flash, so I walk around to the back of the house, which holds the family room. "Hey," I say as I see everyone is there. Matthew sits in the recliner with Karrie in his lap as they watch their kids run around the tree.

I go to the couch and sit next to Cooper, who pulls me in and kisses my cheek.

"Merry Christmas." He smiles as my mother comes with a tray of snacks for everyone.

"Oh, good, you're here." She puts down the tray and the kids run to it, grabbing chips as Matthew and Karrie tell them not too much. "I was just going to start cooking. Want to come help?" she says, knowing I'm just going to sit there and watch as she cooks. I nod.

I sit at the island as my mother chops, cuts, sautés, cooks, stirs, and everything else. Karrie comes in not long after sitting down next to me.

"You need help?" she asks Mom, who just shakes her head.

"So," Karrie says. "What's new?" She looks down at my wrist, "Whoa."

"Yeah, it's my Christmas present." I say as I look down at the watch, the watch that he wrote he loved me on. "He engraved it." I take it off and hand it to her. Her eyes go wide as she reads it.

"He loves you," Karrie whispers as she looks up and I nod. "Do you love him?"

I look up at my mother, who stands there with her knife in midair as I admit to the world I love him. "Yes, very much so." I wipe the tears from my eyes and smile. "I love him."

My mother puts her head to the side and is about to say something when my phone beeps and I see it's a picture from Denise with the sweater I bought her as she poses in front of my Christmas tree. Wait, it's not my tree; it's Max's tree. I close off the phone and look back up as they both look at me.

"When are you going to tell them?" Karrie asks, meaning my brother and father.

"We just started." I try and convince more myself than her.

"I get it," Karrie says as she remembers the secret at the beginning.

"Okay, enough about this. Karrie, get the plates. Aly, set the table with the tablecloth. We are going to be sixteen," she says and I walk to the dining room and start getting the table ready.

I take out the red tablecloth and gold napkins. The placemats are also gold. Karrie comes in with the plates and we go about setting the table. More people start to arrive, like Doug and Vivienne along with her parents. The twins finally come downstairs, kissing everyone hello. I look over at Karrie and Matthew hugging by the tree as he picks Vivi up to kiss her finger. Justin is sitting in the game room watching some movie. Cooper is hugging Mom as she cooks. My phone pings and I open it to see Denise, Steve, and Max hold up their wine glasses. I study the picture, the hurt coming at me. I look around and go to my mom first.

"I need to go," I tell her as she looks at me with a knowing look.

"Where are you going?" Cooper asks. "Is everything okay?"

"I need to go, um. It's our first Christmas together and I need to be with him."

"Who is him?" Cooper asks.

My mother takes off her apron. "I'll drive you."

"No. I'm going to get an Uber," I say, grabbing my phone, and ordering one.

"This is going to be your first Christmas away from home," Cooper says with a sad face, his eyes blinking tears away.

I walk to him and wrap my arms around his waist. "I love him, Dad." I cry in his chest. "I love him and I just left him to be with you guys, but…"

He kisses my head as he rubs my shoulders as I cry into his chest. "He should know how lucky he is."

I nod, wiping away the tears as I try to get an Uber in Long Island to drive me all the way back to Soho.

"Why is she crying?" Matthew asks as he comes into the kitchen, picking up a piece of bread.

"I have to get an Uber," I say, looking down, sending request after request. At this rate, I may have to steal my father's car and drive back to the city.

"Why?" he says as he sits down at the table and I look up at him.

I love my brother and would lay my life down for his in a heartbeat, but I love Max wholeheartedly.

"Because I need to go back. I just have to."

"I'll drive you," he says, not asking questions, not asking why, just doing what I knew he was going to do, make me happy. I'm about to accept when my phone pings.

"Yes?" I say as I see the driver is ten minutes away. "I got one." I throw my hands in the air. "I need to say goodbye." I go to my sisters first, hugging them, and then Justin.

Karrie whispers good luck to me as I go to hug Matthew.

"I love you," I tell him as I hug him.

"He better fucking cherish you or I'm going to skate over his dick with my skates." He kisses my head. "After I ram my stick up his ass."

I laugh, thinking about that picture.

"He does," I say, going to hug my mother next. "Thank you," I tell her and then whisper in her ear, "for everything."

She grabs my face after letting go of me and looks me in the eyes. "He better do good." Then she nods to Matthew. "Or I'll sic that one on him." She nods to the side. "And that one."

I swallow the lump in my throat, nodding as I walk to the door where Cooper is waiting with me with my jacket. "You call me when you get there. You hear?" he says as I put my arms through the sleeves, turning around, the scene bringing me back to when I was six and he was getting me ready for school when Mom was in bed.

"If at any time you want to leave, or come back, you call me and I'll come and get you."

"Okay, Dad," I say, grabbing his hands. "You know how I know that I love him?" I look at his surprised face. "He looks at me like you look at Mom. Like she hangs the moons and stars."

"Honey, she does," he says. "I swear if he treats you bad or breaks your heart, I will rain down the house on him." He kisses my head. "While I have him buried under it. Your mom and I have been watching *The Sopranos*. I know lots of things now."

I laugh at him as my phone shows me that my ride is outside. "I love you, Dad," I say, hugging him, and then running out to the waiting car.

I don't text him the whole time I ride to his house. The road's almost deserted. I look down at the picture that Denise sent me almost an hour ago. The three of them sitting at a table, Max's smile, not lighting up his eyes. My legs start bouncing up and down as I watch the road and get closer and closer to him. My phone pings again with a picture of Denise leaving with four bags of food. I guess he ordered too much. I laugh and look up, knowing I'm finally here. I thank the driver and run up the stairs, trying to get there faster and faster. I dump my bag and grab the key out of my purse, opening it, and swinging it open to see the room dark, almost black, but the shades are open so the lights from outside are coming in, but the lights from the tree light up everything.

"Max," I say, throwing my key on the counter as he comes around the corner from his bedroom, wearing nothing but his shorts.

"Allison," he says almost in a whisper.

"I love you," I say to him from my side of the room, tears now streaming down my face as he stands there looking at me, making sure I'm real. "I love you. I didn't say it before because I was"—I throw my hands in the air—"I don't even know why. But sitting there at my parents' house, with all my family, something was missing. A piece of me was missing." I wipe the tears that are coming down. "It was missing because it was here with you."

"Angel, get your ass over—" He doesn't finish because I'm running to him and jumping into his arms. He goes back a bit, but catches me as I look into his eyes, my hands going to his face. "You came back?" he asks as I nod, smiling, while tears still fall.

"I came back to you, for you." I kiss him gently on the lips. "Besides, you didn't open your last gift." I kiss him again. "Me."

## MAX

I see her and don't believe it's really her. I blink seeing her in front of me and then she says the words I've been dying to hear—I love you. Words only Denise has ever said to me. And here she is, in her new jacket and boots, standing in the middle of my loft telling me she loves me. I don't know what the fuck I did, but I'm not giving her back.

"Angel," I say, my heart beating so fast I think I'm going to run out of breath. It's almost like I'm panting. "Get your ass over here." I don't finish because she's running to me as she jumps and my arms wrap around her waist as I step back. She looks into my eyes, her hands going to my face. "You came back?" I ask as she nods, smiling, while tears still fall.

"I came back to you, for you." She pecks me gently on the lips. "Besides, you didn't open your last gift." She kisses me again. "Me." And with that, she lets go of my face as she shrugs her shoulders. Her jacket falls off as she leans in and bites my lower lip. She hugs my neck as her mouth comes to mine. My mouth opens to hers. It's like coming home. It's like it was always meant to be. Like she was made for me.

I walk to my bedroom, the lights still out since I was in the bathroom when she arrived. My hands go to her ass as my legs hit the bed. My hand roams up to her back as she locks her ankles around my waist. I moan out when pulls away from my lips, as she unwraps her legs from me and places her feet on the bed.

"The whole time sitting there, all I wanted was for you to be there with me." She kicks off first one boot and then another. "Then I got a picture of you here, and your smile." She leans down, crosses her arms, and pulls her shirt up and over her head, tossing it to the floor. Leaving her in her baby blue satin and lace cushioned bra. "It didn't reach your eyes. It fell short." She pulls her pants down her hips as she shimmies them all the way down, kicking them off with her foot. She stands there with her blond hair all over the place in her bra and underwear and she's legit the picture of an angel. "So I knew then and there that my place was here, next to you." She smiles as she gets on her knees, bouncing a bit, and crawling to the edge of the bed, her hand coming out touching my bare chest. "I want to be with you." She kisses my heart, no doubt feeling it pound erratically under her lips. "I want to be with you completely." One hand goes to the place she just kissed in the middle of my chest.

I place both hands on her hand. "Angel." I shake my head. "You don't have t—" Her finger goes to my lips.

"I want you to make love to me. I love you." She smiles big as tears come out again. "Like love love love you." She laughs. "Like Romeo loved Juliet, without the dying." She tries to make a joke of it as my thumb catches a tear that is rolling halfway down her face. "Love me, Max."

"I don't know what I did to deserve you, but I'm going to prove to you that I'm that good guy you keep telling me I am." I advance to her, my hands going to her hips, then my finger going from her belly button to her chin, her eyes following it. "I promise to never hurt you." I peck her lips. "If at any time you change your mind, we don't have to do this."

"Max." Her hand cups my cock that is almost poking out of my shorts. "I promise that if you don't use this on me tonight, I'm taking it anyway."

I laugh at her, putting my hands in her hair. "I wanted to do this differently," I say as I tilt her head to the side, kissing her neck. "Candles." I kiss the other side of her neck. "Rose petals." I kiss her chin. "Music."

"I don't need all that. I just need you."

I snap and attack her mouth, pushing her backward on the bed, as her legs open for me and I lie on my arms as I kiss her with everything that I have. Everything that I have to give her. I kiss her and then slowly trail kisses down her neck as I reach one breast, her chest going up and down. I snake my tongue out, in between her bra and her nipple. While my other hand pushes the bra down, I roll one nipple and bite the other, making her back arch off the bed. The heels of her feet dig into my bed as she is squeezing me closer.

"Max."

Her hands go into my hair. I do the same to her other breast, taking it in my mouth and rolling my tongue around the pink peak. I kiss her center and travel little butterfly kisses till I get to the edge of her panties.

"You're everything that I have been waiting for." I kiss her right above her elastic as I peel them over her hips.

I've done this almost every day, yet I look at her, scared to hurt her, scared to not be the man she deserves. She lifts her hips, telling me she's waiting. My heart beats so fast, my palms are sweaty, you would think it's my first time and in some ways, it is. This isn't fucking. I'm going to make love to her.

"I've fucked up so much in my life." My mouth goes on her, the wetness melting on my tongue like sugar. "I know I don't deserve this gift." I suck in and her head goes from side to side as I manipulate her clit with my tongue, my teeth, as my fingers slide inside of her, first one, then two, then three. "I can't walk away no matter how many times my head tells me to. It's my heart that wins out this time." I twist them as I try to stretch her. I know she's getting close because my fingers are being squeezed so tight I don't think I can move them in again.

"Max, please," she begs me and I know that it's now.

I lean up on my knees, leaning over to the bedside table I keep condoms in. Grabbing one in my hand, I tear open the corner with my teeth as she watches me.

"I'm on the pill," she starts saying as I stop mid tear. "When was the last—"

And I don't let her finish.

"I think it was February," I say, looking into her eyes. "I'm clean. We get tested monthly."

"I know," she says.

"I've never ever done this without one, not even once," I tell her as she nods. "You're sure?" And she nods again. I look down at her, her knees to the side, her pussy open for me. The wetness glistens, so I pull my shorts off. I grab my cock in my hand and rub the head through her folds, wetting me. I line my cock up to her opening as I push the head in a little. Her pussy grips me like a vise. I hiss out and try not to let myself take in the moment. I slide in a little at a time as Allison tenses. "You okay?" I ask her as she nods while she holds her breath. "Does it hurt?"

"No, no, it's fine." She looks at me, pushing her legs back, trying to open up more. I go in a bit more. This time only the head is in. "Just do it in one shot." She grabs onto my arms that are beside her. "Like a waxing."

"I'm afraid if I move I'll hurt you even more," I say through clenched teeth, pushing through till I'm halfway in. I swear sweat is starting to roll down my back. I go back out and push in, this time a bit more. I see her bite her teeth and hiss. I go in and out again, once, twice and then I just push all the way in as she screams, not in pleasure. I stay buried in her. "Fuck. Don't do that," I tell her as I feel her clench around me.

"I can't help it," she says, moaning. "I think my vagina is rejecting your penis."

"I'm going to move now," I say, pulling back out and then in again, this time sliding in with more ease. My arms shake from holding up all my weight as Allison's hands stay on my hips. "You're so tight," I hiss out as she looks at me and I slowly go in and out till she finally relaxes a bit. "Angel, I love you" I lean down and kiss her, my tongue rolling with hers as I fill her, as she wraps her legs around my waist, our lips never leaving each other as we both dive off of the cliff together. I ride out our orgasms together, my thrusts coming slower till I'm just buried in her.

I leave her lips, kiss her nose, and then turn onto my back, bringing her with me. "Are you okay?"

"Um, well, considering you're still in me, yes." She leans down and kisses my neck. "I'm kind of hungry," she says as her stomach lets out a big growl. "I didn't eat dinner."

"Okay," I say, hugging her even closer. "Let's get you fed." I slip out of her and roll off the bed. There's a hint of pink on my sheets, and my eyes just stare at it.

"Sorry about that," she says shyly. "I'll wash the sheets now." She gets up and leans down, trying to take the sheets off as my hand comes out and stops her from doing anything.

"Leave them," I say as she stands back up. "Go get in the bath. I'll bring you something to eat." Pecking her lips, I leave the room. I grab a couple of things from our dinner I was going to take with me on the road: turkey, stuffing, some mashed potatoes with gravy. I fix the plate, putting it in the microwave and go in search of her. I walk into the bathroom as she is just getting into the tub. "It's in the microwave, but I don't know if you can eat turkey and stuff in the tub." I laugh as I see her sit down as she goes down to her neck, the water a color pink. "What's in the water?"

"A bath bomb," she says as she lays her head back against the wall behind her. "Want to come in with me?" She opens her one eye, looking at me. I step into the tub and wince at the hot water. "I like really hot baths."

"This isn't hot, it's scalding," I say as I crotch down and go in slowly. My legs go around her body. "This is why I never take a bath. I can't even fit in here," I say as I see my knees come up from the water. "What did your family say when you told them you were leaving?"

She rubs my chin. "They were sad because it's my first Christmas not there." She smiles at me, no doubt in her eyes. "But"—she shrugs—"they knew I had to go."

"I'm not going to be sorry you're here and not there." I shake my head as I grab her foot and start massaging it. "What happened tonight is the best gift that someone has ever given me. I'm a selfish bastard and I wanted you here."

She stands up, the lingering pink water dripping off of her. She steps out of the tub, grabbing one of the hanging white robes that is hanging near the shower. Something that she added over time.

"Go eat," I say as I get out of the tub. "I need to wash off this pink shit."

She laughs as she comes to me and gets on her tippy toes, kissing me under my jaw. "Okay." She walks out as I start the shower. By the time I finally finish, I find her washing her plate and putting it in the dishwasher. "What time are we leaving in the morning?" she asks as she leans against the counter.

"Five a.m., so we can make it there just before lunch," I say as she closes the lights off and we make it back to the bedroom. "I can't believe you're really here," I say as she slides her robe off and gets in the bed, grabbing the covers that are at the end of the bed. I get in next to her, wrapping my arms around her. "Merry Christmas, angel." I kiss her head as she lies in my arms and falls fast asleep.

## ALLISON

I hear the beeping coming from his side of the bed and I groan out. I open one eye, seeing it's still dark outside. "Shut it off," I say, burying myself deeper in the covers.

"It's four forty-five." He kisses my neck from behind me where he holds me in his arms. "Are you okay?" he asks quietly.

"I'm a little sore," I tell him the truth. "It's not like a bad pain." I turn in his arms, tucking my arms to my chest. "Kind of like throbbing."

"We should have waited," he says, bringing me closer to him as the alarm rings again. "We need to go." He turns and shuts the noise off.

I roll to my side of the bed, getting up, and walking to the bathroom. I stand in front of the mirror and look at myself. Do I look different? No. I turn sideways. Can you tell that I had sex last night? Nope.

"What are you doing?" Max asks from his side of the sink as he wets his toothbrush.

"I'm checking to see if I look different now that I've had sex." I grab my own toothbrush. "Vivi said you can tell when someone has sex," I say, putting the toothbrush in my mouth, and talking while the toothbrush sticks to one side. "I have to send her a picture and see if she spots the difference," I say in between brushing and spitting. Max goes to his closet, coming back out wearing jeans and a T-shirt while I stand here in yoga pants and one of his hoodies I saw on his chair.

He looks me up and down and smiles when he sees me in his shirt. I shake my head. "I'm going to toss the sheets in the laundry before we leave." I grab one corner as he watches me. "What are you doing?" I ask, huffing.

"I'm trying to see if you look different." He smirks at me as I glare at him. "You don't. You're just as beautiful as you were last night, or as you were two days ago." He walks to me, grabbing me, pulling me to him. "Actually, I'm lying, you do look different. You're more beautiful." He kisses my nose. "Now let's go. I want to be on the road by five and it's four fifty-seven." He turns and goes back into his closet, coming out with his travel bag. "I packed a couple extra sweaters for you in case you don't have clothes."

I nod at him as I grab the sheets and walk all the way across the loft to the laundry room. "Okay, I'm ready," I say after I toss the sheets in the basket.

"Grab the bag in the fridge," he says and grabs our jackets. "I started the car, so we don't need our jackets. You ready?"

I nod as I grab my purse and the food bag and follow him out.

We load up the car, getting in. "Road trip," I say as I buckle myself in, taking off my UGGs and tucking my feet under me. "We didn't even pack coffee," I tell him, looking at the streets that are deserted.

We drive away from the city as the sun comes up and I look out the window. "Where are we going?"

"I own a house right over the border, a log house. It was the first thing I bought when I got my contract. I use it as my summer home. It's right on a lake, buried almost in the woods. It has a cabin, but it's iffy and the Wi-Fi is a crap shot." He smiles at me. "No one but Denise knows about this house. It's the basics: kitchen, living room, bathroom, and bedroom. I did have it gutted three years ago and updated."

I nod at him and then lean my head on the window, watching the grass go from green to white. We pass the border in record time. It's so small there is only one guy for both sides. "I called the guy to make sure everything is shoveled before we get there," he says as I look around as he pulls off at an exit. I look down and see my phone go from four bars to three to one. "Told you Wi-Fi is iffy."

I shrug my shoulder. "I don't care. I'm with the only person who matters right now."

He smiles at me and takes turn after turn, going higher and higher as my ears start to block. You don't see any houses anywhere; just pine trees. We pass a store, a gas station, what looks like a diner, and then he turns left into what looks like a driveway. "Are we here?" I ask as he zigzags till it opens up to a stunning house. "This isn't a freaking log cabin, it's a fort."

I take in two wooden garage doors, with the stairs right to the side. The house is sitting on two levels. He parks the car, turning it off as I put my UGGs back on and follow him up the stairs. The right side of me is a sitting area, being held up by stilts. He opens the door and I take it in. It's an open concept like his loft. There is a little room right off the entrance that is where he stores all his jackets and there is a bench. He takes off his shoes and hangs our jackets. A door in the corner shows me it's a bathroom. "Come, I'll show you around," he says as he takes my hand in his. We walk into the house right into a hallway with three doors, but we go to the left that leads up to an open area. Right away, there is the kitchen. The cabinets are a dark brown, lining the whole wall in an L-shape. The sink is facing a window that shows you more trees. But what gets me the most is the windows on the back of the house.

I look up and see that everything looks like logs are holding everything together. As we walk into the middle of the house I look around and the only thing I see is the back wall of the house is just huge windows. All held together with wood logs, the sunlight coming in to the whole house. A two-person table sits right in front of it with a fireplace to the right hand side all in bricks to the ceiling. The rustic leather couch sits in front of the fireplace that has a television hanging on top of it. There is a door to the side with a deer head hanging from the top. "Please tell me that isn't real."

He laughs at me. "I didn't shoot it if it's any consolation." He drags me back to the other side as we walk down the hall where he opens what is the bathroom. The bathtub is in the middle of the room with a window over it. A shower stall is next to the bathtub all in glass. White towels hang and are folded everywhere. He opens the only door left in the hallway. I see windows everywhere showing us the lake in the back. His bed is right in the middle of the room. The brown and white covers look like a cloud. On the side is another fireplace pointing straight to the bed. I walk to the windows and see the outside. "It's a dream getaway."

"It is," he says as he comes to me, hugging me from the behind. "Let's have lunch." He walks out of the room, grabbing his jacket. "I'm going to unload the car." He walks out as I go and open the fridge, which is fully stocked.

"How is it your fridge is fully stocked?" I ask him as he puts the food bag on the island.

"I have a couple who makes sure everything is kept okay during the winter season when I'm not here," he says as he walks to the fireplace, opens it, and starts the fire.

"Are we going to Netflix and chill?" I say as I take out some eggs to cook us breakfast. "Oh, can we have brupper?" I ask him as I look around to see if he has everything that we need in order to do it.

"What the fuck is brupper?" he asks as he gets up and turns around.

"It's breakfast for supper," I say with a smile. "It was my favorite meal growing up. Pancakes, eggs, bacon, sausage. All for dinner."

He shrugs his shoulders. "Whatever you want, angel."

I clap my hands together and say "yes" under my breath. "So you want to have supper for breakfast?" I ask him, taking out the things that he brought for supper, which are leftovers from last night.

"Sure and then I want to have a nap." He winks at me.

"Max Horton, is that code for you want to have sex?" I put my hands on my hips. "Because I really want to nap."

He smiles and then stops. "You think it will be okay?"

I tilt my head. "I mean, we can try and see."

"If it hurts, you need to tell me and we will actually nap."

I wave my hand in the air as I heat us up some turkey. I get up when we are done, bringing the plates to the sink, opening the water while I feel him at my back. His hands go up my shirt, his palms slowly running up my stomach to my breast. The touch causes me to shiver and goosebumps to come out.

"I really want to nap right now," he whispers in my ear as I tilt my neck to the side and give him access to it.

He bends his face into my neck where he bites me softly the same time as he pinches both nipples. My head falls back on his chest as my wet hands go to the tops of the sweater. My hands lie on his that are underneath it. His hands leave me as he pulls the sweater over my head. He turns me to look at him.

"I can't get enough of you." He rips my lace bra off of me, bending down, and taking a nipple into his mouth. He nibbles down and then sucks it in. He does the same thing to the other breast. Taking his hands, he moves down my sides and pulls my yoga pants down my hips, taking the panties with him. "Step out," he says, his voice gravelly.

I do as I'm told as I stand here in front of him fully naked. His eyes roam over my body as he picks me up, turns, and places my ass on the counter. My legs dangle over the counter as he steps in between them.

"You take my breath away each and every time," he says almost in a whisper as he pushes my hair behind me. "I've never wanted anyone as much as I want you." He kisses my lips. I push into him to get more, but he leaves as soon as he pecks me. "You know why I call you angel?" he asks and kisses the side of my lips. "Because you hold the power of me in your hands. You're pure, untouched, and sometimes I swear I can see a halo above your head." He takes one leg and bends it, placing my foot on the counter, and does the same with the other foot. I sit on the counter, my pussy open to him. He takes his index finger and runs it down my center, from my clit all the way to my entrance. "You're so wet for me." He gets on his knees, his face coming right to my pussy. He blows on my clit, making my body shiver.

I look down as his fingers play with me. They go inside me and come out, going up and playing with my clit, my juices sticky on his fingers. My eyes never leave his fingers, watching them go into me. His eyes are also on his hands. I lean back, placing my hands on the counter behind me, and I watch him finger fuck me slowly, my body getting tense when he takes his fingers out and he slowly circles my clit, and just when I feel a tightening and know I'm going to come, he pulls his fingers from my clit and enters me again. I moan out my frustration as he slowly fucks me with his fingers again. This time I take one of my own hands, bring it to my clit, circling it as he sticks his two middle fingers in me.

"You're so close." He leans in and licks my lips, my tongue coming out to meet his as he thrusts his fingers in me.

I let go of his lips, to moan out as the orgasm rips through. I lift my hips as he continues with his fingers. I slowly put my ass back down as he pulls his fingers from me. I watch him put them to his mouth, licking them all clean. He pulls his pants down and his cock comes free.

"This counter is the perfect height," I say as I watch him jerk his cock and squeeze himself.

"Are you sure you're okay?" he asks me and I nod. My feet stay on the counter as he takes his cock and rubs it up and down, wetting his cock as he places it at my entrance and slides in easier now. Our heads are together as we both watch him enter me to the root. "Are you okay, angel?" He pulls out again then pushes into me.

This time the pain isn't there. No stinging or burning now. It's just pleasure. I was a little sore, but it's less and less each time he pushes into me. His cock is going in and out of me as his cock rubs over my G-spot. His thrusts go faster this time, my hips rising to meet him. My clit cries each time his pelvis hits it. I can't stop looking down at us. I can't stop looking at my body taking him, the needs my body is getting to take more of him.

"Angel," he hisses and slams into me now. "Fuck," he says and I know what he means.

I'm coming. My toes curl on the counter as my pussy closes him in, and it hugs him. I toss my head back, moaning out the whole time. When I finally finish he thrusts all the way in as I feel him pulse inside me as he cums with a roar. His hands go to the sides of my hips as my feet finally slip down, and I bury my face into his neck.

"I love you," I whisper before I kiss the vein on his neck where I feel his heartbeat pounding fast.

"Love you more, angel," he says, getting his breathing under control.

"Can we actually nap now?" I ask him, yawning. I don't have to wait for his answer because he picks me up as I wrap my legs around his waist and takes me to bed, where we nap, after round two.

## MAX

We walk into the arena together, first day back after the Christmas break.

We got back last night after spending three days in the country. It was fucking bliss. No outsiders. I could touch her when I wanted, kiss her when I wanted, and make love to her when I wanted. And let me tell you, I wanted it every single second. Driving back home, I asked her to pack a bag and stay with me. I just wasn't ready to let her go and I don't think she was either. So it took her fifteen minutes to pack a huge bag and when we got back home, she set herself up in my closet. Seeing her things hanging with mine made me smirk. I have her. She's here and she's with me.

When we get to her office, she walks in and turns her head to wink. "Skate hard."

I shake my head as she dumps her bag and I walk to the locker room. Half the team is there, so I nod at them and then stop at my place, shrugging off my jacket. I listen to the other guys talk about their holiday when Phil comes in.

"Merry Christmas, you filthy animals," he says and dumps his bag on his seat and shrugs out of his jacket also. "Hey, Max." He sits down and takes off his shoes. "Did you enjoy the woods?"

I laugh at him. "It was perfect," I say as Matthew comes in with Luka. The team is almost all here. I get up and go about my workout, leaving the guys in the room.

When I meet up with them about an hour later Phil is in front of his hook stretching.

"I swear Aly looks different," he says to Matthew, who is taping up his hockey stick. I don't say anything as I go to sit down, finishing off my protein shake. "I saw her before and she's glowing."

"I think she's in love," Matthew says, not looking at anyone. "She left the family for the first time ever to spend Christmas with this punk," Matthew says and I take my T-shirt off.

"Do you know who he is?" Phil asks while Matthew shakes his head. "You think it's someone we know?"

"Nah," Matthew says. "No way anyone is that stupid that they are going to go and date my sister." He puts his stick down. "I'm sure he's some stockbroker or something, maybe even a banker who doesn't get his hands dirty. Fuck, he probably doesn't even know what hockey is."

"Knock, knock, knock." I hear Allison's voice at the door as she holds her hands in front of her eyes. "Please put all penises away. I'm coming in."

I laugh and Matthew groans.

"Three, two, one," she says as she opens the door. "Hey, everyone, just checking in to let you know that everything is set up for Buffalo. We will be having the team dinner with whatever families make it down. All rooms have been booked and they are officially sold out, so if you didn't get an extra room and you needed it you're shit out of luck. We leave as soon as the game ends, so if your family is not coming on the plane but meeting you there, please make sure to tell me so I can have some extra cards made for you."

Phil raises his hand. "You bringing your plus one, Aly?" he asks with a big ass smile while Matthew glares at him.

"You never know, maybe he just might show up." She shrugs her shoulders. "I mean, I need to have someone to kiss at midnight." She shakes her head, smiling.

Charles and Nico, both rookies, raise their hands.

"I can help." Charles smiles while Matthew throws his roll of tape in his face. "Ouch, I don't want her to feel left out."

I snort, get up, and start putting my things on. "The only thing you need to worry about is getting your ass on that ice and making a difference," I tell them both, pointing at them. "Head in the game."

"Okay, well, this was fun. See you guys after the game." She nods and ducks out.

I close off the chatter and get myself ready for the game and dreading the fact that we are leaving again tonight. I get ready and am bouncing on my skates by the time it is ready to skate.

"I'm so fucking tired," Matthew says. "All this holiday bullshit and the eating. I am ready to sleep for a whole nine hours without someone kneeing me in the balls." He runs out to skate.

I follow suit, hearing the fans cheer. I look around, seeing that the arena is only half full for now, which isn't new since it's pre-game. I skate out, testing my blades, going left to right as I look up at the families pouring in now. I see Allison by the glass again, with Matthew's kids. I skate to the glass as little Vivienne smacks the glass while Allison stands behind her. I put my glove on the glass while she hits it, as I wink at Allison and she whispers something in her ear, then the little girl blows me a kiss. I throw my head back and laugh as Matthew pushes me out of the way.

"Stop trying to get my girl to send you kisses."

I laugh at him. "I was just standing here. She was the one who sent the kisses." I take off then, accepting the pass from Luka in front of the goal where it lands on the back of my blade and I tip it up over his pad.

"Fuck you!" he yells as he slams his stick down.

The game is pretty slow for both teams, both of us just basically figure skating and not even caring, till they snow Luka in the face after the whistle. I knock the guy back and the referee calls a penalty for me, leaving the fans to boo. I sit out in the box for two minutes, but my team doesn't let me down by scoring a short-handed goal. One of the rookies, Nico, taps in a rebound. When I finally get out of the box and get back on the bench he leans in.

"How's that for making a difference?" He smirks at me as I squirt him in the face with my water from the bottle in front of me. By the time the end of the game comes around, we skate off with a victory. I take my gloves off, tossing them in my travel bag in front of my bench, taking off my jersey, and tossing it in the big basket in the middle of the room.

"One hour, folks. That is when the bus leaves and the plane leaves in ninety minutes," Allison yells and then walks out. I finish getting dressed in forty-five minutes and walk to her office where I see Cooper and Parker sitting in the chairs in her office.

"Hey," I say, looking down at my phone, pretending to read something, but I'm not.

"Hey," Allison says softly and sits in her chair, putting her laptop away. "I forgot my bag in your car. Do you think you can give me a lift there?" She looks up at me.

"Sure, we can get going whenever you're ready." I smile and nod at her parents. "Are you two coming?" I ask them.

Cooper says, "Yes, but we are flying in tomorrow with the whole crew. Should be fun."

Allison picks up her bag and comes to kiss her parents goodbye. We walk out, going straight for my car, and driving over to the private plane area where I park the car and carry the bags to the plane.

"How many are we going to be?" I ask, looking at the huge plane that is waiting for us.

"About a hundred and fifty, give or take. Doug refused to say no to anyone so some are even bringing their in-laws." She climbs into the plane ahead of me and I swear I'm going to bite her ass tonight.

"Aunty Aly, Aunty Aly." I hear as she walks in and Cooper runs to her. "We take the plane," he says as she throws her bag in the first seat she finds open as I put her bag in the overhead bin.

"You sitting with me?" she asks me and I just nod.

I go in, sitting by the window while she goes in the back and speaks with Karrie.

I have my earphones in when she comes back and sits down next to me.

"Whatcha watching?" she asks as the bus gets here with the rest of the team. They slowly start coming on the plane, and it's an hour later by the time everyone is sitting down and buckled in. Thank fuck the flight is only an hour and fifteen minutes.

When we get to Buffalo three buses are waiting for us. We walk off the plane with her following me in the back as I walk to the first bus and look back and see people carrying kids off the plane. It's a nightmare and I just want to get to my room.

"What's wrong?" Allison asks from next to me as I put our bags under the bus.

I look around, seeing that we are the only two on the bus. "What's wrong is that I haven't kissed you in about seven hours and I'm about fucking done," I huff out. "And I don't give a fuck if we have connecting rooms or not, I'm not sleeping without you."

She puts her purse on her lap as she watches the people outside. "You are so cranky, and"—she leans in and pecks my lips fast—"it's been nine hours, but who is counting, right?"

I grumble out as people get on the bus and the hotel is another shit storm. I go up to my room and see that there is a door on the side wall. I text her, asking her where she is, when a soft knock comes from the door. I swing it open to find her standing there still with her coat. I don't give her another minute as I grab her face with both my hands and kiss her like I haven't tasted her in a week. Her hands go to my waist as we stand here and just fucking kiss. "It's too long," I say as I pull my lips from hers, and I pull her in my room, and yank her jacket off of her. "Too fucking long," I say desperate to feel her on me, desperate for her to be under me, and I don't think I'm the only one because her hands are gripping my shirt while she rips the buttons down.

"I've always wanted to do that," she says with a smirk. "I hope you brought another one, but I don't care." She gets up on her tippy toes and bites my bottom lip while my hands rip her bra cup down and I lean in, sucking it in, and then biting her next to the nipple. I pick her up and toss her on the bed as she lands on her back. Her hair is all over the place as she rises on her elbows to look at me, one tit out, my red mark showing proudly. Her black tights are molding her body, as she sits up then takes off one of her black-heeled booties and tosses it to the side, doing the same to the other one. "You coming to get some of this?" she says and I pounce on her and by the time we are finished, the sheets are wrapped around our legs, our bodies have a sheen of sweat, and we are both panting. "I can't move," she says. "I want to get up and go. My mind is telling me to get up, but my body is like, nah, tomorrow." She yawns.

I curl up, grabbing the tangled sheets, and toss them over us as I lean over her as she tries to keep her eyes open but fails miserably. I kiss her neck as I roll to my side. She turns over, cuddles into me, and we fall asleep with her face in my neck, her hand on my heart, and my hand on top of hers.

I wake up the next day, looking around at the empty bed as I hear the water running and then shutting off. I grab my phone, checking to see that is it almost noon. There is no skate today, so it's a relax day.

She walks back into the room, her hair wrapped in a white towel, and a white towel wrapped around her body. "Morning, sleepyhead." She puts her knee on the bed as I grab her and yank her on top of me.

"Morning, angel," I say, leaning up and kissing her.

"Want to go grab some lunch?" she asks as the towel from her hair comes down. "I'm starving." She rolls over and gets off the bed.

I do the same, going to the bathroom, and starting the shower. "I'll be ready in ten," I tell her as I jump in the shower and she does her hair.

I get out and grab a towel as her phone rings.

"Hello," she answers. "Really? Okay, but I was meeting up with Max for lunch, so if that's okay, we will join you guys," she says to whoever is on the phone. "Perfect, we'll meet you there."

I look at her.

"So my family is having a family brunch and we are going."

"Isn't it going to be weird?" I ask.

"No, we are friends. You drive me to and from the game all the time, so…" She shrugs while she grabs her black tight yoga pants and puts them on over her white lace thong. The pants mold her every fucking curve. "Don't even think about it, Max. My family is waiting."

"What are you talking about?" I ask her, hiding my smile.

"You look like the cat right before he pounces on the bird." She points at me as she puts on the matching white lace bra with a big knitted sweater that's falling off the shoulder. I grab my own boxers and get dressed in jeans and a T-shirt and slip on my jacket and a scarf. I take my beanie hat, throwing it on. "You look hot."

I grab my phone and put it in my pocket.

"Don't even think about it, Allison," I mock her as I open the door and walk out and straight into Karrie and Matthew. I stand here almost with my mouth open, trying to think of a reason why I'm walking out of her room when Allison opens the door.

"Oh, hey, you guys," she says then looks at me. "Thanks for returning my gloves. I almost forgot them again." She saves us as she puts her hand up with the gloves. "Are you guys headed down?"

I see Karrie look at Matthew to see what he is going to say and we are so lucky because Vivienne cries because Franny pulled her hair. I look back at Allison, who looks at Karrie as she says, "Dodged that bullet."

We all get into the elevator as Matthew presses the button for the lobby as he cuddles Vivienne and tells Franny to be nice. We get downstairs the same time as the rest of my family and we walk around the corner to the restaurant that we are going to be eating at. We don't make it two steps before some fans come up to us and ask Matthew and me for autographs. We sign them all and walk to his family that is waiting for us. I sit down next to Allison and I feel out of place, almost like I'm not supposed to be here. I look around at the table, who are all looking at their menus, and I'm one second away from bailing. I don't know how she does it, but she must know because she grabs the hand that is on my leg next to her.

"Did you hear that they have to redo the ice for the game?" Matthew says as he looks at his menu.

"No," I say, "but what do they expect? Outdoor hockey isn't like in the rink."

"Did you ever play outside?" Cooper asks, and I let out a breath I didn't know I was keeping in. I can talk hockey.

"I did, I still do," I say as I take a sip of water that the waitress has just put down. "My cottage is set near a lake, so if I'm down and it's cold enough I lace up with the kids up there."

"I tried to do a rink in the backyard one year," he says, shaking his head. "Let's just say it's a good thing the wife owns one that is covered."

I nod at him as I look at the menu and we all place our order.

"So, Aly, is your guy coming to meet you for that midnight kiss?" Cooper says as he puts his fork down.

"I don't know. He said maybe, so I'm excited," she says next to me, and I turn and watch her smile at her family.

"Max, you drive her home all the time. Have you seen this guy?" Cooper asks as Matthew looks at me, waiting.

"Nope, but I usually just drop her off and leave, so…"

"He's probably one of those stockbrokers who has clean hands and wears polo shirts and pink pants. He probably goes fucking sailing," Matthew says and I laugh.

"There is nothing wrong with any of that," Allison says from beside me. "I love him. He treats me like a princess and that really is all that matters."

"Did you get a PI and do a background check on him?" Cooper asks as Parker gasps beside him and he looks at her. "It's for her own safety. What if he owes the mob money or he killed his last girlfriend?"

"Dad, you really need to stop watching *Dateline* and *48 hours*," Zoe says laughing. "He's probably hot," she continues.

"Okay," Allison says as she gets up. "I'm out. I need to go to Macy's."

"For what?" Matthew asks and she turns and smirks at him. "For lingerie. You know, just in case." She winks at him as he groans and Cooper throws his head back.

"Parker," he says, "talk to your daughter."

"I'd go for red," Parker says as she hides her smile behind her coffee cup. "You know, for the holidays."

I get up also. "I need to go also. I need a shirt." I take out my wallet and look for the waitress.

"My parents paid already," Allison says from beside me. I thank them and say bye to everyone as I walk out, following Allison. "See, that wasn't so bad, right?" she asks as we flag down a cab and make our way over to Macy's.

"I just, I felt weird."

She grabs my hand again and kisses the top.

I turn to her now. "Are you really going to buy lingerie?" I ask her as she shrugs her shoulder.

"I don't know. Am I getting a special present at midnight?"

I pull her close to me. "Oh, I'll give you that something special all right."

## ALLISON

"It's freaking freezing," I say to myself as I walk down the mat to the outdoor arena for the warm-up skate. "Who said this was a good fucking idea?" I ask no one since I'm all alone as I continue to the outdoor rink. The sun is shining, which makes you think it's warm, but guess what, it's a lie. I watch as the guys skate on the ice, getting used to playing outdoors. Some of the guys are taking pictures while others skate around with winter hats on their heads. I look around at the stadium that we will be playing in. Over fifty thousand tickets have been sold and the news crews are setting up their booths. There are people everywhere doing something. I walk to the boards and stand there while Ryder and Nico come over

"Hey, Aly, Nico wants to know if you're dating anyone special," Ryder asks as Nico pushes his shoulder.

"Um," I start saying as I hear a familiar voice.

"Don't you clowns have other things to do?" Max says as he gets to the board and takes the bottle of water and drinks some. "Beat it," he says to them and they just shake their heads at him and skate away.

"Now that wasn't very nice." I lean my hip on the board. I grab my phone out of my pocket and raise it in the air. "Smile, Mad Max," I say as he gives me a brooding smirk. I turn and look at him as he finally smiles and I capture it. "Wow, did that hurt your face? You did smile. Your face might crack."

"So funny." He takes off again and I stand here taking pictures of the team for the website. When I almost can't feel my fingers anymore, I walk back inside and wait for the guys to be finished. I update our Facebook page, as well as our Instagram.

"So you ready for tonight?" I hear Doug from beside me as he comes to my makeshift office, which is a desk and a chair with one wall.

"As ready as I can be. The DJ apparently just got there and is setting up. I spoke with the manager this morning to clarify that it is a dry party, so as long as they are in the ballroom it's water and soda. I can't guarantee for when they leave."

I lean back in the chair. "I just want to tell you what a great job you're doing, and I know we only have you for one year, but hopefully you will love it and want to stay."

I smile at him. "What about Mindy?"

"Let's just say Mindy isn't fond of the traveling, or leaving her child behind."

"How about you ask me after the break? I get through this week and then next week it's Vegas and a five-day break. I think I might stay in Vegas for a bit," I say, thinking about maybe booking us into a nice suite, party by the pool, sex all night.

"Okay, fine, I'll wait for after the break to propose to you another contract." He smiles and then turns around.

By the time we make it back to the hotel it's almost close to five before we walk off the bus.

"Okay, we start at seven sharp," I say to them as they all scatter around. I make it back to my room as Max opens the doors to his and then comes into mine and collapses on the bed.

"I'm ready to say Netflix and chill."

"Well, you can do that, but I'm going to get my shower and then dress up, go downstairs, drink nonalcoholic champagne, and then get that kiss at midnight," I tell him as I get up and start the shower. "How about you come in the shower and I, um, wash your back?" I wink at him as he looks up and jumps up.

"Will you wash it really good?" he asks, whipping his shirt off and tossing it on the bed. He's standing there in his jeans as he tries to kick off his shoes, and I just look at him. The ink that I've been mesmerized by each and every single time.

"I love you," I tell him as he unsnaps his pants button. He walks to me, his hands going in my hair as he pulls my head back. "Never loved someone so much in my life."

He kisses me, consuming me, a kiss that makes my knees weak and makes me a puddle in his arms. He picks me up and carries me into the bathroom, sitting me down as he opens the water, comes back to me as he gets on his knees in front of me, and pulls off my shoes then my socks. He pulls my sweater off me and undresses me till I'm naked in front of him as he kisses my cheeks and then my lips as he undresses himself in front of me, both of us not saying a word. We watch each other, our eyes never moving from each other as he holds out his hand to me and I take it in mine and get up.

"I love you, angel, and if you let me I want to spend every single day showing you," he says in a whisper as he opens the shower door and we step in and he makes love to me, slow, so slow he pins me to the back of the shower, the tiles cold on my back, as he leans down and kisses me as the water from the rain shower runs down around him as our lips never let go of each other. He dips lower as my leg goes up over his hip so he can enter me, slowly, softly. He takes my other leg and my legs lock in the back of his. My back moves up and down as he thrusts into me, my hands going into his hair, brushing it back. I kiss him, giving him all of me, as he pours himself into me.

Our bodies together, our hearts beating together, chest to chest. It is something that will forever stay with me because it is in that moment I know that no matter where he goes I will go with him. No matter what happens, I will be next to him and there isn't anything or anyone that can take me away from him. We come together, both of us moaning out in each other.

We let each other go, both of us not saying a word. I was too scared to talk, scared that I would beg him not to ever leave me, scared to scare him away with my confession of my undying love. It is so much bigger than even I am. So we each get ready, him in his black suit, as I put my black bra and panties on. My gold sequined skirt fits exactly mid-thigh, with the black sleeveless top clenching at the waist and then flaring out. The gold belt finishes off the look. As I sit on the bed putting on my shoes, he comes out and whistles.

"We are coming back here right before midnight?" he asks as I stand up and brush down my shirt.

"Yes." I smile at him. "I'm getting my kiss at midnight!"

We walk out of the same hotel room again, but this time no one is there to see us. We make our way to the reception hall where the noise is already seeping out. Kids running everywhere, chasing each other with balloons. We walk in and I look around.

"Where are you sitting?"

He shrugs his shoulders as his hands go to his pockets. I see Zoe and Zara run up to us.

"Aly, you look stunning. I need to borrow those shoes," Zara says as Zoe adds in, "I need to borrow that skirt."

I laugh at both of them and then they turn to Max.

"Hey, my mom said that you're sitting at our table," Zoe tells him, which surprises us both.

"Oh, there's Nico," Zara says and they both take off.

"Well, I guess that settles where you'll be sitting." I smile at him as he continues to look around. "I'm going to go and see my mom. Want to come?" I ask him as he shakes his head.

"I'll get something to drink." He smiles and then makes his way over to the bar area that is surrounded by all the men.

I walk to where I see my mother standing talking to Karrie. "Hey," I say to them.

"You look amazing," Karrie says while she sips water. "I think I'm going to yack."

"Well, then I guess I look really, really amazing if it's making you want to yack," I joke with her.

"Ugh, your brother knocked me up again," she says, looking like she really is going to throw up. "I just haven't told him yet."

"He's going to be so happy," Mom says from beside her.

"Seriously, you guys need to not take the 'Netflix and chill' so much to heart. Four kids. Four," I say, laughing.

"Yeah, I know, but this one is really an accident," she says as she yells out, "Franny." And we all look at where Franny is trying to pull down a boy's pants.

"So," Mom says, "how long are you going to keep Max a secret?" she asks as Karrie giggles.

"I need to be there when you tell your brother. He is such a dumbass. It's right in front of him." She shakes her head.

"I guess I just want to be us for a little bit longer before I have to gear up for war." I look at both of them. "I hope I have their support, but regardless I'll stand by him proudly," I say, blinking tears away from my eyes, because the thought of having to choose is so big my heart hurts.

"You will never ever have to choose," my mother says as she comes to hug me. "Ever."

I don't have time to answer because the DJ asks us to take a seat for our dinner. I look around the room to see where Max is and he's standing by the bar with all the other guys as they all make their way over to their tables. I see him look up at me as I walk to him, meeting him halfway.

"I think we are table number five," I say as I point to the table in the corner. He puts his hand on the lower part of my back as he escorts me to the table. We sit next to each other as Matthew and Karrie argue over who is at fault for Franny trying to pull the little boy's pants off.

"I told you before it would come back and bite you in the ass, no one pants anyone."

Matthew blows out a big breath and says through clenched teeth and a hiss, "How else was I going to explain why you had your pants down and so did I?"

I throw my head back. "Ugh, I'm going to be sick."

Karrie glares at me as Matthew points his finger at me. "You try having sex with three kids running around. It's damn near impossible."

"Are we really discussing your sex life at a table with Mom and Dad?" I laugh at him as he looks over at Mom, who is shaking her head, and Dad, who tries to look down at his utensils. The rest of the dinner goes off without a hitch, no one blaming anyone for the sex. My phone beeps in my purse, so I take it out to see it's from Denise wishing me a happy New Year.

I check my phone, smiling, while I answer her and then Matthew chimes in. "Are you sexting at the table with Mom and Dad?"

"Actually, no, because my guy just said he will be here right before midnight, so I'll be leaving very shortly to go to him."

"Why can't he come here?" Dad asks and Matthew nods. "What is the whole mystery? I'm telling you I don't have a good feeling about this."

"Okay, fine, I'll talk to him about meeting you guys after the break." I look at both of them. "Now are you happy?"

They don't have time to argue because the DJ starts with the music and the kids pull everyone up to dance with them. The hours fly by and when I look down I see it's almost ten minutes to midnight.

"I have to go," I tell them as I kiss everyone and wish them Happy New Year as I look around to see Max and see he isn't anywhere to be found. I walk to the elevator, taking out my purse, and calling him.

"I'm upstairs in the room," he says and I tell him I'm coming.

I open the door, walking in, and stop as I see the room has a yellow glow. The curtains are open, but it's the hundred candles that he has placed all around the room that give it the yellow glow. The television is on and I see there are seven minutes before midnight. "What is all this?"

"When I was younger everyone used to say that whatever you're doing at midnight when the ball drops is what you're going to be spending the year doing." He gets up from the bed he was lying on. His suit jacket gone, his tie gone, the two top buttons opened, his shoes, and socks also gone. "So I decided that is exactly what I'm going to be doing."

"Really?" I ask, watching him as he comes closer to me. "And what is that?"

"Loving you," he says right before he takes my lips.

I let out a sigh right before my tongue meets his. His hands go to the back of my neck and pull the zipper down on my shirt. I use my hands to untie the belt as I cross my arms to take off my top.

"You are the most beautiful thing I have ever seen," he says again before kissing me, this time my hands working the buttons of his shirt as it opens for me and my hands rub on his chest, and he moans into my mouth. I push the shirt off his shoulders. I stop kissing his lips to lean down and kiss his right side of his chest.

"I love you," I say right before I peel my skirt off and step out of it, I'm about to take off my stilettos when he tells me to stop.

"Leave the shoes on," he says as I nod to him and he pulls down his pants and his boxers all at once. I reach out, grabbing his cock in my hand and moving my hand up and down, my body already calling for him. He leans in and unsnaps my bra, and it falls down my arms as my nipples get hard from the cold. He bends and picks me up, his hand under my legs and one around my waist. He gently places me on the bed and then slides between my legs. Kissing me slowly, my back arches up and he rips my pants off. The delicate lace never stood a chance. My legs open more, allowing him to fit, as he takes his cock in his hand and rubs it up and down my wet slit, sliding into me as if I am made for him.

I put my head back as my body accepts him. He gets on his knees when he is fully inside me. His hands grab mine as he puts them above my head and our fingers wrap around each other as he leans down and kisses me while he makes love to me. My legs go back, tilting my hips so I can get him deeper in me. He slams into me gently over and over as we both hear, "Ten, nine, eight, seven, six, five, four, three, two, one, Happy New Year." And then the sound of popping from the fireworks outside.

"Happy New Year, angel," he says when his lips move from mine.

"Happy New Year, love," I whisper to him as I look into his eyes and he still moves in and out of my body. My body takes over and my hips thrust up, meeting his as I beg him, "Harder." My body shakes for the release he can give me. He finally slams into me, grinding his pelvis against my clit, and I come at the same time that he grows even more inside me and he also goes over.

He pulls me to the side as my head lies on his arm.

"I want to tell my family about us after the break," I say to him as he looks down at me.

"It's time." He nods as he kisses my lips and my eyes close and I drift off, only waking the next morning when there is a knock on Max's door. I sit up as the sheet rolls down my chest, and I grab it to hold it back to me.

Max gets up, going in his room, and closes the door, then comes back with a room service tray. "I ordered breakfast since we need to leave in about three hours and it's going to be a long day."

I smile up at him as he sets down the tray and then goes back to get another two and he finally sits down on the bed and the robe opens. "How many things did you order?" I ask him as he pours two cups of coffee.

"I pretty much ordered everything that they had." He opens the lid to the five covered plates, showing me eggs, pancakes, waffles, French toast, and oatmeal, as well as yogurt with fresh berries.

"This is the best ever," I say, sipping the coffee that he handed me and leaning over to kiss him. The coffee tastes on his lips also. "So," I start saying as I grab a fork and cut a piece of pancake. "Want to stay in Vegas for the break?" I look at him as he is eating the scrambled eggs and he shrugs his shoulders.

"Whatever you want, angel," he says. "Let me know. I'll make the reservations."

"You know reservations is my thing, right?" I look at him and smile. "Where do you want to stay? I'll make the reservations." I take a bite of the waffle. "The pancakes are way better."

"Angel, you want to stay in Vegas, I'll handle it," he says. "End of story."

"You know I'm a planner. I need to know where we are going, what we are going to be doing. I can make reservations for some shows. I can talk to the concierge and see what they sugges—"

He puts his hand on my lips. "Let's wing it."

I put my eyebrows together. "Max, I don't wing it." I scratch my neck. "Just the thought is giving me hives."

"Allison, it'll be fine, like a surprise," he says as he smiles, then looks up at my face. "It's going to fine. Breathe, angel."

I roll my eyes at him as he finishes eating and we start getting dressed to go to the rink. I dress in my warm clothes since the game is outside today. "I don't know how people are going to sit outside with this cold and watch the game," I say as I tie my big boots.

"Now give me a kiss good luck," he says as I stand up and suddenly feel like the Michelin man.

I go on my tippy toes. "Love you," I say as I kiss him. "Break a leg, love."

## MAX

The fucking cold seeps into my lungs. "Remind me never to do this again," I say to the line as I sit down. I am wearing my equipment, which is soaked with sweat but when you sit down it gets almost stiff.

"Stop fucking complaining," Matthew says from beside Phil. "You're having the game of your life. One more and it's a hat trick in front of fifty-seven thousand maniacs."

I don't argue with him there. I came on the ice with a mission to show her that I'm worth that chance.

"Stone," the coach calls from behind us, letting us know it's our turn for our line. I jump over the boards as soon as the winger that I'm replacing comes to the bench and skate to my side as Luka stops a stop and covers up the rebound. We get to the side of him to start his face-off. I'm deep in the corner as I crouch down and wait for the puck to drop. Matthew clips the puck, but it shoots to the other player beside me, but my stick intercepts it as I shoot it behind the net for Nico, the defenseman, who takes it as the Buffalo players skate off for a line change. He passes the puck to Phil, who skates it down the ice while

Matthew skates down the middle. He passes the puck to Matthew, who takes it on his stick by passing the guy who is supposed to be watching him by going around him. I get to the blue line before him, stopping to wait till he is in the zone before I skate in. Once his skate is over the line I skate in with him as he passes the puck back to Phil as Matthew stands in front of the goalie. I stay right next to the goalie, but no one is looking at me as they try to knock Matthew out of the way for the goalie, who is on the left hand side. Phil sees this and passes the puck to the right, giving me the perfect opportunity to tap it into the empty net, which is exactly what I do. When I see it's in I skate to the corner and jump on the glass, as winter caps are thrown on the ice. Phil and Matthew come to me as Nico finally gets to us and jumps on us screaming as Ryan, the other defenseman, meets us at the blue line. We skate back to the bench as we high five everyone. We don't even have time to touch the puck again when the horn rings and we end the game with us winning 4-1.

They call my name as first star of the game as I go around tossing pucks into the crowd. I skate by Matthew's family all on their feet and see the smile on Allison's face. I toss the puck over the glass at her and little Cooper catches it before her, so I laugh as I skate off the ice and head to the locker room. The press is there to interview me. I take off my helmet and run my hands through my hair.

"You were on fire today," the reporter starts off. "How were the ice conditions out there?"

"Yeah, it wasn't the smoothest ice, but since when is it smooth when you play outside," I answer, smiling.

"You had the record high for playing minutes today and you had three goals and one assist. You think this will come into play when it's time to negotiate your new contract?"

"I'm not thinking about that. I'm thinking about the here and now and enjoying every single second. New York is home for me and I hope they keep me." I shrug and look at him. "Time will tell," I say as he thanks me for talking to him.

I talk to four more reporters. By the time I walk back inside the room, half of the team is already in the shower. I get in the shower, but I'm the last one dressed, out of the room, and on the bus. I walk in and I don't see Allison anywhere, figuring she is on the other bus. I sit down in the front, bringing out my phone, and seeing a text from her.

***Franny fell asleep on me, so I'm in the family bus so she doesn't wake up.***

***SO proud of you #MadMax rules***

I shake my head as I answer her.

***You can show me how proud tonight.***

We get to the plane as everyone walks off the buses and we all load up again. It's an hour longer because of all the people, but this time Allison comes to sit next to me.

"Hey," she says as she sits down and I want to lean down and kiss her lips, something I do all the time, but something I've never done with people around and I have to say I'm ready for it to be out.

"Hey yourself." I smile at her as she fastens her seat belt.

"Can we have Chinese?" she asks me as she looks out the window at the plane finally going down the runway.

"Yeah, we can have Chinese," I say and put my head back as the flight takes off. We land before the beverage service is done and with this many people it's nuts. We walk off the plane and as I grab our bags Allison says bye to her parents I walk ahead of her and start the car. I pull up the number of the Chinese restaurant and place our order before she even gets in the car. I look around and see that no one is close, so I lean into her as she kisses my lips twice and then a third time.

"Good job, honey," she says as she puts her seat belt on and I make my way to the restaurant but not before she asks to stop at home and get more things. "At the rate I'm going there will be nothing left for me at the brownstone."

I nod as I pull off, thinking that was exactly my plan to begin with.

When we finally arrive home, it takes two trips to the car to bring in everything and the food. We dump everything, sit at the island, and eat.

"You were on fire tonight." She dips her egg roll in the sauce. "My man." She bites it and licks her lip that has sauce on it.

We finish eating as she recounts what it was like to watch the game.

"It was freezing as fuck," I say as I pack away the leftovers.

"We have one more game and then we take off for eight days, so if you aren't going to eat it, chuck it," Allison says.

I close the fridge and then toss it all out, knowing that I'm not eating this tomorrow or the next day.

"We play Chicago and then we take off for Arizona and then Vegas?" I ask her to make sure and she nods.

"It's going to be a rough couple of days. We leave Arizona that night to fly into Vegas," she says as she walks to the cabinet and takes out Stanley's food. "I need to wash some clothes and then put stuff away." She walks away, picking up her bags and bringing them to the room. "Babe!" I hear her yell as my eyebrows shoot together.

"Babe," I whisper to myself as I walk into my closet where I hear her yell my name again.

"MAX!"

"Yes." I see both our bags in the middle of the room as she starts tossing things in piles. She puts on one of my sweatpants that are rolled at the waist and look like they will still fall off her and one of my T-shirts. "Angel."

"All those clothes need to go to the cleaners. Do you have a bag to put them in?" She looks up and I walk to her, grabbing her face, and kissing her lips.

"No bag. I just put them in a ball and carry them," I tell her as I pick them up to show her. "See?"

"Okay, I have a bag we can put them in." She picks up her empty bag and fills it with all of our stuff. "I need to go shopping for bikinis for Vegas." She starts adding her clothes to the side of the closet that was empty. "I have all my stuff here," she says again, looking at the space that was bare a month ago and is now full of her stuff.

"Good, now you don't have to go back there anymore. Why don't you just give Matthew back the key?" I ask her as I sit in the chair that is in the middle of the room.

"How about we tell them about us, and then move on to we are living with each other." She stands there and I nod.

"Okay," I say, "as long as you know that you're not going back there."

"Really?" she says as she puts her hand on her hip.

"Really." I cross my hand in between my legs.

"And what if I said I wanted to go there tonight and sleep?"

"I would say you bet your fucking ass you're not leaving this house," I tell her, not even blinking.

She shakes her head. "You would never stop me."

"Try it," I tell her. "I dare you."

"Don't you pull that shit with me, Max." She throws the bag at me as I swat it away.

"Angel, the only place you sleep is beside me. So if I'm here so are you."

"We will just see about that. I'm staying at home tomorrow." She starts picking up the clothes to bring to the laundry basket.

"You bet your ass you're staying at home tomorrow, this home!" I yell as she walks out of the room and I hear her growl, making me laugh to myself. She gives me the silent treatment for the rest of the night, going to bed with her back to me. I curl up to her as she wiggles her ass. "I love you," I say to her neck as she huffs out. "I love you, too, caveman."

"Only when it comes to you." I kiss her neck softly and she turns in my arms. "Mine." I kiss her lips.

"Only yours." She rolls me to my back and shows me exactly how much she is mine.

"One more fucking period and we get five fucking days off. I'm going to arrive tonight and not leave my house," Matthew says from his side of the room. I just nod, thinking about how different our five days off will be. I haven't told Allison yet, but I rented a three-bedroom suite at the Cosmopolitan hotel. It comes with a wraparound terrace and I can't wait to just hang by the pool with her. Hold her hand in public, kiss her in public. The period flies by and we get our asses handed to us. Everyone slowly makes their way out to load the bus. "Where are you going?" Phil asks as he picks up his bag.

"I'm going to stay here," I say.

Matthew says, "I think Allison's dude is coming to meet her. Hey, if he picks her up here, can you send me a picture?"

I nod as they both leave the room. I make my way down the corridor to where I see Allison. I had our bags already sent to the hotel. It's shocking what they will do when you are dropping eight grand a night on a room.

She leans against the wall as she waits for me and once she looks up and sees me, she comes to me, "Okay, where to?" She tries to get the hotel name from me.

"The car should be waiting. Let's go," I say as she follows me and groans.

"Max, this isn't funny anymore." She almost whines as we walk out and I see a black Lincoln car waiting for us.

The driver gets out as he nods to me. "Mr. and Mrs. Horton."

I just nod and look over to see if Allison is going to correct him and she just gets into the open car door that he is holding.

I get in next to her as he takes Allison's laptop case and my backpack. She sits down and he gets into the car and takes off. We arrive in no time, since the arena is close. She smiles as she looks up at the hotel.

"Well, well, well, Mr. Horton, you did good." She smiles as she takes her bag from the chauffeur.

I walk beside her, my backpack hanging on one hand as she grabs my hand and joins our fingers together. We don't stop at the desk since I've already got the room number and there is someone waiting for us upstairs. We walk through the casino where it looks like diamonds are hanging from the ceiling. I see Allison looking around.

"This was always my favorite hotel." She picks up my hand and kisses my fingers.

We take the elevator to the sixty-first floor. Once the elevator doors open the butler is there waiting for us. "Mr. and Mrs. Horton, welcome to the Chelsea Penthouse in the Cosmopolitan hotel. My name is Andre and this"—he gives us his card—"is my direct line for whatever you need during your stay here. Twenty-four hours a day." He laughs as he looks at Allison's surprised face. "No one sleeps in Vegas." He turns and walks to the door. "The floor can only be accessed by the key card or security." He opens the door and the chandelier in the middle of the room lights up the floor made up of white marble and the walls have floor-to-ceiling mirrors. "Follow me," he says as we put our bags down on the table that is against a wall and walk down a hallway that opens to a big room.

Allison lets out a gasp beside me. I see what she is gasping at. The whole room is cream, but the whole back wall that is floor-to-ceiling windows shows us the view of all of Vegas and all the lights lit up.

"This is what we call the great room," Andre says as he steps into the room.

There is a cream sitting area with two couches on one side of the room with a high top table right in the back of it with six sitting stools. I look behind us and there is a fully stocked bar on one side and a kitchen on the other side. To the left side is another living room in front of a television and then to far left side of the room is a dining room table for eight.

"All the remotes to the functions are on the table right here." He picks up the remote, which is an iPad. "You can control everything on here."

I nod as Allison walks to the windows and Andre presses a button and a door opens to the terrace outside.

"It's a wraparound terrace, so you can get to it from each bedroom."

Allison turns around. "Each bedroom? How many bedrooms are in this room?"

"This is the three-bedroom suite." He looks at me. "I will show you the master bedroom."

I look over at Allison and she mouths, "Three bedrooms, what the fuck?"

I shrug my shoulders as I follow Andre to the right side of the room where the door is. It's actually two bedroom doors, so he opens both. The king-sized bed sits in the middle of the room and we see that it has the same windows as the 'great area.' The bed is up against the wall with two doors on each side. A sofa is right in front of the bed with a table that faces a wall with another television. Allison walks to the door and opens it, standing outside.

"I see the fountains," she says as she leans over.

Andre waits for her to come back inside before going to one of the doors by the bed. We walk into the white marble bathroom. The bathtub is in the middle of the room facing another window looking outside, the drapes up. The shower in the corner is a classic marble shower. The vanity is a two-person vanity.

"You can access the bathroom by both sides of the bed. There are closets on each side before you come into the room." He points to the hidden doors that we didn't see. "If you want we can take the terrace to the other two bedroom, so you can see the view," he says as Allison and I both nod.

We step outside, this time seeing the other side of Vegas as he walks around the corner and we see the Strip now and a sitting area with couches. We pass our bedroom, then the great area, and see another sitting area right before we stop at what is the second bedroom that has two double beds. "This room has two double beds and its own bathroom," he says, pointing in, and then walks farther down to another bedroom with a king-sized bed. "This is the last bedroom. It also has its own bathroom."

We don't bother going into them. He turns back, going into the door of the great room. "Now what can I get you guys to eat?" he says as he turns and looks at us.

"We can go downstairs and get something," Allison says and I just nod.

"As you wish," he says. "I have taken the liberty of putting your things away in each closet," he says, making his way out. "Let me know if you need anything."

"We will," I say to him as I watch Allison look around the room. "So?"

She turns to me. "So? SO? SO? This is insane. Holy shit, this room is for a group of eight people."

I shrug my shoulders. "There was nothing else available anywhere. From what they told me it's the biggest week of the year."

"Are you tired?" she asks me and I try to shake my head, but she smiles. "You just tried to hide a yawn." She laughs. "How is this? We order room service from Andre, eat in bed, sleep in a bit tomorrow, and then start anew."

"That sounds like heaven," I say as I go sit on the velvet couch. "Why are there two couches in one room?" I ask her.

"One is a sitting area, the other is the living area," she tells me like everyone should know. She picks up the binder. "What do you want?" she says as she brings the binder to me, sitting next to me.

"You," I answer her. "You, only you."

"That is the perfect answer, so how about we order up some food and then you can have me before it gets here?" She cuddles closer to me, as she gets on my lap and my cock springs to action. "We can actually fuck right here." She grinds her pussy on my cock, the binder falls on the floor, and she attacks my face with her lips, all notions of ordering food are thrown out the window.

Because we are in Vegas, she is dressed in a skirt, or what looks like a one-piece romper. My hands go to her skirt as I raise it up and my hand trails her legs, till my hands cup her ass.

"Fuck," I say between kisses, as she unties the sash around her waist and just pulls it off over her head. Her lace half-bra is just covering her nipples. I lean down, biting a covered one, and then sucking it in. Her head goes back as one hand goes to my belt buckle and the other to the knee behind me as she arches her back, still grinding against my cock. The heat from her pussy seeps through my pants.

"Fuck," she moans out and I know she is close to coming as she rubs against me.

I undo my button, pushing her off of me, as I pull the zipper down. I look at her eyes that are dark blue now, her lips puffy from me kissing them. I free my cock as she takes it in her hand, moving her small hand up and down my shaft, squeezing him, making my balls go tight. Pre-cum drips out. She scoots back a touch so she can bend over and take the tip into her mouth. The wetness of her tongue makes my eyes close in ecstasy. She takes me as far as she can, moving her head up and down three times till she stops. She moves closer to me.

"I'm in charge this time." She pulls her panties to the side. I see her pussy dripping wet already. She grabs my cock, raising over it as she slides down it. Her hands go to the sides of my head where she holds the couch for leverage as she rides me. Her tits are in my face as my hands come up and squeeze them, pulling the cups down so I can ravish them. I roll a nipple around my tongue as my fingers roll the other one. Her pants get deeper and louder as her pussy starts to get a bit tighter.

"My girl wants to do all the work, right." I pinch both nipples, knowing it drives her crazy and she doesn't let up, this time her hands going to the back of my legs, making her lean back a bit, making me go deeper. Her tits are moving up and down as she continues; I move her panty to the side and see her clit, pink and glistening. "My angel needs me to touch her here." I move one finger over her clit, gently, as her eyes close and she takes in the feeling. My hips thrust up the next time she comes down on me, making her move up faster. "Can't get enough of you," I say through clenched teeth as her pussy gets tighter and tighter. "Want me to keep playing with your clit?" I ask her as she pants out "yes." My finger plays her clit from left to right and when I know she is almost there I change to circles, making her moan out in frustration.

"Max." Her head goes from right to left as her thrusts get shorter and shorter.

"I got you, angel," I tell her as I put my hands on her hips. "Play with your clit, I'll finish."

She moves one hand from my knee and then goes to her clit where she goes in little circles, as she watches me as I thrust up hard. We both moan as my hand moves her up and down over my cock. I know I'm not going to last long, since she is getting tighter and tighter.

"Yes," she chants out, "yes." Her chest heaves as she finally cums on my cock, her hand moving faster on her clit. Till she is almost at the end and that is when I cum inside her, planted all the way to the root. She collapses on top of me, as I hug her waist.

"Hold on," I say as I get up with her hanging onto me. "Shower time," I say as she wraps her arms around my neck.

"Wait, call Andre," she says, reaching for the phone next to her.

Picking it up, I press zero, which brings me to the front desk. I ask for room service and it brings me straight to Andre. "Sorry about that, Andre, I was trying to reach room service."

"You have reached them. I'm them. What can I get you?"

"Pizza and wings," I say, knowing that it's almost her favorite.

"Right away, sir, it will be twenty minutes."

"That's fine, just leave it on the table," I say, thinking that this shower might be more than twenty minutes now that my cock has gotten a chance to rest, and I'm not wrong, the shower lasts as long as the hot water does. Our fingers are shriveled like prunes as we get out and put on the white fluffy robes. I follow her outside to the great room, seeing the food all over the table, two pizzas and four plates of wings. We bring the food into bed with us as we watch television till I finally hear some snoring from her side of the bed. I close it off, following her into her dreams.

## ALLISON

I feel soft kisses on my neck. I turn and my head goes deeper in the pillow that feels like a cloud. "Hmm," I say as I reach out to hold him only to find the bed empty. I open my eyes and see that he's standing over me while he kisses my neck.

"Hey," he says in a whisper. "I didn't want to wake you, but it's almost noon." I look at him shocked.

"No, it's not." I look to the side and see that it's a quarter to twelve.

"This bed is heaven. We need to get one like this for home," I say as my eyes close again as I dig deeper in the covers.

"Come on, I ordered you pancakes," he says as he presses the button on the iPad and the drapes open slowly, letting the sunlight come in.

I roll out of bed, grabbing the white robe I was wearing last night. I walk into the room to see that all the shades are up and there is a table set up outside on the terrace.

"I thought we could eat outside." He points to the table as I follow him.

I sit in the chair, picking up the cup of coffee that is already poured for me. "You're the best." I smile at him as he sits in front of me and we eat, discussing what we are doing today. I grab my coffee cup and get up to go lounge on the outside couch, seeing that the fountains are starting. Max follows me, sitting down, putting my legs on top of his. "Want to go visit the shark reef?" he asks as I look at him. "Supposed to be something to see," he continues.

"You want to go to the aquarium?" I ask him, smiling. "Okay." I watch his smile come out.

"Let's go." He throws my feet to the side and holds out his hand to help me up. "I already got us tickets," he says with glee. "And they are closing it for an hour, so it's only us. That Andre can do so many things."

I laugh as we go into the room and I slide on my white tight fitting jeans, torn in the knee with a white tank top that flares out, tucking it in the front. I take my lilac-colored knitted sweater. He comes into my closet as he is dressed in black shorts and black button-down short-sleeved top, a cap on his head.

"Ready?" he asks as I look at him, smiling, nodding.

I put my gold flip-flops on and grab my cream purse as we leave the room. We take the elevator downstairs and walk out holding hands when he stops mid-step and I stop with him. "What's the matter?" I ask him, thinking he might have forgotten something, when he lets go of my hand and his hands go to my face.

"Nothing," he says the second before his lips find mine, as my hands go to his arms. His kisses leave me dizzy, wanting more.

"I've never had the chance to kiss you in public." He grabs my hand again and continues walking to the door. "Well, after next week you can kiss me every single time you want," I tell him as the driver opens the car door for us. He stops us.

"I want to kiss you every single day."

I get in and turn to him after he gets in the car. "I want to kiss you also, every single day." I nod as he puts his hands around my shoulder, bringing me close to him as we look outside and see the sights as we drive all the way to the end of the Strip where Mandalay Bay is. We get out and follow the signs to the aquarium as we walk through people, our hands always linked. We stop at the entrance where it is written closed for the day.

"I thought you said we had this for an hour?"

He shrugs his shoulders. "I didn't want to rush." He nods at the guy as he gives his name and I watch as the man moves aside and we take the escalator up and walk down the hallway that looks like stone.

"It looks like real rock," I say as I touch it. "It is real rock." I turn as he watches me. "It sounds like we are going into a jungle," I say to him as I look up at the trees hanging from the ceiling. I look down and jump when I see what looks like a crocodile. "Oh my God." I hide behind him as he stands there looking at him, pointing out little things about him, but I see nothing but the crocodile. We walk through another hallway, this one darker, with ponds at the bottom, but the dry rock on the top, and I see a snake. "Seriously you said aquarium not fucking jungle rock."

He laughs as he puts his hand around my shoulders. "I'll never let anything hurt you, angel."

I lean back, looking at him, seeing that in his eyes. His lips come down to mine softly. We continue walking down the path, looking at the tropical fish, some turtles. Till we get to a circular pillar in a dark room that has jellyfish floating in the water. "This is so cool," I say as I place my hand on the tank as the jellyfish float all around the tank as I watch Max watch them.

We continue walking as we enter a tunnel. The side and all the way to the top is all glass as we see sharks swimming above us. I stop in the middle, turning around as I watch all the fish just swim around. "I always wondered if sharks could be tamed," I ask as I look around.

"Do you know for them to mate the male has to bite the head, or the gill?"

I throw my head back laughing, shaking my head. "Of course you would know how they have sex." I look at him as he puts his head back and laughs also, crossing his arms over his chest. The muscles in his arms make his tattoos look huge, making his sleeves of his shirt stretch. I walk to him, the sleeves covering half my hand as I reach for his face. "I would like you to bite my head to mate with me."

Smiling up, he leans down and kisses my lips. "Marry me," he says and my hands drop.

"Wha—" I say as I step back, not sure I heard him. My hand goes to my mouth as I take in Max, who is now bending down on one knee as he holds my left hand.

"I have no idea what I'm doing right now," he says with a nervous laugh, and continues, his voice soft, "but this morning, when you said we should get this bed for home it made me feel complete, like all the pieces in my puzzle are finally all in place. You're my home. Wherever you are is my home." He shakes his head now as I see the lone tear come down his face. "You, Allison Grant, are my home." I smile as he says this as tears are now running down my cheeks. "I've done despicable things, and I'm not the nicest person out there, but with you I feel like I'm worthy. With you I feel like everything I did just led me to you. You make me want to be that better person." He shakes his head again, looking down and then up. "It's crazy, right? We just met, we just started dating. Fuck, your family doesn't even know about us, but I don't give a shit because I want you as my wife. I want to build a home with you, I want to come home to you, I want our kids. Fuck, I want kids with you. This has to be the most unromantic proposal of all time. But I love you, heart, body, and soul. It's yours, angel. Forever. Marry me. Be my home. Let me be your home. Till my last dying breath I promise to be your home."

I stand here looking down at this man who I started off hating, who got under my skin, time and time again, who weaved his way so far into my heart I don't think it would beat without him. So I do what any normal, sane person who has been dating a man for a month does. I nod. "Yes," I whisper as I get down on my knees in front of him and bury my face into his chest while he holds me and he waits for me to raise my head so he can kiss me.

"I love you," he says against my lips. "What are you doing tonight? Want to wake up a Horton?" he asks jokingly, but I get up and just go with it.

"Yes."

He gets up, taking me with him as he picks me up, and spins me around. "I have no idea how we are going to do this. But I think Andre has an idea." He kisses my lips, puts me down, and drags me out of there, my laughter echoing the whole time. We get outside where the driver is still waiting for us. He gets out of the car when he sees us coming, opening the door as Max tells him to bring him to the best jewelry store in Vegas.

"First thing we need to do is get you a ring." Max takes out his phone and calls Andre. "Allison and I are getting married tonight. I need the best jewelry store in all of Vegas," he says and listens to what Andre says. "Tonight, think you can make it happen?" he says into the phone as the driver drives down the Strip to our hotel. "Which jeweler are you taking me to?" he asks the driver.

"Joes on Beverly Hills."

I'm sitting there and the rest of the day is almost a blur of happiness.

*We walked into the jewelry store and Max asked for the manager and said he needed a rose gold engagement ring and wedding band. I sat down in the chair in front of a woman who brought out a black cloth, putting them all down on them. I picked them up, but I didn't go past the second ring when Max picked up the last ring in the long line. A rose gold square diamond ring with white diamonds on the side.*

*"This one," he said, looking at me. "Do you like this one?"*

*I looked at it as he slid it on my finger and it fit perfectly. I looked back up at him, nodding. He then asked for the matching wedding band that was a simple band with white diamonds.*

*"Are you getting one?" I asked him as he nodded and asked for a silver band. But I knew exactly which one I wanted to slip on his hand. I got up from my seat and pointed to the black thick band, outlined with rose gold. "That one," I said as I waited for her to give it to me. Taking his left hand, I placed it on his finger to see if it fit, and it was perfect for him. "Made just for you."*

*I said as he looked at his finger, nodding his head. They wrapped up the rings in record time and by the time we made it back to the suite Andre was there waiting with a man and a woman. He nodded when he saw us.*

"This is Isabelle and Henry. Henry has tuxes for you in one of the guest rooms and Isabelle is here with dresses. Your makeup and hair will be here within the hour. You have an appointment at eight-thirty this evening. I have all the papers here. I just need a signature in order to speed things up," he said and pointed to the papers on the table as Max stepped in and signed and so did I.

"This is really happening," I said with a smile. And then I was taken away to my room where there were four racks of dresses, everything from Cinderella style to stripper style. But one dress caught my eye. They say you know when it's your dress and I knew just by running my hands over it. The flower details in the halter part had been crocheted by hand. Tiny pearls were around them. It was short all the way down with a chiffon wrap starting at the waist with two slits down each leg.

"This one," I said as I picked it off the rack, seeing that it was backless, which made it more romantic. "That is my favorite also," she said then asked me, "Which shoe would you like?"

But it wasn't even a choice. It had always been my dream to have the blue shoes from Sex in the City. "Do you think you can get me the blue Manolo Blahnik?"

She nodded as she took her phone and asked me my shoe size.

There was a knock on the door as the hair and makeup people came in and looked at the dress.

"I would do a low loose bun, let it flow around your face," the hairdresser said and the makeup artist had already set her things down and opened it on a neutral palate. By the time I was done, there was a knock at the door.

"Five minutes." I heard Andre say as they all waited for me to get up.

I slipped the dress on, the back fastened by Isabelle, who held the chiffon part in her hand and tied it around my waist. I sat down as I slid my feet into the shoes that arrived ten minutes ago.

"I'm ready," I said as I turned and finally saw myself. My hand went to my stomach as the butterflies started, and tears started to form with happiness. I blinked them away as I turned to open the door and there he sat in his black tux that looked like it had been tailored for him. His blue eyes clear, his hair perfect, and the best part was the shock and awe on his face when he saw me. The smile that came out as he took me in as I stood here in front of him wearing my wedding dress. His eyes glazed over with a sheen of tears that he blinked away as he walked to me and I walked to him, meeting him halfway. He stopped right in front of me as he got down on one knee again. "This time with the ring," he said as he slid my engagement ring on my finger. I looked down and I knew I would never take it off.

"Sir," Andre said, "the car is waiting in the garage in order to not draw attention."

I wrapped my fingers into his as we walked out of the room, the chiffon flowing all around my legs. I picked up the side of the dress as the elevator arrived and we got in. Once the door closed, he turned as he looked at me.

"I've never seen a more beautiful bride in my life." He touched my cheekbone with his finger. "Is this real? Are you real, angel?" he said as his thumb traced my face to my jaw, all the way to my lips. "Forever," he whispered as I placed my hand on his.

"Forever," I repeated his vow.

The doors opened as we were swept to the little chapel.

So here I am standing behind the closed door as Max waits for me on the other side. "You'll be fine, dear," the lady says as she grabs my hand and squeezes. I'm sure she is grossed out by the clamminess.

"Excuse me," I say as I open the door, peeking my head in. "Psst," I whisper to Max, who looks at me, and I motion at him with my hand to come here. He walks down the aisle to me, a worried look on his face.

"Are you okay?" he asks as he takes me in and I start walking back and forth, pacing.

"I…" I start to shake my hands.

He comes to me and grabs my hands. "Angel." His voice calms me.

"I don't want to walk down the aisle alone. I know I get the whole I'm walking to you and blah." I throw one hand in the air. "But I want to walk down together, both of us, giving ourselves to each other." I look up at him. "Is that stupid?"

"No, angel," he says, bending to kiss my lips. "Let's do it together," he agrees and the butterflies slowly slide away.

The nerves settle in my stomach as I wrap my hand into his arm and we walk down the aisle together. I turn my face to look at him as I find him looking at me. It's the moment I think I will remember forever. It's like it's just the two of us. We get to the front of the aisle where the judge is.

"Dearly beloved, we are gathered here today in the joining of Max Horton and Allison Grant," he starts saying as I stand here looking at him. The smile I've grown to love, the smile I dream of at night. The smile that I want to keep on his face forever. "Allison, will you repeat after me," he starts and I stop him.

"I know that we said traditional vows, but I want to do my own." I look at the judge and then at Max.

"For as long as I could remember I've always wanted to be a princess. I had every single princess dress that you could possibly think of. I had the bed, the room, the shoes. I had it all but the prince. I would sit in my gown and dream of my prince. That he was tall and handsome. I would dream that he would kiss me like a princess should be kissed. He would fight for me, hold me, cherish me, and most of all love me. Then I grew up and I waited for that feeling. Each and every single day I waited to see if it was a myth or a reality. I saw my mother fall in love with her prince, I saw my brother find his princess, and there I was waiting, dreaming, hoping that my fairy tale would come true. Then I bumped into you," I say as a tear rolls down my cheek, and he wipes it away with his thumb, "or you ran into me. But either way it was fate. I mean, I didn't like you." I smile thinking about it. "You were a big ass." I shake my head. "There were many times I wanted you to suffer horrible things."

He smiles at me.

"But then you came out, the real you." I take my hand, pressing my palm on the tears. "The soft Max. The Max who opens my door, the Max who makes my coffee without me asking. The Max whose kisses make me want to lift my foot like a princess. The Max who holds me all night just because. The Max who will fight for me and will fight with me. The

Max who loves me. Loves me so much I feel it all the way to my soul. The Max who treats me like a princess." My breath hitches now as the tears flow freely. "I promise to be true to you. I promise to love, honor, and cherish you till my last breath. I promise to be by your side, holding your hand in good times and protecting you in bad. I promise to share my life with you and be the best wife and mother that I can be."

He leans down and kisses me, as the judge clears his throat.

"I promise you all that, my prince. My happily ever after. "

"Okay, then, Max, if you will repeat after me," the judge says and Max shakes his head.

"I know we said traditional and after hearing all that"—he points to me—"I"—he takes a deep breath—"I'm known for a lot of things, but none of them ever good. From when I was growing up to my teenage years, it was all 'oh, Max, he's the wrong type of kid. Don't play with him, don't go next to him.' I kept my head down and my heart cold. I had one goal and one goal only, to show them I would be better than them."

I squeeze his hands.

"I tried but then the bitterness took over." He shakes his head, blinking away tears. "I never thought anyone would want me or that I could love, only because I didn't know what it was. I didn't know how. Till you." He brings my hand to his mouth. "Till you bumped into me. And then called me an asshole." He smiles. "Then you were everywhere, in my face, in my thoughts, in my dreams," he sighs out. "I fought it for so long, thinking there was no way that someone so perfect could love me, could want me. But you stood there, in front of me, giving me a chance, showing me how to love, showing me what it felt like to love someone, showing me that for the one you love you sacrifice. I would sacrifice everything that I have to make you happy, to see a smile on your face. I watch you when you sleep. Not in a creepy stalker way, but just to make sure you're real. Just to make sure you're there with me. I promise to be true to you. I promise to love you till my last dying breath. I promise to provide for you and our children, and I promise that you will never go a day without knowing how much you are loved. I promise that I will never take you for granted. I promise that I will strive to be the man you deserve, the man you are worthy of, the man you can be proud of. I promise to make you not just a princess but to make you my queen. I promise to give you your happily ever after you deserve and to be the man worthy of you."

"You are that and so much more," I tell him as I look back at the judge. "Can I add to mine? I promise to make sure you see how worthy you are of me every single day."

"Are we done?" the judge asks us as we both nod. "Great, now the rings," he asks as Max takes them out of his pocket and hands them to him. Giving him my ring, he says, "Repeat after me. With this ring I thee wed."

Max takes my hand and slides the ring onto my finger. "With this ring I thee wed." Then the judge hands me Max's ring and tells me to repeat, so I take the ring and place it at the tip of his finger and repeat.

"With this ring I thee wed." I smile as it sits on the base of his finger.

"By the authority vested in me by the State of Nevada, I pronounce you to each other, husband and wife.

"You may now kiss the bride," the judge says right before Max grabs my face in both of his hands. His hard-big hands, holding my face gently.

"I love you," he whispers right before his lips land on mine, soft, gentle, and full of love. My hands go to his waist as I close my eyes and take in the safety of my husband.

"I love you with everything that I am," he whispers against my lips as I smile and look into his crystal blue eyes. "I love you more," I say as he lets go of my face and we shake the judge's hand. He grabs my hand as we walk out of his chapel while my chiffon train trails us.

As soon as the door to the chapel opens, my chiffon dress blows up almost like Marilyn Monroe, the hustle and bustle of Las Vegas almost non-existent since we are off the Strip. I see someone in the distance snap a picture because his flash goes off.

"I think someone just took a picture of us," I tell him while we make our way to the car that is waiting for us.

"Angel, it's Vegas, everyone is taking pictures." He waits for me to get in before climbing in after me. "So, my wife, where do you want to go?" Max turns to me and smiles while his thumb rubs the hand he's holding.

"Back to our room," I say, looking at our hands. "I want to go back with you, lock the door, and just be with my husband."

"I was hoping you would say that." He pulls me to him as his arm goes around my shoulder, and I fit perfectly in the crook of his arm.

We watch the city lights come into focus again once we get on the Strip. Walking through the lobby, I hold on to my husband's hand as I watch his ring glisten in the light. I watch as Max unlocks the door for us. Walking in, I head for the living room that is now turned into what looks like a small reception. Gone are the couches, and in their place is a cast iron square with blush pink roses wrapped all around it. Tea lights make it across. I go into the middle of the room as I turn around and see that all the furniture is gone. The only thing in this room are blush roses, which are my favorite.

"This place looks like a fairy tale," I say as Max walks to me holding a bouquet in his hands.

"For you." He hands it to me as our song "Dive" comes on.

"Dance with me?" I ask him as I walk to him.

"Every single day of my life," he says as he wraps a hand around my waist.

He takes his phone out and raises his hand as he snaps a picture of us. I'm looking at the camera while he looks at me. "Stunning," he says quietly as his phone starts pinging.

"Angel, don't freak out." His voice is curt, tight.

I don't have the time to say anything because my phone buzzes with a text from Matthew.

***Allison, when you get this you better call me.***

"Oh my God." I look at him. "What did we just do?" He looks at me shocked and steps back and away from me. "Max," I say, reaching out to him while he dodges me.

"A mistake!" he whispers, his voice trembling.

I don't know if he's asking or telling. My heart hurts as I see his eyes go dark as he turns and walks out of the room as the front door slams after him. As I stand here in my wedding dress, a tear rolls down my face and I look down and see my glistening wedding band.

## CHAPTER 30

### MAX

The door slams behind me, the click making my heart go to my throat. I close my eyes, only seeing the confusion in hers. "Oh my God. What did we just do?" The words echo in my head.

I walk to the elevator and press the button, my feet moving like lead. My chest hurts. I think I'm having a heart attack as my palm goes to the center and I rub it. I put my hand up on the wall and hang my head.

"A mistake," I say out loud. "She thinks it was a mistake."

"Like fuck I do. I never said that word; you, you said that. Putting words in my mouth, nothing about us is a mistake, nothing." I hear her voice and turn to see tears stain her face. "You." She points at me. "You aren't going to get away that easy." She walks out as the elevator doors open. "Go ahead," she says, her hands crossed over her chest. "I fucking dare you to get in that elevator."

I don't move and the doors close.

"You just vowed to love me in good times and bad and the minute bad comes you fucking leave." She throws her hands up.

"I didn't fucking leave. You didn't see the pain in your eyes. You didn't see the turmoil I saw," I tell her. "I vowed to make you happy!" I yell.

"You think making me happy is my husband leaving me on my wedding night? You think making me happy is my husband not being at my side?" She turns and walks back into the room as I follow her this time.

"I wasn't leaving. I was"—I throw my hands up in the air—"I don't know what I was going to do to make it right. I was going to call them and tell them of my intentions." I'm pulling at straws here. "I had no idea what I was going to do besides punch a hole in a wall or something. I was going to call Parker and ask her to help me. I just want…" I look at her, my beautiful wife. My wife. "I promised to make you happy."

"There is a shit storm brewing out there." She points to the window. "And tomorrow when we wake up we have to face it head-on. But tonight I want to dance with my husband. I want to drink way too much champagne and I want to eat cake, because today I married my prince and that is what they do."

"Angel," I say to her, "the shit storm is going to be a tornado. It's a level five hurricane, but tomorrow we face it head-on together," I agree with her and I go to her, wrapping my arms around her waist while I kiss her wet cheeks. "But tonight my wife wants to dance with me, drink too much champagne, and have me eat cake off of her."

She smiles at me. "I didn't say that."

"I'm improvising." I kiss her lips and she kisses me back. "I'm sorry I made you cry on our wedding day. I'm sorry I let the fear of losing you take over."

"You love me?" she asks me.

"More than my life," I answer her without missing a beat.

"Then let's have tonight. I'm not letting anyone ruin my wedding." Her hands go to my neck. "Including my husband." She winks at me.

"Holy shit, I'm married." She laughs as she throws her head back and laughs again as she lets me go, picks up her dress as she runs outside, and yells to all of Vegas, "I'm married." Then she looks at me. "I'm married."

I stand here watching her glow. "You're married."

I don't know what happens, but all of a sudden, our song is playing again. I stick my hand out for my wife. "Dance with me again?"

She puts her hand in mine, her engagement ring glistening in the light, as I take her in my arms and dance with her on the balcony sixty-one stories on top of Vegas, with the lights shining and the fountains shooting up. We stand out here as we sway to the music that stops after a while. We kiss, soft little kisses. We come inside and drink way too much champagne and I get to eat plenty of cake off of my wife. And I love every fucking second of it. Till the pounding at the door the next day. I raise my head from the pillow, the sunlight coming in as I look over and see it's noon.

"What is that?" Allison gets up on her elbow as the pounding continues. "Is that construction?" she asks as I get up and put on a robe that is embroidered with Mr. on it. Allison is putting hers on that is marked Mrs.

The pounding starts again and this time I hear voices shouting, "Open that door or we will break it down."

"Oh my God." Allison gasps out when Andre opens the door and four people follow him. Matthew, Karrie, Cooper, and Parker.

"Sir. They…" He tries to explain, but Matthew is pushing him out of the way.

"You." He points to Allison with his finger. "Get your shit. We are leaving." Then he turns to me. "And you, conniving little swine."

"Matthew," Karrie says from behind him, holding his arm as he rips it away.

Allison stands next to me.

"I said pack your shit." He raises his voice and it's enough.

"You better watch your tone with her," I say as I put my hand in front of her.

"You don't say a fucking word." He points again at me. "You married a rapist. A fucking rapist," he spews out of anger and the three women in the room gasp out while Cooper puts his hand on Matthew's shoulder.

"Son."

"Get out," Allison says softly from beside me.

I turn to see that tears are streaming down her face, but she doesn't stop.

She charges him, her hands flying to his chest as she pushes him, yelling, "Get out of here or I'm going to call security."

I run after her, grabbing her around the waist to stop her from charging him again.

"I'll leave when your shit is packed!" he yells even louder. "Fuck it, we don't even need it. Get your purse."

"That is the last warning you are going to get from me. I don't give a fuck how you talk to me, how you treat me, but you will not talk like that to my wife," I say as calm as I can. "Ever," I say between clenched teeth. "You treat her with the respect she deserves or I'll have no trouble knocking your ass to the floor," I say to him as he advances and we square off, face-to-face, chest-to-chest.

I have Allison behind me gripping onto my arm. Karrie is gripping onto Matthew's arm, and then Cooper steps in between us.

"Stand down, son," he says and we both don't move.

Parker stands by the door, looking around at what was our reception area. "Is this where you got married?" she asks as she looks around with a hand in front of her mouth.

"No," Allison speaks calmly, "this was after."

"Did you get any pictures?" she asks as she sobs out and Cooper goes to her, taking her in his arms as Allison sniffles away her tears.

"Yes."

She nods at her daughter. "You must have been so beautiful."

"She was," I finally say. My eyes are still on Matthew as the fury looms in them. "You can either stand down and talk to her calmly or you can get the fuck out. Choice is yours."

"You don't get to tell me how to talk to my sister," he growls out.

"She's my wife now," I growl out. "And you won't talk to my wife like that."

"Matthew," Allison says as she pushes him away from me, or tries to, and when that doesn't matter, she pushes me back. "If you want to talk about this civilly, we can, but if not, Max is right, you need to leave."

"Allison, you've just ruined your whole life. You will be associated to him forever now."

"Good," she says, throwing her hands up. She pushes him again. This time he goes back a bit. "I'm fucking thrilled. I'm happy. I shouted it from the rooftops last night and I would do it every single day if I have to. I love him," she says to Matthew and then to Cooper. "I love him, all of him. His past, his mistakes, his screwups, and his triumphs, because that is what makes him the man I want to be with for the rest of my life." She shakes her head as she looks down and then up again as she sobs out, "Don't make me choose, because it's him I will choose."

I can't take it anymore. I spin her around and bring her to me as she buries her face in my chest, my arms wrapping around her as she cries in my chest. I whisper to her that everything is going to be okay, except I don't know if it will. I look around the room, seeing the women with tears running down their faces.

"Aly," Cooper finally says, "we just want the best for you." Then he looks at me. "You took away so much from her by doing it this way. You took away the chance of choosing her dress with her mother. You took away me or Matthew walking her down the aisle."

"I'm sorry for that," I say, looking at Parker as she gives me a small smile and a nod. "But I will not apologize for making her my wife and marrying her. I will never be sorry for that."

"Matthew," Cooper finally says to him, and Matthew turns around. "He's her choice."

He shakes his head.

"Nothing you can say will change her mind."

"Matthew." Karrie comes in front of him. "Look at me. What would you have done if everyone hated you and wanted to take me away from you?"

Matthew crosses his hands, rolls his eyes, and pffts out. "I'd take you anyway. But—" he says as Karrie puts her hand in front of his lips.

"But nothing. You can either accept it and have a place in your sister's life or you don't accept it and lose her."

"I'm not losing her. He's—" Matthew starts and then this time it's Parker who stands up.

"That's enough," she says as she comes to us. "You got us all riled up and on a plane at five-thirty a.m. You came here and didn't even talk to your sister. You ordered her around instead."

He puts his hands on his hips.

"I don't know Max, but I know your sister, and if she is risking everything she has and loves him he must be worth it."

"Mom." He takes his cap off, scratching his head. "I'm looking out for her and protecting her."

"That's my job," I say. "The moment she said she loved me that became my job. Fuck, it became my job the minute she looked at me. I don't want her to choose me or you. It would kill me to have her do that. It would kill me because I know it would kill her."

"Matthew, son," Cooper says. "Don't make her choose."

"Fuck!" he yells out again, "why couldn't you date the stockbroker, or I don't know, a farmer, or fuck, the guy who sharpens the skates? Why him?"

"First off. Fred is fifty-nine." She turns in my arms, looking at him as my arm wraps around her neck. "And you don't choose who you fall in love with. It just happens!" she says, putting both her hands on mine.

Karrie gasps. "Oh my God, that ring is gorgeous." She steps forward to grab her, and while Parker comes over, I let go of her as her mother takes her in her arms.

"I want to see all the pictures and then we should go out tonight and celebrate. You can wear your dress and we can have a small reception." She cries again. "And then when we get home we can do a bigger one."

Cooper and Matthew moan at this as they look at each other.

"Baby, I told you we have nowhere to stay," Cooper tells her as Andre finally pipes up from his corner.

"There are no available rooms in all of Vegas tonight. It's the biggest week of the year."

Karrie turns to look at Matthew. "Did you just drag me on a six-hour flight promising me some fun in the sun? 'Don't worry, babe.'" She throws her hands in the air, mimicking him. "'It'll be fine, babe.' 'Don't worry, babe, I packed your saltines.' 'You can't have morning sickness already.'" She stops talking as her eyes go big and Parker gasps out. "Surprise," Karrie says. "I'm pregnant."

"You can stay here," Allison says as I look down at her. "I mean, we have three rooms." She then looks at Matthew. "You can stay if you're not mean to my husband. If you can't follow that one rule, go sleep in the lobby." She then turns and looks at me. "Is that okay?"

"Whatever you want, angel," I say as I lean down and kiss her.

"Oh my God," Matthew says out loud. "Oh my God," he says again as he gasps out in horror, his hand going to his mouth. "Oh my God." He looks at us then points at Allison. "You're the one who gave him a hickey on his junk." He closes his eyes and puts his finger on them. "I'm going to be sick," he says as Allison finally relaxes in my arms. "Sick."

"There is a room with two queen beds, and one with one king."

"We will take the one with two queens," Karrie says as she grabs her bag from the floor. "You can sleep on the freaking terrace. Bringing me here with no reservation, acting like a crazy person," she huffs out as she collects her breath, "I told you to calm down, told you to talk but does he listen to me, NOOO, not Matthew Grant, he has to come in guns blazing. Like a dragon foaming fire from his mouth." She storms away down the hallway as Mathew yells "babe" as the door slams and you hear knocking.

"Babe." And then another slam.

"Can I see pictures now?" Parker asks, sitting on one of the chairs.

"Sir," Andre says from the door again. "If you would like, I'll have room service come to set up something on the terrace so we can get the room back to normal."

"Thank you, Andre," Allison says as she hands her mother her phone with the pictures we took last night. "I'm going to get dressed." She turns, leaving the room.

I see Parker looking at the phone and then showing them to Cooper with tears.

"She's..."

"I wasn't lying before when I said she was the most beautiful bride ever." I walk over, grabbing my phone, then handing it to them as they swipe through the pictures I took of her on the terrace. "I'm really sorry that we didn't tell you and kept it a secret." I shake my head. "I don't come from a family who loves and supports each other like you guys. I have Denise and I know I would kill for her, but"—I take a big breath—

"it didn't dawn on me everything she was giving up to marry me the way she did."

"I wouldn't change a thing," Allison says as she walks toward us. She has yoga pants and my T-shirt. I laugh thinking it's her way of saying she's all in. "We need to put out a press statement and I'm sure Doug will not be happy about all this. Why don't we call him while you get dressed?"

I nod at her as she tells her parents that we will be right back.

The door closes behind her softly as I go to the bed and sit down on it, my head falling down with the weight on my shoulders. I close my eyes, replaying everything that just went down. I feel her hand through my hair. She places herself between my legs.

"You okay?" she asks as I raise my head to see her.

"I know how much you love your family, and I hate to put you in the position," I start out saying as she leans down and kisses my lips.

"I love you more." She stands up, taking her phone, and calling Doug, putting him on speakerphone.

He answers on the first ring, "This better not be a call that Matthew is in jail for beating your husband up." He laughs out as I hear kids fighting in the background. He moves the phone from his mouth and I hear muffling. "Cooper, you need to share." He comes back. "Sorry about that. I got the kids for the week."

"You're on speakerphone," she mentions. "Max is here also."

"So you two decided it was a good idea to go off and elope?" Doug says, his voice changing to serious.

"It wasn't like that," I chime in. "It happened and it was the best thing to ever happen to me. I know this will not go well with the association." I look at my wife. "But it is what it is. I don't give a shit if we tell the press or not."

"It's too late about that. There was a picture circulating already. I just want to congratulate you both and wish you nothing but happiness. Allison, I take it you will handle the press?" he says. "Now I have to go. Somehow the kids seem to think that finger painting my walls with my shaving cream is a good idea." He hangs up.

"So which one do you like better?" she asks as she shows me two pictures of us. "I like this one," she says as she shows me a picture of the two of us standing on the terrace, her hand on my chest with her ring showing, as my hand hangs from her shoulder, my ring showing also.

"I don't care, angel."

She starts typing and then shows me.

#MadMax is officially off the market. Max Horton wed girlfriend Allison Grant yesterday in an intimate ceremony. The couple is excited for this next chapter in their life.

"Send the picture to Denise also, please. She is probably pissed that we didn't tell her," I say as there is a knock on the door.

"Come in," Allison says and Parker comes in and closes the door behind her.

"Andre said to tell you that everything is set up." She wrings her hands together nervously. "Max, I know that we don't know each other, and I know that we started off on the wrong foot. And I totally understand if you don't want us here. You just have to understand that Matthew is used to protecting her, so it's hard for him to let go," she says with tears.

I look at her and then at Allison, who is wiping away a tear. "I have a sister also. Our mother, she's a drunk. Our father took off when we were kids," I start out saying as Allison sits next to me and holds my hand. "She got married to not only a drunk but a drug user. When my sister was sixteen he tried to rape her." I look at Allison, who puts her hand in front of her mouth. "It's not my story to tell, but she called me and I went there. It was right after the rape charges. I was already skating on thin ice with the Stingers. Well, I went there and I beat him to a pulp, his face all bloodied and broken, my knuckles bleeding and sore. I just couldn't stop hitting him. The only thing in mind was the sound of Denise's wails. My mother, who yelled and screamed the whole time, called the cops on me. Doug came, bailed me out, and made sure that Denise was taken care of. From that day, it's been just the two of us. I have no idea where my mother is or even if she's alive, but I know that I would have done the same thing Matthew did if Denise went off with someone and eloped."

"Max," Parker says from her standing place, "will you make sure that my daughter is happy?"

I nod. "Every single day."

"Would you do whatever it takes to protect her?" she asks.

"With everything that I have."

"Do you love her, so much that your heart hurts when you are fighting? Do you love her so much, you would try and give her family a chance to be part of your life? Do you love her?" She stands there, five foot two, back straight, head high, asking me these things.

"With your daughter I can breathe easy. With her, I can smile just because. With her I know what love is." I look down at Allison. "With her love I know that I can face anything, even the wrath of Matthew and Cooper."

She is about to say something else when there is another knock at the door. This time Cooper walks in.

"So Karrie is sitting down at the table and has already started eating. I will add she is eating for two, but I'm afraid there will be nothing left if you guys don't get out there." Then he looks at the tears on his wife's face and then at the tears on his daughter's. "What's the matter?" he asks as he takes his wife in his arms.

"I'm just asking my son-in-law some questions." She smiles at her husband. "I'm starving and exhausted. Let's leave Max to get dressed and go make sure she doesn't eat all the food."

They turn to walk out of the room, opening the door, and the sound of Matthew's voice comes in.

"Dammit, Karrie, I said I was sorry. Stop throwing things at me!" he yells as you hear him say ouch, before the door is closed.

"Are you sure you're okay with this?" my wife asks me, as I look down at our hands together.

"It'll be interesting, that's for sure," I answer her.

She leans in and kisses me, her left hand going to my cheek.

"Thank you for loving me and for being something so irresistible," she says as she leans in and seals it with a kiss.

## MAX

*Six months later*

"You may now kiss the bride."

I lean down and kiss my wife again, for the second time in my life. The shouts and cheering is very different than when we first did it. When I let go of her face, I see our family and friends—okay, more her family than mine—gathered in the backyard of my in-laws' New Long Island mansion. I just have Denise, who stands next to me as my best man. She agreed to be the best man, but drew the line at wearing a tux. Instead, she stands next to me with tears rolling down her face wearing a strapless champagne dress. She looks beautiful, but not as beautiful as my wife as she stands beside me wearing another dress, this one picked out with her mother. It's not as beautiful as her original dress, but she is still the most beautiful bride ever. This time her dress shines more. A soft breeze blows her veil back as we walk down the outdoor aisle, nodding to everyone as we pass them.

My mother-in-law beams with Cooper next to her. She got her wish.

She planned the wedding that she has always dreamed of. Cooper got to walk his daughter down the aisle, even joking when they asked who gives this woman to be wed and he said "her mother, brother, and me."

When we got back from Vegas the dust settled. Well, most of it did. Phil still got a kick out of pointing out to Matthew that it happened right under his nose. Which usually got me a glare and a grunt. Did my brother-in-law and I get along? Well, let's say that we tolerate each other.

Allison finally moved all her stuff out of the brownstone and now it's all over our loft, which I have to say I fucking love. Our pictures are also scattered around. We travel together and sleep in the same room now, which makes me happier than I can put into words.

"You happy, angel?" I ask as we get to the walkway leading to the big white tents that are set up for the reception. The ceremony was only fifty people, those closest to us. The reception, however, is five hundred of our closest friends and family. I tried to have them cut the list just a bit, but when Copper started puffing up his chest with my first daughter is getting married it's a celebration and then my mother-in-law with the fake tears, you made her elope, I threw my hands up in defeat, not caring who they invited.

"Every day with you I'm happy," she says as she kisses me.

We follow the pathway to the reception area, which is lit by jars of candles. The tent has a veil all over the tented roof with lights strung all up. Long tables fill up most of the yard with white linen cloths and gold chairs. Soft light pink and champagne flowers are all around.

"My mother went a touch overboard." She grabs a champagne flute from a passing waiter.

I shake my head and by the time we look around it's almost the end of the night. I stand next to my wife as she takes the microphone, tapping it to make sure it works. My hand is around her waist as I hold her hip in my hand.

"We just want to thank you all for coming and helping us celebrate our wedding. Well, second wedding," she jokes as I lean in and kiss her neck. "I know we said we didn't want to do certain traditional things, but there is one tradition that I can't not do. And that is the father daughter dance. Where is my father?" my wife asks as she looks around. "Dad?" she asks as she spots him. "Come up here."

Cooper stands up, coming to us as she hands me the mic and nods to the DJ, who starts to put on the song "Butterfly Kisses" as my wife dances with the man she calls dad. Her real dad didn't bother getting an invitation, this after he called her after news of our elopement hit the media. He was less than pleased that she was irresponsible for all of her actions. The only thing my wife said was fuck you after hanging up on him and blocking his number. I watch as he hugs her and they sway. At the end of the song, she leans up to give him butterfly kisses on his cheek.

The dancing goes on till the wee hours of the night. Now here we are in the car, making our way to the house in the woods. She sleeps most of the way there, curled on the seat as my hand reaches across the console.

Once we finally get there and unload ther car, we sit on the dock, watching the water stream down.

"It's so peaceful," she says from her Adirondack chair. She looks over at me. "It's perfect." She gets up, coming to my chair, and sitting on top of my lap.

I wrap my arms around her, kissing the top of her head, and she buries her head in my neck and we watch the sun set.

## ALLISON

*Five Years later*

"I don't wanna go to Gramma and Granpa, I wanna stay and fish," my three-year-old blue-eyed monster Michael tells me.

I smile at him and lean in, kissing him. "But they are excited to see you," I tell him, as he crosses his little arms across his chest and pouts. Yup, just like his father.

Michael sits in his car seat as I wait for his father to come to the car.

"Max," I yell, "let's go, please."

I look up at the house and see my husband coming down the steps with my baby girl Alexandria in his arms, her tiny pigtails slanted on one side, her gummy smile looking up at her father. She has him wrapped around her tiny little finger and she's only ten months.

"Dada, Dada, Dada," it's also the only thing she says. Even though I carried and breast fed, he's the star of her show.

"Let's go, my little princess," he says as he opens the door and puts her in her seat, bending down to blow bubbles into her neck as she giggles. He closes the car door, wrapping his arms around my waist, bringing his lips down to mine, and then slowly trails kisses to my cheek and then down to my neck. He groans as I push him away from me.

"No," I say, smiling. "That's what you get when you bring your daughter in the bed with us, blue balls." I open my door, getting in, and watch him walk around, opening his door and getting in.

"She was crying," he says as he turns the car on and starts driving while he looks into his rearview mirror, smiling at his son, who looks exactly like him. He sees Alex from the mirror he has placed in front of her as she tries to eat her toes.

"She was playing you. That wasn't a cry, it was a whimper," I tell him as he looks over.

"She's teething, you said so yourself," he says as I look out at the window, leaving our summer home behind as we gear up for the next year. After we got married, Doug presented him with another five-year contract. It's Max's last year, or so he says. Somehow I don't believe him, but I will support him for however long he wants to do it.

The same time he gave Max his contracted he offered me the same one. It was a no-brainer for me until I got pregnant and had Michael. Max and I both decided that it would be too hectic for the baby with all the traveling and I didn't want to leave him anyways. So I was now a stay at home mom, and I love every single second of it.

Training my replacement however was more fun than I care to admit, Olivier came highly recommended and let me tell you he was over the top.

We make it home a little after seven, having to stop more times than we would like with the kids. I get out, stretching my legs. I look at our home that we bought in Long Island. Gone is the loft. Well, not gone. Denise lives there now, but with the kids, we wanted—or Max wanted—a huge yard, so they can run and play, so we settled on a six-bedroom house. I shake my head as I open the door to get my baby girl out, who smiles at me as she reaches out her arms to me.

"Hi, princess," I say as I put her on my hip.

She is content till she sees her father walk around the car and lunges for him. He catches her and throws her hands in the air.

"There's my girls." He tosses her in the air, catching her as she laughs.

We don't make it far before Mom and Dad get here and honk the horn. "Gammy, Gampy," Michael says as he runs to them, Cooper squatting down as he grabs him and tosses him up.

"You got so big," my mother says as she gets to Cooper's side and he puts Michael sideways so my mother can plant him with kisses.

"No more," Michael begs as they walk to us and my mother sees Alex.

"There is my favorite baby girl." She tries to get Alex, who hides her hands in her chest as she lies on her father, hiding in his neck. "Well, I see she hasn't lost her love for dad." She laughs as she kisses Max on the cheek. "Hey, son." It didn't take my mother long to fall in love with Max, and as soon as Matthew and Cooper saw that she accepted him, it was a little easier convincing them.

"Come see Mommy," I tell Alex while I try and grab her. "So Daddy can bring in the things."

She grunts out her displeasure in leaving her father. "Dada, Dada, Dada."

I roll my eyes as I carry my whiny daughter inside the house as the boys unload the car. I place her down in the family room as she crawls over to her toys that she hasn't seen in a while. She puts everything in her mouth.

"You look like you lost weight. Are you okay?" my mother asks and I just nod.

"Yeah, I'm fine. It was a hectic summer. Alex was all over the place. I spent half the time running after her," I explain to her as the front door swings open and Michael runs in.

"Uncle Matthew is here with Auntie Karrie," he says as Matthew walks in with Karrie following behind him as the kids around them, all going to see Alex in the room, who shakes her hands up and down in excitement seeing all the kids.

"We brought pizza," he says as he puts down the five pizza boxes he is holding on the island as Karrie smiles and places paper plates she is carrying beside them.

"Welcome home. Nothing says welcome home like twenty people

showing up, right?" She looks at Matthew, who rolls his eyes.

"I wanted to come and see my niece and nephew. Kiss me," he says as he walks into the room, picking up Alex, who grabs his face, pinching him as he tosses her in the air, blowing bubbles on her stomach.

"You look just like your mommy."

She laughs, not understanding what he says, so she counters with, "Dada, Dada, Dada."

"I look like my dad," Michael says from beside him as Matthew looks down at him, putting Alex back on the floor and taking Michael, tossing him up.

"You may look like your dad, but you're all Grant inside."

"Horton," Max says as he comes into the room. "Ignore your uncle. His old age is getting to him."

I see Matthew whisper fuck you to him.

"You're older than me."

"Your sister keeps me young." He winks at him and then Matthew throws his head back, groaning.

"Sick, sick, sick." Then he turns back to Michael. "Did you practice your stick handling while you were gone?"

Michael shakes his head. "We went fishing."

"Okay, fine, but tomorrow you come over and we can play hockey." He puts him down, coming into the kitchen, grabbing a plate, and putting pizza inside.

"Did you get the e-mail Oliver sent everyone?" Matthew asks while chewing his pizza, "he is insane."

"Why?" I ask as I cut a tiny piece of pizza and give Alex some as she sings da da da da.

"For the Horton Grant Pediatric foundation picture, he wants us all to be in our tux suits, with no pants." Max tells me, leaning over and kissing Alex.

I laugh at the thought, "I mean it might be really really good."

"You know some of the guys cover their junk when he comes in the room right." Matthew says, "when you came in they would stand up and lift a leg to have it hang, meanwhile now they just cover it. It's hilarious."

Our quiet night becomes a welcome back party as everyone drops by. Even Zoe and Zara, who come in with candy for the kids. Luckily, I intercept it before they can give it to them. By the time everyone leaves, Michael is dragging his feet to his bed and Alex sleeps on her father's shoulder, her hands under her. He places her in the crib as she fusses a bit.

"It's okay, princess, Daddy is here." He taps her bottom as she falls back to sleep.

I tuck Michael in as Max comes into the room, kissing him goodnight as he turns on his side and falls asleep before we walk out the door.

"You tired, angel?" He throws his arm around my shoulder and my stomach still gets butterflies.

I turn up, looking at him, the best thing to ever happen to me. The best thing that I could ever have wished for. My prince. Or now as he calls himself the king.

"What do you have in mind?" I ask as my hands already slide up his shirt.

He moans out as he picks me up and my legs wrap around him. "I was thinking a nice long shower." He kisses my neck as his hands squeeze my ass. "A little back rub after that." He closes the door behind us and goes to the monitors, turning them both on in case the kids get up. He is the best father in the world. "So what do you think?"

"That plan sounds so irresistible, just like you." I lean down, kissing him, thinking that no matter how much we fought it, it would have always ended up like this. I would have always been his wife.

It was just something so irresistible.

# BOOKS BY NATASHA MADISON

**Something Series**

Something So Right

Something So Perfect

Something So Irresistible

**Tempt Series**

Tempt The Boss

Tempt The Playboy

Tempt The Neighbor – 2018

**Heaven & Hell Series**

Hell and Back

Pieces of Heaven

**True Love Series**

Pefrect Love Story – March 2018

Unexpected Love Story – April 2018

Broken Love Story – May/June 2018

**Novellas**

Cheeky

Until Brandon –April 2018

**Madison Rose Books**

Only His

# ACKNOWLEDGMENTS

Every single time I keep thinking it's going to be easy. It takes a village to help and I don't want to leave anyone out.

**My Husband**: I love you, I don't tell you enough. Thank you for letting me sit in bed most of the day writing, and for not busting my chops when I don't cook. Oh wait you do!

**My Kids**: Matteo, Michael, and Erica, Thank you for letting me do this. Thank you for being proud of me, I love you honey bunches and oats!

**Crystal**: My hooker and bestie. What don't you do for me? Everyone needs someone like you in their corner and I am so blessed than you chose to be in mine. I can't begin to thank you for the support, love and encouragement along the way.

**Rachel:** You are my blurb bitch. Each time you do it without even reading this book and you rocked it. I'm so happy that I ddin't give up when you ignored my many messages.

**Meghan:** I'm so so proud to call you my friend. Thank you for making me make that list, and making me see I can actually achieve it.

**Jamie & Sarah:** Thank you for being in my corner, and always having my back.

**Lori:** I don't know what I would do without you in my life. You take over and I don't even have to ask or worry because I know everything will be fine, because you're a rock star, I'm also scared of that whip!

**Denise:** The hole finder. I can't put into word how honored I am that you took Max and made me make him even more Epic! I can't wait to bring Denise to life!

**Melissa:** My cover girl, I have more covers than stories, but I know you won't let me stop. Thank you for sending me covers while I sleep so I don't yell at you before you go to bed. I love you.

**Beta girls:** Teressa, Natasha M, Lori, Sandy, Yolanda, and Carmen, Yamina. For three weeks I bombarded your messages with chapters and you ate it up. Thank you for holding my hand, telling me when things sucked and for being by my side.

**Madison Maniacs:** This little group went from two people to so much more and I can't thank you guys enough. This group is my go to, my safe place. You push me and get excited for me and I can't wait to watch us grow even bigger!

**Mia:** I'm so happy that Nanny threw out Archer's Voice and I needed to tell you because that snowballed to a friendship that is without a doubt the best ever!

**Neda:** You answer my question no matter how stupid they sound. Thank you for being you, thank you for everything!

**Julie:** Thank you for taking my book with all it's mistakes and making it pretty, or as pretty as it can be.

**BLOGGERS**. THANK YOU FOR TAKING A CHANCE ON ME. You give so much of yourself effortlessly and you are the voice that we can't do this without.

**My Girls:** Sabrina, Melanie, Marie-Eve, Lydia, Shelly, Stephanie, Marisa. Your support during this whole ride has been amazing. I can honestly say without a doubt that I have the best Squad of life!!!!

**And Lastly and most importantly to YOU the reader,** Without you none of this would be real. So thank you for reading!

Printed in Great Britain
by Amazon